Fritha looked shocked.

That was good. Perhaps she would leave him alone and let him keep his secrets.

"I'm only trying to help," she explained.

"I don't need your help," Urien countered.

God's blood, why didn't she leave?

"I just don't want any harm to come to you."

He looked away. He was not worthy of her love. Not worthy of any woman's love. "I can take care of myself," he said harshly. "I don't need you to tell me how to do that."

Still she didn't leave. Why wouldn't she see that he didn't want her? That he couldn't? What would it take to make her understand?

The truth.

He faced her squarely, looking down into her beautiful, trusting eyes, dreading the way they would change....

Dear Reader,

This month, we are happy to bring you the next installment in Margaret Moore's Warrior series. *A Warrior's Quest* follows the path of the disillusioned Urien Fitzroy, a mercenary soldier who is no longer content to live his life by the sword.

Julie Keane has no use for an indentured servant more suited to be the lord of the manor than a common laborer, but Zachariah Hale soon proves his mettle in *Bound by Love,* from the writing team of Erin Yorke.

Web of Loving Lies by Barbara Leigh is a heartwarming tale of two sisters whose lives become inescapably intertwined with a man who falls in love with one sister, but is forced into marrying the other.

From author Beverlee Ross comes the story of a weary gunslinger, Clint Strand, who finds himself amazingly willing to be saddled with *Annabelle,* a feisty young woman who isn't afraid of anything.

Next month marks the release of our Western historical short story collection—UNTAMED. With authors Heather Graham Pozzessere, Joan Johnston and Patricia Potter contributing, this is one collection you won't want to miss!

Sincerely,

Tracy Farrell
Senior Editor

A Warrior's Quest

MARGARET MOORE

Harlequin Books

TORONTO • NEW YORK • LONDON
AMSTERDAM • PARIS • SYDNEY • HAMBURG
STOCKHOLM • ATHENS • TOKYO • MILAN
MADRID • WARSAW • BUDAPEST • AUCKLAND

Harlequin Historicals first edition June 1993

ISBN 0-373-28775-5

A WARRIOR'S QUEST

MARGARET MOORE

says that the first great love of her life was Errol Flynn. "Naturally, I was devastated to learn that he died when I was three years old," she admits, but adds that her interest in historical-romance writing developed from that early fascination. Margaret lives in Scarborough, Ontario, with her husband and two school-age children. When not in her basement at the computer, she enjoys reading and sewing.

With thanks and love to my parents, Donna and
Clint Warren, who taught me the meaning
of ''home.''

Chapter One

The dark-haired man sitting astride the huge horse made his way through the market crowd as if the people were no more than stalks of grain in a field. Indeed, most made way for him, although a few brave souls hesitated a moment before averting their eyes and moving aside.

It was obvious to all that no one but a man, whose business it was to fight, rode such a horse, in such a way, with such a keen eye to watch them.

Urien Fitzroy's gaze came to rest on the castle looming above the town of Bridgeford Wells. It was large, newly built, strong and surely expensive. He had seen many fortresses in his travels, but this was one of the finest.

He glanced around the market. The people seemed wary of him, but not overly frightened. As he had good cause to know, townspeople unsure of their lord's protection tended to look especially apprehensive at the arrival of a stranger.

The goods being sold were many and varied, and that too was a sign of security and prosperity. Obviously he had not made a mistake coming to this place.

Perhaps what he had heard about the lord of Castle Gervais was true as well, that the nobleman was always seeking experienced soldiers to train his men.

Some time ago, Urien had discovered he no longer wished to earn money doing whatever a lord demanded. For the past few years, he had managed to survive on his winnings from participating in tournaments, but it had been months since he'd been able to join in a hastilude as more and more noblemen were demanding that only they be allowed to participate.

Tired and thirsty, Urien halted his horse outside an inn on the other side of the town. It was a small establishment with a stable along one side of a muddy courtyard. Two wattle and daub structures formed the other sides of the yard, one no doubt for lodging and the other for cooking and storage. An old man sat on a bench outside the inn's open door.

A healthy-looking lad came out of the stable. Urien dismounted and said, "My horse needs to be fed and watered."

"Stayin' the night?" the boy asked shyly.

"I don't know yet."

The boy nodded and led away the horse while Urien approached the inn.

"Fine day," the old man offered in a surprisingly strong, if somewhat squeaky, voice. His measuring gaze was shrewd and his thin arms well muscled.

"Yes," Urien replied as he went past. He wondered if that man had been a soldier once, too, or a farmer. He had good reason to know that a farmer could be as strong as any warrior. And twice as merciless.

The inn was cool and dim after the hot afternoon sun, and it took a moment for Urien's eyes to adjust to the darkness.

"Good day, sir!" a female voice said, addressing him from one of the corners. "Lookin' for lodgin'?"

"Perhaps."

By now he could see the speaker—a plump, middle-aged woman with a cheerful face. "We're cheap and we're clean," she said as she approached him. "There are a few more places in the town, but we're the best."

Of course, Urien thought. They all said that.

"Good grain for your horse, too. And my Tom'll brush him down right fine. You'll see."

Urien's lips twitched in what, for him, was a smile. The acknowledgment that the treatment of his horse was at least as important as their treatment of him tipped the balance. "I'll stay, for tonight at least."

The woman grinned and nodded.

"I want some wine. The best you've got."

"Certainly, sir."

"Bring it outside."

"Aye, right away, sir."

Urien went out into the sunlight. Since the time spent in the north of Wales a few years ago, he enjoyed the warmth of an English summer. He sat down on the bench beside the old man, who slumbered, his soft snores audible but not enough to be disturbing.

The woman came out with the wine and set it beside Urien. "There you go. The best to be had in Bridgeford Wells."

Urien reached into his purse and tossed her a coin. Her eyes widened for an instant, then she grinned. "It's not so much as that, sir."

"Take the lodging out of it, too."

"Oh, aye, to be sure." She eyed his purse again, but blushed when she caught him watching her and hurried back inside.

The wine was good, very good for a place so far south of London. A horse—not his—whinnied softly in the stable. A bee, drawn by the sweet scent of the wine, hovered nearby. With a flick of his wrist, Urien sent it buzzing off. Then, letting himself feel the tiredness of his long ride, he leaned against the wall.

A girl, not too young but not what a man would call old, either, came sauntering into the courtyard. She carried a large basket covered with a cloth balanced against one hip. Nice hips, he noticed, watching her progress beneath his lowered eyelids. She also had slim, shapely ankles beneath the homespun dress and tunic. More than that he couldn't see without opening his eyes wider.

As she drew closer, the boy he assumed was the innkeeper's son came out of the stable and smiled. "Fritha! Mam'll be pleased to see you!"

"Not more so than I am to see her, Tom."

The girl's voice was pleasant enough to be intriguing, so rather than let them know he was listening, Urien stayed just as he was.

"How is she?" the girl asked softly.

"Not too bad, most days. It's the nights that get her low. That's when she misses him."

"Well, she's got you, at least."

He could almost see the boy's chest swell with pride. Indeed, who could blame the lad for being proud, when a voice like that, filled with simple admiration and respect, said such a thing.

"Who's that?" the girl whispered, gesturing toward Urien.

"Don't know. He come in a short time ago."

"I don't think I like the looks of him."

"Why not? He's a well-made man," Tom said.

"He has a handsome enough face. But he could probably cause plenty of trouble."

"He's not armed."

"Not that we can *see.* I think he's dangerous."

"What do you suppose he's doin' here, then?"

"I suppose he's come to see if Lord Gervais will hire him."

"Oh. Think he will?"

The girl paused, and Urien realized he was holding his breath, which was foolish. He made himself breathe slowly, as if sleeping.

"Yes, I believe he would want him. I've never seen such strong-looking shoulders and arms. He could probably take on half Lord Gervais' soldiers all by himself."

"Aye." The boy's voice was full of awe.

"And show them no mercy, Tom."

"Oh, aye." The lad sounded suitably chastised as they walked past the bench and into the inn. Urien had heard enough. "Handsome enough" face, indeed! And who was *she* to make it sound as if he robbed and raped for a living? He was a hired soldier, which was nothing to be ashamed of. Granted he'd done some unsavory things in the past, but that was long ago.

He sat up and took a lengthy drink of the wine. Impudent wench.

Impudent, shapely wench.

He heard the muted voices inside and wondered if they were still discussing the stranger in the courtyard.

Not that he cared. He was used to being stared at and having people speculate about his past. Usually he let them imagine what they liked. They always came up with infinitely more interesting stories than the rather mundane and simple truth: that he was born a bastard to a poor young woman who died shortly after, leaving him to the not-so-tender care of a drunken lout of a farmer.

He took another long pull of the wine, trying to drown the bitterness in his mouth that always came when he thought of those days. Still, that farmer had made him strong, and determined. The moment Urien was able, he had run away, hiring on with the first lord who would take and train him. Since that time, he had made his own way in a world that had little use for bastards, but much for a good fighter.

The talk ceased and the girl came out the door.

"Good day," he said, pleased to see her give a little start of surprise. When she turned to him, he saw that the promise of the hips and ankles was made good by the rest of her body. Her breasts were not large, but firm and round above her narrow waist. Her white creamy skin continued up the slender neck to a finely featured face, with full, red lips, pink cheeks and hazel eyes that surveyed him coolly.

Perhaps he could forgive her insolent words.

"Good day," she answered, turning to leave.

"What have you in the basket?"

With a toss of her nut brown hair, she looked back at him over her shoulder. "Nothing that would interest you."

"How do you know? I might find your... wares... very interesting."

She smiled coyly, and his lips curved upward. He could almost taste her kiss as she sauntered closer. "Do you think so, sir?"

"I think so, indeed."

She reached into the basket and brought out something wrapped in a cloth. Slowly she undid the cloth and produced a honeycomb. "Is this what you're after?"

"Not exactly, but something just as sweet."

Suddenly she threw the comb, hitting him square on the cheek. The honey stuck to his face, oozing out of the comb and down his chin.

"Why you...!" he cried, leaping to his feet. But she ran out of the courtyard with a peal of musical laughter, her skirt swinging around her slim legs.

"Curse the wench!" he muttered as he sat down on the bench and found that he had knocked over the wine when he had jumped up. "God's teeth, I should find her and make her pay for that."

"For what, sir? For lettin' you know she didn't appreciate your invitation?"

Urien's eyes narrowed as he turned to the old man, who sat shaking with silent laughter.

"Don't take it amiss, sir. You just met your match in that game, is all," the old man said.

"What are you talking about?" Urien growled.

"That's our Fritha. She don't take lightly to impertinence."

"She's a relative of yours?"

The old man seemed to find that the funniest thing yet. It was some minutes before he was calm enough to reply. "God's wounds, sir, no. Not at all. She belongs up there." He nodded toward the castle.

Urien felt a sharp stab of envy. He could easily imagine how good it would be to be lord over such a castle—and such a wench.

"Fritha won't put up with no nonsense, not from men and that's for sure."

Urien raised one eyebrow. Could it be that she would refuse even a lord's attentions? He couldn't quite believe it, unless the lord was married to a woman who would make life a misery if he were caught dallying with a serving wench. Or perhaps the girl's husband was a big, brawny fellow any man would think twice about angering.

The old man wiped the laughter tears from his cheeks and sighed. "But she's a fine girl. The whole town thinks so, and that's sayin' somethin'. Anybody got a bit of trouble, there's Fritha. Always willin' to help—and not makin' it seem like she's doing you a service, neither."

"Her husband must be rather neglected."

The old man gave him a measuring stare. "She's not married."

"What's wrong with her?"

The old man grinned. "Not a thing. A very fine girl, like I said. 'Cept she wants to choose her husband. Very particular, our Fritha."

"Many offering?"

"A few, but not worth a cow's cud, most of 'em. She sends 'em off, right quick. She's got a tongue, she

has. She can almost flay the skin off a man's back with
it, if she takes a notion."

"Or blind him with honey?" Urien asked sarcastically. He wondered why he'd let the man go on as long
as he had. He wasn't interested in the local blabber of
marriages and betrothals. He was a fighter, here to see
if he could get work.

The man grinned. "Oh, I wouldn't be too angry
about that, sir."

Urien responded with a derisive grunt as he wiped
the last of the sticky honey from his cheek.

"If she'd really taken a dislike to you," the old man
said firmly, "she would have thrown a rock."

Fritha hurried through the outer courtyard of Castle Gervais. Lady Gervais would be angry that she was
late, but Fritha had wanted to see Meara, whose husband had died of a fever a few months ago.

After that encounter with the rude, arrogant
stranger, Fritha wished she had gone another time;
however, when she recalled the look on his face and
the honey slowly dripping down his chin, she was
tempted to laugh out loud.

And she had to admit he did have a very fine chin.

She reached the gate into the huge inner courtyard
and hesitated, peeking out of the shadows. Mercifully, there were only a few scattered soldiers standing about, aside from those on watch on the
battlements.

She had no wish to encounter the persistent, per-
plexing Sir Tallentine. Frowning, she hurried across
the open space and into the door of the hall.

"Ah, Fritha!"

She bit back a curse at the sound of Sir Tallentine's nasal tones. She turned to find him leaning against the wall near the corridor to the kitchen. He pushed himself forward and walked toward her.

As usual he was dressed as if it were a special feast day, with a brocaded tunic trimmed with gold, a dazzlingly white linen shirt beneath it, linen *chausses* and soft, smooth boots of expensive leather. She glanced at his face, which seemed as soft and smooth as his boots.

His eyes, however, were anything but soft. They always reminded her of a ferret's: tiny, darting about as if searching for prey. She considered them much more indicative of his personality than either the rest of his face or his languid, drawling tones.

"Back from the market?" he inquired.

"Yes."

"And flushed from hurrying. I must say, it becomes you."

"If you'll excuse me, my lord, Lady Gervais is waiting for me."

"Of course."

Without waiting, she hurried toward the staircase leading to the upper bedchambers. At least he had been a little less talkative than usual, although she failed to see why he bothered with her at all. She gave him absolutely no encouragement, and her dowry would be sufficiently small that he should have been discouraged by that alone.

To be sure she was nobly born, but her father had been a minor earl with little money. Her mother had died when she was very young and her father had sent her to be fostered in Lord Gervais' household. Then he had apparently forgotten all about her. He had never visited, or sent presents, or even inquired if she was well.

For her part, Fritha barely remembered him at all, and when word of his death arrived, she had felt little sorrow.

It was Lord and Lady Gervais who had been parents to her. They had been the ones whose good opinion she valued, the ones she sought to please. In return, she had begun, even as a child, to perform whatever tasks she could about the castle.

When Lady Eleanor had died ten years ago, Fritha had felt as much grief as if it had been her own mother.

She knew many in the town had hoped Lord Gervais would take her for his wife, but their relationship had always been a familial one; it would have been unthinkable to either of them.

Last year, when Lord Gervais had returned from visiting a distant lord and spoken highly of a woman he had met there, Fritha had been happy for him. Lord Gervais had truly cared for Lady Eleanor, but it was time he took a new wife. He deserved to have children, and she knew he would make an excellent father.

So he had married and brought home his bride.

Fritha had known from the day Lord Gervais brought Adela home that her life would never be the same again. Whenever men were nearby, Adela was a lovely, soft-spoken, demure wife. With Fritha and the servants, she was harsh, demanding and vain. Fritha kept all this to herself, however, because she loved her foster father. If Adela made him happy and he did not discover her true nature, she would not disillusion him.

She reached the bedchamber and knocked softly.

"Come in," came Lady Gervais' gentle voice.

Fritha opened the door of the huge and well-furnished room. The tapestries on the walls were the finest to be had, the bed the softest, the linen without equal. The large clothes chest, intricately carved, had come all the way from the East and had cost Lord Gervais enough gold to feed a family of tenants for several months. Adela even had a mirror.

At this moment, however, the room was in complete disarray. Costly gowns lay upon the bed, the ebony chairs, even the floor. Girdles and other finery were scattered about. Lady Gervais, beautiful, golden haired and slender, sat in a chair in front of the mirror brushing her hair.

"Oh, it's you," she said bluntly as Fritha set down her basket. "I can't find that purple girdle with the gold links anywhere."

"I put it in the chest on the right-hand side," Fritha said, keeping the impatience from her voice. It seemed Lady Gervais could never search for anything without making the chamber appear as if a huge wind had flung everything about.

"I looked."

Fritha went to the chest, lifted the lid and peered inside. The girdle was there, under a cloak, on the right-hand side just where she'd laid it. She lifted it out.

Lady Gervais, seeing Fritha's reflection in the mirror, said, "Good." She went back to brushing her thick hair. "Where have you been this time?"

Fritha began picking up gowns and folding them. "I went to see Meara."

"Who?"

"The innkeeper's wife. He died just after Christmas."

"Did he?"

"I wanted to see if she needed anything."

"And you kept me waiting for that? You barely have enough time to arrange my hair before dinner."

"I'm sorry, my lady."

"I don't want you to be late again, or I shall have to speak to Lord Gervais."

"Yes, my lady."

"Now, leave those things and fix my hair."

When Fritha picked up the brush, she had to suppress the urge to hit her mistress over the head with it, but she didn't even dare to show her displeasure on her face.

She knew all too well that her fate was in Adela's graceful hands as much as Lord Gervais'. Adela wanted to see her gone, married off to whomever would take her.

Fritha simply couldn't imagine leaving Bridgeford Wells, and not only because of Lord Gervais. The townspeople were like family to her, and she appreciated their affection. This was her home, and she had no wish to leave it, even supposing she met a man who tempted her.

Not that she had ever met a man who was even remotely tempting. There had been some who eyed her like a horse at a market fair and some who were a little more subtle, like Tallentine.

And then there were men like that impudent fellow at Meara's. At least he had been honest about what he wanted. No doubt Sir Tallentine wished to make much the same proposition, but he couched it in flowery language and obscure flattery. Maybe that was why she found herself less insulted by the stranger's words than she was by just the way Sir Tallentine looked at her.

Lord Gervais was always looking for soldiers. He would surely be interested in the stranger, for everything about him was like a finely crafted weapon. He had the broad, muscular shoulders that came from years of training with lance and mace. His strong arms could probably swing a sword as easily as another man a scythe. His long, powerful legs seemed made for hours in the saddle. Even his lean, sharp features had a wary and predatory look to them.

She should consider herself lucky that he hadn't chased after her. He might have caught her, taking hold of her with his strong, sinewy hands...

"What's the matter with you today?" Adela demanded.

"I'm sorry, my lady," Fritha said, starting, as she finished arranging Adela's heavy golden locks.

The next morning Urien found it surprisingly easy to enter Lord Gervais' castle. He knew better than to wear a sword or carry any obvious weapon. However, the guards resting against the cool, gray walls in the shadow of the great arched entrance seemed more intent on watching the women than looking for potential enemies.

Urien was not impressed.

As he approached the inner gate, he heard the familiar clash of weapons and voices that told him he was listening to nothing more than a mock combat. He went beneath the portcullis and came upon a vast courtyard.

Several young men stripped to the waist were practising with wooden swords. No doubt they were sons of noblemen sent to Lord Gervais to learn the arts of war.

Urien watched for a little while. As with most men who were not engaged in actual fighting, their movements were slow to the point of sluggishness, although wooden swords were much lighter than metal ones.

It would be better for the squires to train with real weapons, Urien thought, letting them get a feel for how the sword's weight would affect its movement. After all, these were not pages, but young men who might be called upon to fight in battle. They wouldn't be using wooden swords then, and one miscalculation could cause serious injury, or death.

In another corner of the field, mounted men were aiming lances at a small quintain. The man-sized dummy spun around on its turning table whenever a lance hit what was supposed to be a small shield. The dummy's other "arm" held a mace, which swung around, too. The quintain could be a useful device to teach men to react quickly, but it was devoid of the cunning a human opponent would possess. After a time, it even became quite predictable.

Over in the opposite corner, Urien saw a group of archers shooting at straw targets. He could tell, even from the gate, that their bows were old and brittle. If

he had learned one thing about fighting from the ac-
cursed Welsh, it was the value of good bows and better archers. Lord Gervais would do well to provide
newer weapons.

In the center of all this activity, there was a man
seated on a very fine white horse. He was young—not
more than twenty—with extremely rich, extremely
clean clothing. His tunic alone would have cost Urien
at least three months' wages in a good year. Occasionally the man would bark some comment to one
of the youths, but mostly he just sat there, looking . . . pretty.

Urien's lip curled in disgust. He had no use for men
who were too afraid of dirtying their clothes to get
down in the mud with the men who might one day save
their land, and their lives.

At that moment, the door to what had to be the hall
opened, and an older, well-built man stepped out.
Urien stared. Once, years and years ago, he had been
in a tournament. His opponents had been led by this
man now walking firmly through the courtyard. His
opponents had won, with good, honest fighting. No
wonder the name "Gervais" had seemed somehow
familiar.

Urien could respect a lord like that.

The activity in the courtyard ceased immediately.
The fool on the white horse dismounted and stepped
daintily toward Lord Gervais. They spoke quietly for
a few moments, the pretty boy shaking his head and
raising his hands in a gesture of hopelessness.

Urien glanced around the courtyard. The young

men were watching the two noblemen, giving each other covert, disgruntled glances.

Urien couldn't blame them. He wouldn't want a man like that young fool to be his master, either.

He took a deep breath and stepped out from the shadow of the gate. He strode across the courtyard, ignoring the stares of the men. When he was a few feet behind the younger man, Lord Gervais stopped talking and looked at him.

"I know you, don't I?" the lord inquired.

Urien nodded. "It was years ago at Lord Marchebank's tournament—"

The other man turned quickly. "Who are *you?* Don't you know better than to interrupt?"

Urien ignored him and kept his gaze on Lord Gervais. "I remember you, too," he said simply.

Lord Gervais smiled slowly. "Why are you here?"

"I heard you were hiring soldiers."

"*My lord,*" the young man corrected.

"He's not my lord . . . yet," Urien replied coolly.

Lord Gervais' gaze never left Urien's face. "Are you asking me to hire you?" the nobleman asked.

"Yes—unless I am to be under this man's command."

"You scoundrel! How dare you—"

"Tallentine tells me he's unable to teach my squires anything and dismisses them as hopeless dullards," Lord Gervais continued, ignoring the younger man. "Could *you* teach them how to fight?"

Urien slowly surveyed the youths in the courtyard. They were all different shapes and sizes, some obviously having lived too well, and some coming from more frugal homes. But he had seen enough from the gate. "Yes, I can."

"Good. You're hired." Lord Gervais turned to go.

"But, my lord!" Tallentine began.

Lord Gervais stopped and turned back. "What is it?"

"You don't know this man!"

"I know *of* him, and what I know is enough for me."

"You would put him over me?"

"No, Tallentine." Lord Gervais' mouth betrayed impatience. "You are no longer in charge of the squires."

"*What?*" Tallentine squawked.

"*My lord,*" Urien added helpfully.

Tallentine scowled fiercely. "You knew him years ago, my lord. Perhaps he is no longer quite so skilled as you recall."

"Shall I test him, do you think?

"Well..."

"As you wish, Tallentine. You fight him, and if he beats you, I'll hire him. You can then return to your own estate."

"But my lord!"

"Now, Tallentine."

Urien didn't smile, but he was vastly pleased. Without hesitating he stripped off his tunic, handing it to a very skinny youth who stepped forward to take it without uttering a word. The youth also handed him a broadsword. Urien swung it a few times and passed it from hand to hand. He liked the feel of it.

"Well, surely, my lord, all we need to do..."

Tallentine's protests faded. Lord Gervais wasn't responding, and he realized he would have to fight or be disgraced. With a peevish expression he turned around, beginning to undo his fine brocade tunic. No one came to help him, until he called to a brawny young man who then stepped forward.

The rest of the men formed a ring with Lord Gervais at one end. When Tallentine had drawn his sword, Lord Gervais lifted his hand and let it fall to begin the contest.

Urien decided to get things finished quickly. It was too simple. Two blows to the dolt's sword, a trip into the mud, and it was over, with Urien's blade at the man's throat.

Lord Gervais stepped forward. "Well, Tallentine, he's an excellent fighter."

"Whose loyalty goes only to the man who pays for it," Tallentine said, his teeth clenched. Urien pressed his sword a little closer to the smooth white throat.

"Then I suppose I should pay him well. Come..."

"Fitzroy. Urien Fitzroy."

"Come, Fitzroy, and we'll discuss the amount over some wine. You've earned that, too."

The thin youth holding Urien's tunic handed it back to him and took the sword. Urien almost expected the boy to stagger from the weapon's weight, but he didn't. He looked at the boy's face and saw a determined gleam in his gray eyes that impressed him.

Urien put on his tunic quickly, nodded his thanks and followed Lord Gervais.

As they walked into the hall, Tallentine, still lying on the muddy stones, glared at the rest of the youths in the ring, who one by one began to walk away. "You oafs!" Tallentine cried. "Isn't somebody going to help me up?"

Nobody did.

Chapter Two

Fritha glanced around the huge hall as everyone waited for the entrance of Lord and Lady Gervais for the noon meal. The room was nearly filled, for Lord Gervais was a popular and respected nobleman. Knights who owed him service were only too willing to send their sons to be trained under his watchful eye, and many paid visits to Castle Gervais throughout the year.

Dogs roved under the tables, waiting for the scraps of food that would fall to them. The pages stood ready to begin serving the meal, joking and laughing. The squires sat, proud and disdainful of the younger boys who were doing precisely what they themselves had done only a short time ago.

Everything seemed quite ordinary, until Fritha caught sight of the stranger whom she had hit with the honeycomb. His cheek was slightly bruised and she felt a sudden rush of embarrassment, which she struggled to subdue when her gaze encountered his mocking, dark eyes.

Fritha looked away quickly. Everyone in the castle had heard of the man who had beaten Tallentine and was now in charge of the squires' training. His name was Urien Fitzroy, but beyond that—and the fact he had defeated Tallentine as easily as a barn owl kills a mouse—no one knew anything about him. Judging by the hard line of his mouth and the guarded look of his eyes, Fritha doubted that anyone would ever learn much more of him, unless he chose to tell them.

Perhaps she shouldn't have thrown that honeycomb. For one thing, it had been a waste of good honey.

Lord Gervais, regal and powerful, and Lady Gervais, demure and beautiful, entered the hall and took their places on the dais. As usual, Fritha stood among the servants. Lord Gervais once protested her choice of such a lowly place, but she truthfully said she preferred it. It enabled her to discuss household matters. And she preferred to sit away from Adela.

The priest gave the blessing and everyone sat down to begin the meal.

Fritha glanced at Urien Fitzroy and saw that he was staring at Adela as if he had never seen a woman before.

Fritha tore her bread into tiny pieces. It was nothing to her if he stared at Adela. Most men were captivated by her beauty. Why should she expect him to be any different?

She popped a piece of bread into her mouth and ate the rest of her food hurriedly. She could think of several things she needed to do, all of them in other parts of the castle.

As soon as she could do so, she stood up and went outside, not looking at anybody else in the hall. Once in the courtyard, she berated herself for acting childishly. After all, Adela was like a beautiful flower—who made everyone else look like a straggly weed.

Fritha headed for the stables. There was something honest about animals, she reflected, and, except for the guards, everyone was still in the hall. She could be alone there.

As she approached, she heard an unfamiliar neigh. She entered the dim, warm building, and at once noticed the huge horse tethered inside. She approached the animal slowly, saying soft, gentle words, reaching out to stroke its muscular neck. It was a powerful animal; it would take a powerful man to control it. "You're a fine one," she whispered. "I'd like to try you someday. Would you let me?"

"Who could resist such an entreaty?"

Fritha started and looked behind her. Urien Fitzroy leaned against the stable door, his muscular arms crossed.

Her heart began to beat rapidly as he looked at her, but not with fright. She could summon help in a moment, should it come to that.

"I was speaking to your horse," she said coolly.

"Pity." Urien replied, pushing himself off the wall.

True, this female was nowhere near as lovely as Lady Gervais, but she certainly had a fine body.

Fritha stepped to the other side of the horse. "What are you doing here?" she demanded.

"Getting my horse. I must say that's a fine way to talk to the man who's just been hired to train Lord Gervais' squires." He moved casually around to her side of the horse, where she would have to go past him. He was rather surprised that she didn't seem the least bit impressed by his last words.

The girl realized what he was doing and went the other way. His lips twitched with a grin as he side-stepped to intercept her. "Leaving so soon, Fritha?"

"How do you know my name?"

"The old man at the inn told me."

"Did he?" She began to go back the other way, facing him all the while.

"Yes, he did." He moved to the other side.

Suddenly she stopped and put her hands on her hips. "Aren't you a little old for this childish game?"

"Aren't you?"

"Yes." With that, she walked straight at him, as if willing him to get out of her way.

It was not Urien's custom to get out of anybody's way, especially not serving wenches with shapely bodies and lips that deserved to be kissed often, and by a man who knew how.

He caught her around the waist and pulled her to him. "One kiss and I'll let you go."

She looked up at his face, and he saw that she had lovely teeth, full red lips and fine, smooth skin. Her bold hazel eyes gazed into his own with an expression he took for interest. His blood stirred, hot and throbbing with desire. He hadn't had a woman for several days—and nights—and this comely maidservant would certainly—

Then he felt the pain as her foot came down with great force on his and she shoved her knee at his groin, connecting with excruciating accuracy.

With an oath he let her go and she ran toward the door.

Unexpectedly she paused at the threshold, her eyes flashing. "I suppose you're used to women who would find such insolence irresistible. *I* am different." With an indignant toss of her chestnut curls, she walked away.

"By all the saints, you're different," he muttered, hobbling around until he felt the pain lessen. "You're a witch!"

After a few minutes, when the painful throbbing stopped, Urien took his horse and headed for the inn.

He delivered his mount to Tom's care and sauntered back out into the town. Surely there were some whores in a place this size.

A short time later, he spotted a likely looking alehouse and heard loud, boisterous laughter spilling onto the street from the open door.

The establishment was on the main road through the town, where the road turned to follow the river. Lots of people would pass by on the way to the marketplace outside the castle walls, and it was far enough away from what looked to be the more unsavory part of the settlement down by the river that he doubted its patrons would be the targets of cutpurses. Nonetheless, he moved his money farther inside his tunic to prevent tempting thieves and went in.

There was a fire in a large hearth in the center of the room, with benches and tables around it. The beams in the ceiling matched the dark, scarred wood of the tables.

"By Jove's thundering balls! I don't believe it!"

Urien turned toward the booming voice on the other side of the room, his eyes widening in surprise. "By Zeus' fertile loins!"

In a twinkling, he was enveloped by a huge, muscular man who tackled him, sending them both flying backward out the door. They rolled around in the dirt, playfully pummeling each other until, exhausted, they sat up panting.

Urien was the first to speak. "Bern! What in the name of Zeus' shaft are you doing *here?*"

Bern grinned and rubbed his misshapen ear, the result of too many blows in too many fights. "They've got the best ale you've ever tasted in this town and I was getting a bit stiff in the joints, so I decided to stay. What about you? Been fightin' wild Welshmen all this time?"

"No, not after the first year." Urien stood up and pulled Bern to his feet. "I'd like to try some of that ale. And some of the women."

Bern looked rather sheepish, which surprised Urien almost as much as the unexpected appearance of his old friend and comrade-in-arms. Although Bern's nose had been broken numerous times, he was still a good-looking fellow, and had been as famous for the number of women he had as for his prowess in battle.

Suddenly a high, piercing female voice rent the air. "Bern! What do you think you're doing?"

Urien turned to see a small, stocky woman standing at the side of the alehouse. Behind her stood a gaggle of children, the oldest of whom looked no more than five.

"The wife," Bern whispered, tugging on his tunic like a lad. Urien raised one eyebrow, but Bern's attention was on the woman. He took a step toward her. "Lurilla, my dear, come meet an old friend of mine."

Lurilla frowned skeptically. The children peeked at Urien from behind her voluminous skirts. "Another old friend?"

"This is Urien Fitzroy."

Lurilla's face lit up with a bright smile. "Ah, him! Well, well, I'll let you two have a drink then, seein's as it's him. But mind, not many, because supper'll be ready soon." She curtsied. "I'm happy to meet you, Urien Fitzroy."

Then she turned and bustled off, barking at the children to hurry when they tarried to stare at Urien.

He looked at Bern expectantly.

"I told her how you saved my life."

Urien raised his eyebrow. "*All* about it?"

Bern flushed and his toe moved slowly in the dirt. "Of course I left out the part about us bein' in a brothel at the time."

Urien began to chuckle. "Of course!" He slapped Bern on the back. "Let me buy that drink. I've got to hear the incredible story of how you managed to get married. We all were so certain you'd die in bed—with a whore!"

"Ah," Bern said with a bit of a sigh as he led the way into the alehouse, "those days are over, my friend. Not that I miss them—much. She's a fine woman, my Lurilla. And it's a great thing to come home to a warm house, a warm meal and..." he winked "... a warm, willin' woman."

A serving wench poured them two large mugs of ale. She was shapely, but her teeth were rotten and she was easily past the first blush of youth.

"She's not in that line of work," Bern said, punching Urien playfully.

Urien rubbed his now-sore arm. "Know anybody who is?"

Bern laughed heartily. "One time I would have, but not anymore. Now, tell me, Fitzroy, how do you come to be here?"

"I went to Wales, but the man who hired me was a dishonorable snake. So I left."

"And since then?"

"Oh, I've been here and about. I went back to London, but you weren't there."

"No, by the time my leg'd healed, I'd had enough of the place. Went looking for work, and found Lurilla instead."

"I'm glad things are going well with you."

"So how'd you wind up here?"

"I heard Lord Gervais was hiring soldiers, so I thought I'd try my luck."

"And?"

"And he remembers me from that tournament at Marchebank's."

"No!"

"Yes. Anyway, since I beat that fancy-dressed fool of his that was supposed to be training the squires, he's given me the job. Seems there's to be a tournament in a month. He tells me the squires have a hastilude of their own the first day."

Bern nodded.

"I'm to prepare the squires for it, and if he likes what he sees, he'll take me on for as long as I care to stay."

His friend let out a low whistle. "By Jove's member, he must have been impressed. What about Tallentine?"

"The one I beat? He's to go back to his estate, I gather."

"Glad to hear it. He seems to think a man's first concern should be how he looks. What an ass! Saw him once at a tournament. Carried on as if he'd beaten ten armies single-handed till he realized he'd got cut. Nothing to speak of, but Jove's juice, it bled. The man was sick. All over his fine boots, too!" Bern laughed for a moment, then became more serious. "The girls in the town will be happy, too, knowin' he's not wanderin' around."

"He's like that, is he?"

Bern shrugged. "Not *yet*," he said meaningfully.

Urien wondered if that maidservant at the castle had caught Tallentine's attention, and if so, if she had been so quick to spurn the noble's advances as she had his.

But whose attention the woman attracted was not important. "How about Lord Gervais? I haven't seen him in years. I liked what I saw at Marchebank's, though."

"Oh, he's fair, and well liked. A good man. Have you seen his new wife?"

Urien nodded. Seen her. And admired her. Her astounding beauty. Her quiet, demure grace. Her lovely green eyes. Only once before had he seen a woman like her.

"The townspeople aren't sure what to make of her. She looks like an angel, I hear."

"She's very beautiful." For some reason, the image of that tempestuous shrew, Fritha, came to his mind. He changed the subject, not wishing to betray more than a casual interest in his lord's lady, or any other woman of the castle. "Now, how about you? I suppose you're one of his better fighters."

"No, not me, old friend. Taken up another business, I have."

"What?"

"Brewster. How'd you like my ale?" He laughed when he saw Urien's face. "Good, eh? Actually, Lurilla's father had the business. He taught me quite a bit after I married her, so I took it over when he died."

"Were all those children yours, too?"

"Aye. There's our oldest girl, Adelissa, then the twins, Hale and Lud, Hildegard, and Eldrida's the baby."

"By Zeus, you've been busy!"

Bern nodded, his face lit with pride. "Aye, you could say so."

"The girls have rather unusual names."

Bern grinned and leaned forward over the rough wooden table. "Lurilla said she wasn't having no names of girls I...you know. Well, that narrowed the choices quite a bit, didn't it?"

Urien smiled. He was enjoying himself, which, in his life, was a rare experience.

"Come and have some food, why don't you? Lurilla'd be pleased."

"Oh, I don't think..."

"Why else do you think she mentioned a meal at all? Come on, Fitzroy, do a favor for an old friend. There'll be hell to pay if you don't."

"Perhaps I should. Then maybe I'll believe that you've settled down and become a brewster."

"Aye."

Urien followed his friend to the back of the alehouse where the kitchen was. Lurilla moved about getting some stew and bread as Bern and Urien reminisced about old times.

They had first met long ago, when they had both been soldiering for the same wealthy lord. The two had struck up a friendship, recognizing in each other a man you could trust to watch your back. It had pained Urien to leave Bern behind when he had left for northern Wales. But Bern had broken his leg jumping out of a window when an irate husband had appeared and the money Cynric DeLanyea had offered had been too tempting to refuse, even for the sake of Urien's friend.

Unfortunately, DeLanyea had soon shown that no amount of money was worth remaining in his employ, and so Urien had left, traveling again in search of a lord needing a good fighter.

"Lurilla," a feminine voice called, "may I have some ale to take to..." The speaker paused when she saw Lurilla's guest, halting on the threshold.

"For old Peter? Certainly, Fritha, come in while I pour it. There's somebody here you should meet. He saved Bern's life once, back when he was a good-for-nothing soldier."

Urien felt like diving under the table, although he couldn't exactly figure out why.

"It's all right. I'll wait out here while there's still sunlight."

"Suit yourself. Have a seat there on the bench."

"I shall. Oh, and if I look like I'm falling asleep, I'm not. I'm just resting my eyes."

Urien tried to stifle the flush spreading over his features. It was ridiculous, to think that she could embarrass him by reminding him of his feigned sleep in the courtyard.

He was relieved when Bern began a long story about the time after London, and even more so when Lurilla took the ale outside and bid their visitor farewell.

Bern, who was slow but not stupid, had seen that Urien was affected by Fritha's appearance. "Now, don't be making any mistakes, Urien. She's certainly not in that business."

"She made it rather clear."

"Jove's orbs! You didn't . . ."

"Not exactly."

"Thank God! Lord Gervais'd have you thrown out of the town—at the very least."

"Why? Does he want her?"

Bern gave him a shocked look. "Fritha's like his own daughter. As well as being a *lady.*"

Urien kept his voice calm, as if he hadn't been trying to seduce the girl. "She doesn't dress like it. Simple enough for a man to make a mistake. Is she Saxon?"

"Aye, but she's been fostered in Lord Gervais household since she was a wee thing. He treats her like his own daughter, and she does more than most daughters. Runs the household, and the town, too, in a way."

"The bailiff's delighted to have an interfering woman in the castle, I'll wager."

Bern chuckled. "Bridgeford Wells doesn't have one of those damned nuisances."

"No bailiff?" Urien asked, surprised.

"No. Between the steward and Fritha, Lord Gervais doesn't need the extra expense—although he'd never call Fritha a bailiff, of course."

"No wonder she's not married."

"A few have tried for her, like that young Sir Tallentine." Bern rubbed his bristly chin. "He's a good-looking fellow, but she's given him nothing but sneers. Lord Gervais would never be able to get her to wed anybody but somebody *she's* willin' to have. She'd battle the notion as fierce as any knight."

"I don't doubt it."

Bern leaned back, scrutinizing him. "You said something to her, didn't you? What'd she do?"

"Practically blinded me with a honeycomb, for one thing. And lamed me, and just about castrated me, too, by the feel of it."

"Before or after you spoke with Lord Gervais?"

"The honey was before. The rest later."

"By Jove's bolt, you'd better hope she doesn't tell Lord Gervais about it, or there'll be no work for you, here or anywhere around here—and that's provided he doesn't toss you in the tower to teach you some manners."

Urien frowned.

"Still, I would think you'd have been sent off by now if she'd told him."

"Thanks for the comforting words."

Bern rubbed his chin thoughtfully. "I wouldn't have taken her for a girl to suit your fancy. You always liked your women . . . placid."

Lurilla suddenly coughed and waved her ladle at the children, who had been listening with openmouthed fascination.

Later that night, after being stuffed full of stew and nearly drowned in fine ale, Urien lay unsleeping on a pallet in the inn, thinking about Lady Gervais.

She was without a doubt the most beautiful woman he had ever seen, with hair like spun gold, skin as smooth as ivory, ruby-red lips and large, luminous green eyes. She was even more lovely than Lady Roanna, the only other woman who had moved him in the same way. Like Lady Roanna, however, this woman was married, although it remained to be seen if Lady Gervais was happily wed, as was the Lady Roanna.

What if Lady Gervais was *not* happily wed?

Urien rolled over. It was no good letting his thoughts tend that way, for it could only lead to trouble.

Finally he fell asleep, but when he dreamed, it was not of Gervais' golden-haired wife, but of a tempestuous, brown-haired wench with lips that tasted like honey.

Adela moved away from her husband, shifting slightly in the large bed.

Her lips curled with vague distaste. As usual, his lovemaking had been fast and frenzied, over before she could feel any pleasure herself.

Not that she hated him. She tolerated him, knowing that he was necessary. For a noblewoman, there was no influence to be gained except through marriage.

With Levander Gervais as a husband, she could wield enormous power, provided she manipulated him with such care that he had no notion of her planning.

She didn't consider that much of a risk. Men were easy beings for a beautiful woman to maneuver.

She already had Sir Tallentine's loyalty. All that had taken was a vague suggestion that she felt her husband didn't sufficiently appreciate his qualities, with the unspoken implication that *she* did. She had no doubt he would do whatever she asked.

Unfortunately, he had expected her to help him, too. He had come to her yesterday whining like a child, complaining that her husband had sent him away. She had explained that there was little she could do—for now.

In truth she was most displeased that Tallentine was leaving. He had only just begun a more aggressive pursuit of that nuisance Fritha.

Ever since Adela had arrived, Fritha Kendrick had been sticking her nose into everything she did, interfering and spying. Perhaps she had erred that first day when she had berated Fritha for speaking before being addressed, but how was she to have known that the girl in the plain rustic gown wasn't just another servant? Adela wouldn't be surprised if it had been Fritha's intention to trick her that day, to embarrass her.

Of course it was convenient having the girl take over the odious task of running a household, but there were plenty of other servants in the castle. It would not be difficult to find someone to take Fritha's place, someone who wouldn't question whatever the lady of the castle did.

As long as Fritha remained her husband's favorite, getting rid of her was almost impossible. Sir Tallentine had seemed about the best chance.

She wondered how she could get Tallentine back.

Sir Ollerund, the steward, was not a young man, and old men were liable to die at any time. Tallentine would make an excellent steward, at least as far as she was concerned.

Yes, that was a good idea, replacing Ollerund with Tallentine. She could manage that, somehow. That would give Tallentine plenty of opportunity to help rid her of Fritha.

He might even be persuaded, on the vague promise of more substantial gratitude, to get Fritha with child, with her cooperation or without it. That would certainly compel Gervais to send the girl away. Adela happily envisioned Fritha in a convent, one filled with nuns who prided themselves on the mortification of their flesh. Fritha would no doubt try to tell them all what to do, too—to her peril.

Perhaps Tallentine was not the best choice to seduce Fritha. He'd already had time. And, if he chose to use force, it was quite possible that Fritha would get the better of him, unnatural creature that she was.

She recalled the man in the hall, the one Gervais had pointed out as the man he was putting in charge of the training of the squires. He was a bold-looking fighter with a handsome face and a rugged body. If she were any judge of men—and she definitely was—he could overpower Fritha as easily as he had beaten Tallentine. And he would probably welcome the opportunity to earn some money, in a not unpleasant manner.

Remembering his strong arms and powerful hands was enough to make heat surge through Adela's unsatisfied body. She grew hot and desirous, the blood throbbing through her, pulsating in every limb. She shifted under the linen, moving deeper beneath the fine covers.

Adela depended on no one else, not even to satisfy the needs of her body.

Fritha peered out of the kitchen into the inner courtyard. Sir Tallentine, mounted on his white horse and surrounded by carts containing his baggage, sat despondently in the middle of the yard, waiting to depart.

She almost pitied him. The story of his defeat had spread through the town, told with snickers and grins. How galling to be so easily defeated! And yet, how funny it would have been to see Tallentine sprawled in the mud.

Stepping out, she decided the least she could do—for the sake of Lord Gervais—would be to say goodbye. After all, Tallentine was making no secret that he was most displeased at having to go. He had some powerful friends, and she didn't want him nursing more of a grudge than he already had.

With that thought, she took a deep breath and went toward him. He saw her and dismounted, a forlorn expression on his face.

"I came to bid you farewell," Fritha said, keeping her tone light and trying not to reveal the extent of her relief.

"I wish you well, too," he said sorrowfully.

"Surely we'll be seeing you soon, at the tournament?"

"Naturally I shall be here for that. And if Lord Gervais wishes my services sooner, I'll be glad to come."

Fritha nodded, ready to leave him now that she had said enough to be considered polite. She turned to go, but he put his hand on her arm. "Fritha! I am going to miss you very much."

"Well, um, we shall all miss you here, too, Sir Tallentine."

Suddenly he bent down and kissed her on the lips. A sloppy, wet kiss. It was like being licked by one of the huge hunting dogs' puppies.

It took all Fritha's willpower not to wipe her mouth with the back of her hand when he stopped. Instead, she forced herself to smile as she pulled away.

"Farewell, Sir Tallentine," she said, turning to leave.

"Until I see you again," he replied.

Thankfully, she heard him mount his horse.

Only when she had gone several steps did she realize she was walking toward the stable.

And that Urien Fitzroy, with a speculative expression on his handsome face, was watching her.

Chapter Three

As Fitzroy's look turned from speculation to mockery, Fritha's embarrassment became indignation. She prepared to march right past Fitzroy as if she had important business in the stables.

Her plan didn't work.

"The things one sees in a courtyard," he said coolly as she drew abreast of him.

She paused, surprised and angry that he had the effrontery to comment on what had happened. After all, it had not been her fault, and it was not his place to pass judgment on her.

She eyed him slowly, using the gaze that had repelled several unwanted suitors. She began at the toes of his well-worn boots, up his long, muscular legs, past his broad chest and ended at his handsome face. "Do you like what you see?" he asked, still unbelievably nonchalant.

"Not particularly." Which wasn't a lie, exactly. He was much too annoying for her to *like*.

To her chagrin, he surveyed her in the same manner.

She had had enough. First Tallentine's unwelcome kiss, and now this...this insolence. With her head held high, she strode past him into the stables—and then wondered what she was going to do. She had several tasks to either supervise or do herself, and none of them could be accomplished in the stable. Still, she couldn't simply turn around and go out. It would be as if she were admitting that his presence was enough to confuse her.

She heard a noise at the door. *Was he coming inside?*

She glanced around, but there wasn't even a stable boy to be seen. She certainly didn't want to be alone with him again.

After tucking her skirt into her belt, she swiftly and quietly climbed up into the hayloft.

She waited for what seemed an interminable time. Tallentine's cortege departed, but she waited a little longer, until she could be sure Fitzroy would be gone. Then she climbed down and went into the courtyard.

As usual the squires were marshaled in the yard, but today each one held a large, heavy broadsword, and they were formed in a circle around something or someone. A few visiting knights also seemed interested in what was transpiring within the circle.

It took her a moment to realize whose firm, embarrassingly familiar voice was shouting commands in the center of the circle, but when she did, she hurried toward the hall, hoping to go unnoticed.

As she drew near, the heavy door opened and Lord Gervais, accompanied by Sir Ollerund, came out. "Ah, Fritha, my dear! How are you this fine morning?"

She smiled at Lord Gervais. "Very well, thank you."

"I was about to take Sir Ollerund to meet Urien Fitzroy."

"Who, my lord?" she asked with feigned ignorance.

"The man I've just put in charge of my squires. Saw him once at a tournament and never forgot him. What a fight! What a swordsman! If *you* had ever seen the way he handles a lance, you wouldn't forget him, either."

Sir Ollerund smiled at Fritha. He was Gervais' oldest and dearest friend and knew as well as she did that Gervais *never* forgot a good fight, or fighter. Somehow Fritha already felt that she, too, would be unable to forget Urien Fitzroy, and not because of his prowess with a sword.

"Come and meet him. I'm hopeful he'll be able to get the squires ready in time to beat that braggart Trevelyan. I'm tired of my men dashing about like terrified rabbits!"

Fritha and Ollerund glanced at one another with suppressed smiles. Gervais and Trevelyan's rivalry at tournaments was well known, and although Gervais always sounded extremely angry whenever he talked about it, it was entirely good-natured. If Gervais were ever threatened, Trevelyan and his men would be the first to come to their aid, and Trevelyan knew he could count on Gervais for the same thing.

"I really should see if Lady Gervais needs anything..."

"She's fine, fine. Still in bed. Come on and meet this fellow. What shoulders!"

Fritha realized there was no escape and walked beside Lord Gervais.

"I was just telling Ollerund, Fritha, that Fitzroy has some ideas for training that might cost us a few coins."

"Oh?"

Ollerund nodded, his face showing that he understood that he would never be able to talk Gervais out of spending money for training soldiers. However, Ollerund also understood that it was money well spent, and money that the very wealthy Gervais could easily afford.

As they got closer to the circle, Fritha felt more and more uncomfortable. She cursed herself for ever speaking to Fitzroy as the young men parted and revealed the back of the warrior who had so impressed Lord Gervais. He stood with his feet wide apart, a broadsword held with amazing ease in one hand. And he was half-naked, from his dark hair brushing his shoulders to his narrow waist.

Fritha didn't know where to look, so she kept her gaze firmly on the ground.

"Now, if all else seems to fail," Fitzroy was saying, "you lunge at the man's pride and joy."

From the chortles of the young men, she knew exactly what he meant by that expression.

"I've never met a man yet who wouldn't jump back if he thought you were aiming there."

Lord Gervais cleared his throat. She saw Fitzroy's feet turn.

"My lord?"

"Fitzroy, this is Sir Ollerund, my steward. He's been instructed to get whatever you think the men need as quickly as possible."

"Thank you, my lord."

Fritha was surprised by his humble tone. Was this the same man speaking?

"And this is the Lady Fritha Kendrick."

"I am charmed, my lady."

Fritha glanced up, met his mocking dark eyes so at odds with his deferential tone, and looked away quickly.

"Well, what do you think of the lads, eh?" Gervais asked.

There was a short pause, during which Fritha knew the youths were holding their collective breaths.

"They'll do," Fitzroy replied, "with a lot of work."

Perhaps Fritha imagined it, but she thought they all sighed with relief.

"Good, good." Lord Gervais raised his voice. "I expect us to win the tournament. You've got a month—don't disappoint me."

Although he sounded harsh, Fritha knew the worst that could possibly happen to the squires and knights should they lose was a less-than-lavish banquet afterward. She also knew that Lord Gervais was well liked and respected, and that the young men would do their best. Hopefully, Fitzroy would ensure that their skills with weapons improved.

"Back at it then," Lord Gervais said briskly, turning to go, followed by Sir Ollerund.

Fritha, too, began to walk out of the circle, not daring to look at anyone—least of all the tall, handsome soldier with the dark eyes.

Urien Fitzroy turned back to his charges as though he had never been interrupted.

* * *

"What do you say, Bern? Would it be asking too much, do you think?" Urien rubbed his chin thoughtfully as he sat in the kitchen of the alehouse that evening.

"Naw, not a bit. I tell you, Gervais wants to win. Bad. Trevelyan and his men have beat him two times now. He won't care about the cost."

"What about that steward of his?"

"Ollerund? He's a good man—and he understands Lord Gervais. He won't make a fuss."

Urien nodded, relieved. He had worked for men who would sooner slit their own throats than spend money on weapons, claiming that their knights should provide everything. It was something new to have a generous lord.

Lurilla came bustling in, with the children in tow as usual. She looked at the heavy pot on the hearth, the contents bubbling over into the fire.

"Bern," she said fiercely, "couldn't you have moved that while I saw to the garden?"

Urien, who had seen Bern fight six men single-handed and win, watched his friend's contrite expression with amusement. "Sorry, Lurilla, we got to talkin'..."

"Yes, I know. You men get to talking and that's the end of it." Lurilla put the baby in her cradle and handed Hildegard a small doll made of grain stalks. Adelissa, who looked like a miniature version of her mother, began cutting a loaf of dark bread. "Well, at least the stew's not completely ruined. You'd best go and see how Elva's making out in the alehouse. She might need another keg tapped."

"Oh, aye." Bern was up and out to the alehouse with all speed.

"Urien, can you stay to supper?"

"I'd be pleased to," he said, quite happy to miss a meal at the castle. The food there was good, but he found it a bit of a trial to eat, between trying not to stare at Lady Gervais and catching the disapproving looks of Lady Fritha Kendrick.

"Good."

The twins began punching each other for some unknown reason. "Take the boys outside, will you, so we can get the food on?"

Urien wanted to protest, but he recognized the tone of command. With a shrug, he took the collar of a boy's tunic in each hand and marched them outside.

"Wrestling! Let's wrestle!" they cried in unison. Urien sat down under a broad apple tree. "No," he said bluntly. "I'm too tired."

"Swords! Play swords with us!"

"No."

The boys looked at each other. "Knights and thieves?"

"No."

The boys frowned. One of them—Urien thought it was Hale—came and sat beside him. "Tell us a story then."

Lud joined them, sitting on the other side of Urien. "Yes, yes! A story, with fighting and princesses and knights!"

"I don't know any stories."

The boys gave him a skeptical stare. Lud said, "You and dad was tellin' lots of stories the other night. We heard you."

"They're not for children."

"We're big!"

Urien had to stifle the urge to laugh at the boys who were not yet five years old, but he knew they were quite serious. Since he didn't know when Lurilla would announce that the food was ready, he decided a story was the best idea.

"Very well." He leaned back against the tree and tried to think of something the boys would find interesting.

"We want one about a boy," Hale demanded.

"Who fights."

"And rescues a lady."

"And makes his fortune."

"And gets to be a knight!"

"Is that all?" Urien inquired when they seemed to have exhausted their list.

"He should be good and brave and strong, too."

"Now are you finished?"

The boys' smiles beamed and they nodded, snuggling up against him.

Urien had never had children so close beside him. He found the sensation . . . not unpleasant.

"Once there was a boy—"

"What was his name?"

"Raymond. Once there was a boy named Raymond. He had no father and his mother died—"

"How come he had no father?"

"Did his dad die?"

"Raymond didn't know. Anyway, Raymond was an orphan. A farmer kept Raymond to work on his farm. He had to work very hard."

"Was the farmer nice?"

"No. He beat Raymond, and some days Raymond didn't get anything to eat."

"Ooh!" The boys' faces were full of sympathy.

"Well, Raymond decided he didn't like working for the mean farmer, so he left to—"

"Seek his fortune!" the boys cried in unison.

Urien nodded. "Yes, to seek his fortune. He became a soldier—"

"Did he like it?"

"In the beginning. It was the first time in his whole life he found something he was good at."

"How good?"

"Very good."

"Did he kill people?"

"Sometimes."

"Only if they was bad."

Urien shifted uncomfortably. "As he got older, he realized that he didn't like fighting quite so much. But he didn't know how to do anything else, so he traveled to many lands. He was always looking for something—"

"A lady!"

"A dragon!"

"A witch!"

At that moment Lurilla called them inside for supper. The boys moaned with disappointment, but Urien had had quite enough of being a storyteller, especially with that particular story. He got to his feet.

"He found his fortune, didn't he?" Hale asked, tugging on Urien's tunic.

"Yes," Urien said, walking toward the kitchen.

"And he rescued a lady and got made a knight?" Lud asked, his tone implying that if that were not the case, there was no justice in the world.

Urien sighed softly. "Yes, he rescued a lady and got made a knight."

Together they all went in to the kitchen.

Fritha, standing in the shadow of the alehouse wall, didn't move for several minutes. She had brought some old linen to Lurilla, hoping she knew someone who might need it, but had stopped when she overheard Urien.

Fritha had no doubt that Raymond's story was Fitzroy's own. Suddenly all her notions about the man turned completely upside down. He was not merely another arrogant warrior, but a lonely, ill-treated boy grown into a man with a strong will and hidden pain.

She turned and walked slowly back to the castle, the linen untouched in her basket.

Adela leaned close to her husband. "Is Sir Ollerund quite well, my dear?" she asked, concern in every syllable.

Lord Gervais glanced at his steward with some surprise, then turned to Adela with an indulgent smile. "He's as fit as I've ever seen him."

"Perhaps he's merely tired, then, my dear. He's not very young after all, and it must be quite a task keeping up with a man as vigorous as you are."

Gervais glanced at Ollerund again as he reached for his goblet.

Really, Adela thought, it was too easy to make a rich and powerful lord blush like a boy. And to plant a seed of doubt in his mind.

She brushed a crumb from the sleeve of her fine gown, the fabric as soft as goose down and the color of ripe cherries. She was looking particularly beautiful tonight, she knew, with a cloth of the same color cloaking her bountiful blond hair. Occasionally she would let the cloth slip back to expose a little more of her cheeks. If she did it at the right moment, with just the right expression, such an action could be more alluring to a man than removing a garment.

She smiled to herself, hoping that what she suspected would soon prove to be true. If she were with child, and that child was a son, her hold over Gervais would be complete. All those years of learning the ploys to win a man, learning to mask her thoughts so that men saw only what they wanted, denying herself the younger men she might have married as she waited for someone richer and more powerful, would not have been wasted.

She glanced around the hall. Fritha was there, laughing and talking with the servants like any peasant. Well, let her. She would be a disgrace at the high table. Besides, there was plenty of time to deal with Madame Mischief.

"My dear," Adela said after she surveyed the hall, "where's the fellow who's going to be training the squires?"

"Fitzroy?"

"Yes. Shouldn't he be here?"

"Perhaps he chooses to eat elsewhere."

"I don't see why he would do that. We have the finest cooks."

Gervais patted her hand companionably. "Well, he's used to rough ways, I'm sure. Maybe he feels awkward in such a fine place, with such a gracious hostess?''

Adela smiled at the compliment, then suppressed a frown at a burst of laughter from the people sitting with Fritha. "Really, Levander, I think your people need to realize we're not in an alehouse," she said with deceptive calm.

Her husband chuckled. "Oh, they're merely enjoying themselves. Fritha can make even the simplest things amusing, you know. You should hear her tell about the time we went riding and my horse—"

"I already have, my love." Adela looked around impatiently. "Are the musicians ready yet?"

Gervais nodded at the door to the upper gallery. "Here they come now."

As the musicians took their places, Adela watched for the minstrel who had arrived that day. He was a good-looking young man whose lips, she guessed, excelled at more things than singing.

Not that she planned to be unfaithful to her husband. She would be a fool to take such a risk, at least now, when he was still strong and virile. Nonetheless, a woman could dream...and ask the minstrel to travel her way another time.

Nor would she approach Fitzroy to hint at the task she had planned for him until Gervais was away from the castle for a few days. That would not be soon, for unlike many lords who traveled from estate to estate, Gervais preferred to stay in Bridgeford Wells and let the stewards from his various estates come to him. She had asked him once—when a particularly interesting young knight had arrived for a visit—if he wasn't concerned about being cheated by the stewards, but Gervais had said he trusted his men completely.

Well, she could be very patient, and Fitzroy would not be going away soon. She could tell he was too shrewd to leave such a generous lord.

Ostensibly listening to a complaint about the fish that morning, Fritha watched Adela. The woman was very subtle, but Fritha saw the way she glanced at the minstrel.

Fritha looked away, hoping she was imagining things. It could be that her dislike of her new mistress was making her see things that weren't there. At least, she hoped so. If Adela were ever to betray Lord Gervais, the knowledge would break his heart.

She stood up as the musicians began to play. She enjoyed some music, but not in a stuffy hall. Given her choice, she would rather listen to Tom and Meara sing a simple country song together, or hear old Peter talk about his dog, which he claimed was more intelligent than most people.

It was a fine clear night. She would go and visit them. Adela liked to listen to music and talk with the knights for hours before she retired. There would be plenty of time before Adela would need her.

Fritha left quietly. Outside, the air was fresh with the scents of early summer. The guards leaned against the wall casually, nodding as she passed. As she walked through the town, her steps slowed as she drew near Bern's alehouse.

She should get some ale for Peter. The elderly man stayed at Meara's, although he was no relation. Peter had no family and had spent all his life as a field worker. Now he was old and quite poor, but he always had a kind word or a funny story for Fritha, so it was no trouble to provide him with some fine ale now and then. She turned down an alley that provided a shorter way to the alehouse.

Her reasons for going there had absolutely nothing whatever to do with the fact that Urien Fitzroy hadn't been in the great hall and had probably supped with Bern and Lurilla, she told herself.

She turned down another alley. No, despite the sympathy she now felt for him, she really wanted nothing whatever to do with him. He was too arrogant, too mocking....

It occurred to her that she could smell the river. Stopping, she looked about, then frowned. She realized she had been so preoccupied by thoughts of Urien Fitzroy that she had taken a wrong turn. Now she was in a part of the town where the buildings were old, rat infested and falling down. With a sense of dread, she also remembered that some people said outlaws hid in these buildings when they came to Bridgeford Wells.

Annoyed, she took a deep breath and began to hurry back the way she thought she had come, although she hadn't been paying much attention.

She walked swiftly, telling herself that she need have no fear. Everybody in Bridgeford Wells knew her, and she knew the town well.

There was the back of the fishmonger's house, she thought with relief. I have only to reach the end of this alley and turn to my right.

Then a man stepped out of the shadows and blocked her path.

Chapter Four

"What have we here, then, eh?"

Fritha stood without moving, peering ahead and wondering who the man could be. If he were from the town, he would know who she was.

"Somethin' soft and invitin', if you ask me," a slurred, higher pitched voice said behind her.

She whirled around. A thin man dressed in a motley collection of rags slouched toward her. "Looking for somebody, out all alone?"

Fritha tried not to panic. Help would come the minute she yelled. She opened her mouth, but before she could utter a sound, a huge filthy hand clapped over her face. "Now, don't be like that."

Fritha tried to kick, but the big man who held her was very strong. She twisted fiercely, her dress tearing at the shoulder. The thin man came close enough for her to see his piglike eyes and smell the stench of his unwashed body. He was a better target. She lashed out with her feet, striking him in the thighs.

The man's companion laughed drunkenly. "Oh, I do like a woman with spirit, eh, Duff?"

"Hold on a minute. This's—" the thin one said. Then suddenly he sucked in his breath, his eyes widening.

The man holding Fritha loosened his grip, as surprised as she was. She pulled away just as Duff fell forward, a dagger protruding from his shoulder. The other man turned and ran heavily down the alley. Fritha wanted to run, but there was somebody standing in the shadows where Duff had been moments before.

"I am Lady Fritha Kendrick," she said shakily, "and if you touch me, Lord Gervais will kill you!"

"Don't worry, my lady, I have no desire to touch you."

It was Urien Fitzroy. She felt so relieved her knees went weak—but only for an instant. She cleared her throat. "What are you doing here?" she asked coolly, holding the torn seam of her dress. She lifted her foot to step past the now-moaning figure of the ruffian in the dirt.

"Did you know that fellow?" Fitzroy asked, jerking his head in the direction the other man had gone.

"Certainly not. I'm sure he's not from Bridgeford Wells. Now, if you'll excuse me, I'll be on my way."

Fitzroy moved forward suddenly, his expression intent. "I think the big one's coming back."

Fritha reached down and quickly yanked the dagger from the wounded man, which made him moan still louder. She hurried to Fitzroy's side, but when she looked down the alley, it was empty.

Fitzroy crossed his arms and looked at her, an amused but somewhat respectful expression on his face. "You weren't planning on using that, were you?"

The realization that he had been pretending the other man had returned, probably hoping to see her turn into a quivering mass of terrified female flesh, infuriated her. "I was—and I might yet, if you try anything like that again."

Fitzroy held out his hand for his dagger. She gave it to him, slapping it into his palm with as much force as she could.

He didn't even wince. "We'd better get this fellow some help, or he'll bleed to death now that you've pulled out my knife."

Before Fritha could say anything, Fitzroy lifted the man onto his shoulders and began walking toward the alehouse. "You'll live," he growled to his groaning burden, whom he carried as easily as a farmer carried a small bag of grain.

She had to trot to keep up with his long, easy strides.

"Shouldn't we take him to the guards?" she asked, trying not to pant.

"What for? He's only guilty of bad judgment, if you ask me."

"He tried to attack me, him and his friend."

"He's drunk. And you were alone, in a part of the town that's not exactly..."

"What?"

"Well, he probably thought you were a whore. I don't think he should be imprisoned for making an understandable mistake. Good thing I happened to be passing by."

"I could have managed," she said boldly, telling herself it wasn't a lie.

"Oh, I beg your pardon, my lady."

"I was going to see Meara and Tom," she replied defensively. "I've walked this way a hundred times and never been accosted before." She wasn't going to tell him she had made a mistake and gone the wrong way.

"Perhaps you've been lucky."

Fritha was about to deny that, but it occurred to her that he might be right. She had been afraid when she realized where she was, but she hadn't been prepared for what had nearly happened.

For the past few months she really hadn't been paying attention to changes going on within the town. These buildings had fallen into even more disrepair, and it could well be that men outside the law had been drawn to the cluster of empty near-ruins like flies to dung.

Instead, all her attention had been taken by Adela and the alterations to her life in the castle. Maybe other things had been changing, too—and not for the better.

A flush of embarrassment at her own ignorance spread over her features, and she was very glad it was dark. "I shall tell Lord Gervais about this. He'll soon have his men searching for that other fellow."

Fitzroy only grunted in response.

"What were *you* doing there?" Fritha asked after a few minutes.

"Looking for a brothel," he answered coolly.

Her eyes widened in amazement. It was one thing to resort to such a place, but it was another to announce it as calmly as one might say, "looking for the smithy."

Why should she let anything he said affect her in any way? "There's one on the other side of the town," she replied.

He glanced at her, and she triumphantly noticed that now *he* looked shocked.

They had reached the alehouse. Fitzroy didn't say anything to her, but called for Bern, who came out wiping his hands.

"By Jove's fiery rod, forget your weapon?" Bern asked jovially. He stopped and stared a moment, then bellowed, "Lurilla!"

They went around the back and Urien laid the ruffian on the ground. Lurilla came bustling out. "Oh, dear Lord!" she exclaimed. "Poor old Duff! What happened?"

"I was coming here to take some ale to Peter when this Duff and his friend attacked me," Fritha said. "Do you know him?"

"Well, know 'im to see 'im. He doesn't come here much. But I didn't think he was the kind to do somethin' like that. Are you all right?"

"I'm not hurt."

"He wasn't alone," Fitzroy said. Briefly he described the big man who had gotten away.

"That'd probably be Covell," Lurilla answered. "No harm in Duff—he's a bit simpleminded—but that Covell! Everybody knows he's a thief and a poacher, but he's never been caught at it."

"Does he live here, or nearby?" Fitzroy's voice was calm, but with an underlying intensity.

Bern shrugged his shoulders. "Don't think so. Couldn't say for certain, though."

Fitzroy glanced at Fritha, then turned away. He didn't ask anything more, and she wondered if he had betrayed more interest than he intended. He went toward the door.

Bern shook his head. "Maybe this will get it through Duff's head that he'd better steer himself away from Covell."

"Well, I'll bandage Duff," Lurilla said. "I think he'll be fine with a little rest." She nodded at Fritha's shoulder. "You can mend that while you're here."

"I'll take the ale to the old man," Fitzroy said.

Fritha didn't want to be beholden to anyone, but she didn't see how she could refuse. If she went back to the castle with a torn dress, Adela would be sure to ask questions. And if she found out what had happened, it would be a good excuse to restrict Fritha to the castle. "That would be kind of you," she said rather reluctantly.

Fitzroy nodded and went into the alehouse with Bern.

Lurilla fetched some linen and a basin of water while Fritha went inside and took off her dress. She mended the torn seam quickly as Lurilla washed Duff's wound. Fritha could hear the man moaning and Lurilla telling him that he was going to be all right, as long as he quit lounging about with Covell. When Duff was bandaged, Lurilla called Bern to carry him to the barn.

"He'll sleep it off in there," she said to Fritha when she came in, "but his shoulder will be plenty sore."

She checked her sleeping children, then sat beside Fritha as she put on her dress.

"How do you like Urien Fitzroy?" Lurilla asked suddenly.

Fritha tried to sound nonchalant. "He's good with the squires, as far as I can tell."

"To hear Bern talk of him, you'd think he was the greatest fighter ever born."

"Oh?"

"He saved Bern's life, you know."

"Really?"

"Aye, in a terrible fight it was. They'd come to a town and were sitting in a tavern, just minding their own business. Suddenly, this gang of ruffians jumped Bern while Urien was out fetching the horses. Bern got two down, then took a blow to his shoulder that made his right arm numb. That would have been it, except Urien took them all on and wounded every one of them."

"Good Lord!"

"Aye, what a fight that must have been! The boys've been after Bern to tell them about it every night before they fall asleep."

They both turned when they heard a sound at the door. It was Fitzroy, and as Fritha looked at him, she realized he was annoyed.

"How was Peter?" she asked.

"Fine."

"Thank you for taking the ale," Fritha said to him. "And thank you, Lurilla, for the needle and thread." She stood up. "It's time I returned to the castle. Good night."

She pushed past Fitzroy, intending to hurry home along the main road. She wouldn't tarry, because although there was some light from the nearby buildings, it was still dark enough for someone to hide in the shadows.

When she had gone several paces, she began to hear footsteps behind her. She listened carefully, not wanting to stop, all the while telling herself they existed only in her mind.

But they didn't. When she quickened her pace, so did the person behind her.

She thought the footfalls too heavy to be those of a woman. A man. Covell, trying to keep her from telling Lord Gervais? Some other outlaw, seeing a woman alone at night?

He kept the same distance behind her. Fear tightened her throat. If she began to run, she might get back to the castle before he could catch up with her. On the other hand, as she had discovered tonight, there were several dark alleys opening out onto the road. He could grab her and drag her away....

And perhaps she was dreading nothing. Perhaps the one episode had filled her with unnecessary fear. She didn't want to have to face that fear every time she found herself in the town at night.

She wouldn't.

She took a deep breath and wheeled around, her hands bunched into fists.

It was Fitzroy.

"What do you think you're doing? You scared me!"

"I'm walking back to the castle."

"I don't need an escort. I'm quite capable of taking care of myself, thank you."

"I happen to be returning to the castle, as well."

"Oh."

They walked on. He didn't say anything, but she couldn't deny that she felt safer for his company.

She was beginning to feel rather foolish, too. How must she look to him? Like a ninny who was wandering around the town without thinking about where she was going one minute, then scurrying home like a terrified rabbit the next.

Unfortunately, it was true, although it was Fitzroy's fault, in a way. If she hadn't been thinking about him, she might have seen Covell in the alley, and if he hadn't followed her like a skulking thief, she wouldn't have been so terrified.

She gave him a sidelong glance as he walked beside her. The shadows made his face more enigmatic than ever.

She *had* been rather ungracious. After all, she might have had a difficult time escaping from Covell if Fitzroy hadn't arrived.

"Did you really save Bern's life?" she asked casually, determined to sound interested but not overly curious.

They walked past a window, and in the brighter light she could easily see his handsome profile. To her surprise, his expression was almost sheepish. That made him seem much less imposing.

"You didn't save his life?"

"I did."

"Then why be embarrassed?"

"Perhaps I'm simply a modest man."

She eyed him skeptically. The way he acted in Meara's courtyard and Lord Gervais' stables refuted that estimation of his character. "Somehow I doubt that. There weren't really twenty huge brawny fellows?"

"No. Only five."

"You didn't wound them all?"

"Yes, I did."

"You're still hiding something," she accused.

"I don't have to answer your questions."

"Then I believe the whole story is a lie." She said it flippantly, trying to goad him into telling her the complete story now that she knew it was true.

"I *did* save Bern's life in a fight when we weren't expecting one."

"Of course you did. And I'm the secret daughter of Richard the Lion Hearted."

He stopped and glared at her. "Very well, my Lady Sharp-Nose. I saved Bern's life, but it wasn't in a tavern. It was in a brothel, but for some reason Bern didn't think Lurilla would find that part of the story very entertaining. Now are you quite satisfied?"

Fritha began walking away, her eyes suddenly filling with hot tears of shame that she didn't want him to see. Maybe what had really happened was none of her business, but she didn't think he would get so enraged. And he had called her "sharp-nose," too!

Fitzroy caught up to her quickly. "I don't know who you think made you the guardian of everybody, but some things are best left alone."

"I'm not the one sticking daggers into poor harmless fools," Fritha replied, knowing her words were irrational, but wanting to say something so that he wouldn't know he had hurt her.

"Oh, I see. I should have left him alone. You could have protected your honor all by yourself."

"Yes, I could have. I've done it before—and without your help."

"Perhaps you have some skill fighting off men who are drunk and want to woo you."

Woo her? How could he even think those men had *wooing* on their minds? "I suppose a man like you would call attacking a woman *wooing.*"

Fitzroy's lips tightened. If Fritha had known him better, she would have known that she had angered him. "I mean, my *lady,*" he said, his tone sardonic, "that you can hold your own against men who are thinking of pleasure and not expecting to have to fight."

Fritha put her hands on her hips. If Urien had known *her* better, he would have recognized a sign of trouble ahead. "I see," she replied calmly. "You think that because you and other louts are only thinking of satisfying their lust that it's easy for me to stop them. Is that right?"

"Yes." Urien crossed his arms. He had expected some show of gratitude, and instead she treated him no better than an annoyance, then questioned him like a prison keeper trying to extract information from a thief.

Who gave her the right to probe into his life?

What would she think of him if she knew about his past?

"I don't suppose you'd care to put that to a test?"

He had no idea what she was talking about. "What, fighting or wooing?"

"With you I'm sure it's the same thing."

"*Most* women are only too glad to have my attention."

"Poor things. They must be desperately lonely. But I meant the fighting."

"You want to fight me?" he asked, staring at her incredulously.

"Yes."

He threw back his head and laughed. He'd probably fought more men than she'd ever met in her life. "I won't."

"Afraid?"

"It wouldn't be fair."

"Do you want to concede?"

When he realized she was completely serious, he frowned. "I never yield."

"Then meet me on the riverbank tomorrow, after the evening meal when it's still light out. There's a thicket just past the mill with a clearing in the middle. You may bring any weapon you choose."

"Lord Gervais—"

"Will not know anything about it. This is strictly between you and me, Fitzroy."

He bowed with a grand flourish. "As you wish, my lady. I shall count the hours until we meet again."

And when I win, I shall demand a prize only you can give me, he finished in his thoughts as she marched ahead of him toward the castle.

The next day the squires quickly realized that their teacher was preoccupied. However, they had already learned not to underestimate his ability to catch the smallest lapse of attention on their part, so they wisely kept quiet and did as they were told. All afternoon Fitzroy worked them hard. He was also mercilessly critical of their sword handling, horsemanship, and even the way they removed their mail.

Urien was in no mood to praise anybody as he watched the squires mount and dismount, learning to do it smoothly and quickly despite the cumbersome mail.

He was still angry about last night. Fritha should have known better than to walk unescorted through such a part of town. Being a noblewoman would get her no special protection there.

In a way, perhaps she *was* special—or at least unusual. Any other noblewoman would have reported such an attack at once, with weeping and wailing and demands that the culprits be apprehended at once. Duff—and Covell, had he been found—would have been hanged with all speed.

Apparently, however, Fritha had said nothing. He had little doubt that Covell was far away by now, if he had the sense of a flea, so the soldiers would only have Duff for their trouble. It was kind of her to spare him.

And he had never met a noblewoman who would even admit that such things as brothels existed, let alone tell him where he could find one. His lips twitched at the remembrance of her surprise when he had told her the honest truth, the way her hazel eyes widened like an innocent child's, while her lips parted like a lover expecting to be kissed.

God's wounds, if he kept thinking like this, he would have to find that brothel in the middle of the day.

"Enough!" he called out, as much to stop the squires from their exercise as to stop himself thinking about Fritha Kendrick.

"Fetch your maces," he barked. He pointed at the thin squire whose name, he now knew, was Donald. "Bring mine."

As he watched the squires move off toward the weapons store, he began to wonder if it wasn't better that he hadn't had the chance to exact his revenge on that lout Covell.

Here he had a chance for steady work. Better not to risk that by beating somebody to death, tempting though it may be.

When the squires came out of the weapons store, he wondered again if he should go to the river that night to meet Fritha. She was quick-tempered and had probably challenged him with no intention of going there herself. Even if he did go, did she really think he'd fight her? He was a trained, seasoned warrior, and she was a young woman who'd probably spent her whole life doing nothing more dangerous than sewing. She had challenged him just to goad him.

Fritha was very good at goading.

He **had** to admire her courage, though. He couldn't imagine any other woman he knew who would pull a dagger out of a man and prepare to defend herself with it.

Suppose she did meet him in the clearing, fully intending to do battle with him?

By now the squires were lined up in front of him, maces in their hands. Donald handed Urien his.

"Move apart or you'll knock each others' heads off," he snapped, putting his past and Fritha Kendrick out of his mind and once again concentrating on the weapons of war.

Urien was no closer to deciding whether Fritha would be at the clearing or not by the time the evening meal drew near. He dismissed the squires, giving them time to wash before attending to the knights, who had spent the day hunting. He himself washed quickly in the large room all the squires shared and went to the great hall.

Fritha did not come for the meal. He looked around for her, but she was nowhere to be seen. He wanted to laugh. She was no doubt regretting her hasty challenge and was now too frightened to show her face. He'd go to the clearing, but she wouldn't be there.

Unexpectedly he felt a twinge of regret, until he realized he could chide her for her cowardice. No doubt her eyes would flash with passionate anger. She would probably call him a fool for going there. He would respond with feigned annoyance, knowing that he had won this strange battle.

His lips curved up in a smile of anticipation. He would enjoy baiting her very much.

Lord and Lady Gervais came into the hall and took their places, and all thoughts of Fritha disappeared for a few minutes as Urien admired Lady Gervais' beauty. Her skin was pale and smooth, almost translucent and he yearned to see her blond hair uncovered. Looking at her, he felt as rustic as a peasant standing before a queen.

Then Lord Gervais signaled him to come forward. Urien stood up and straightened his tunic. At once he decided that he would buy himself some new clothes with his first wage.

He approached the dais, aware that Lady Gervais was watching him. "Yes, my lord?"

"I've spoken to Sir Ollerund about the weapons you wish me to purchase. I will supply everything, as long as the lads don't get carried away. Simple weapons, no foolish ornamentation. Agreed?"

"Agreed, my lord. You are most generous."

"Nonsense. I want my men to be well equipped."

"Yes, my lord."

Lady Gervais had been watching her husband as he spoke, but now she turned to Urien and smiled.

He was completely certain he had never seen a more beautiful woman in his entire life. She was angelic.

He bowed and made his way back to his place, but he had no more appetite. He felt as if he'd just seen a vision.

Then the true state of things intruded into his mind. Lady Gervais was beautiful, but she was his lord's wife, and therefore forever untouchable, as beyond his reach as if she really were an angel.

Urien got up and went back to the soldiers' quarters. This was his world, a world of fighting and weapons, of hard muscles and iron, not beauty and grace. He picked up his sword and drew it from the scabbard. How many times had he used this to kill a man? He'd lost count years ago.

A woman like Lady Gervais wouldn't want a man like him.

He put his sword back and stared out the narrow window, down toward the river. The mill wheel turned slowly as the sun sank lower in the sky. In another hour or so it would be twilight.

The river. The mill. Before nightfall.

Fritha.

He turned and went outside. She wouldn't be there, but a walk would do him good. Clear his head, if nothing else.

The river flowed gently past the mill, and the wood was quiet, disturbed only by scampering squirrels and the occasional bird call. It was easy to find the clearing.

Urien looked around. The spot was about twenty feet across and deserted.

Then something moved at the base of one of the trees. Fritha Kendrick rose slowly. "I thought you weren't coming. What weapon did you bring?"

Urien surveyed her clothing. She wore the same thing she always did, a simple gown covered by a tunic slit at the sides, held in place by a plain leather belt. The sleeves were narrow, but the skirt was full. "You're not intending to fight wearing that, surely."

"No doubt you are about to suggest I remove my clothing."

"No, I wasn't, but that's an interesting idea."

She took a step forward. "If I'm going to prove to you that I can take care of myself, I should be attired in my usual garments, don't you think?"

"This is ridiculous."

"I'm going to show you that I can defend myself against any unwanted advances. What weapon did you bring?"

"I have a dagger, but—"

"Good. Prepare to fight, Fitzroy."

"Wait a moment! You don't have a weapon."

She held up her right hand. She had a wooden ladle.

"You're mad."

Without another word, she ran toward him and brought the ladle crashing down on his shoulder as she rushed past. Amazed, he put his hand on his aching shoulder and stared at her. "God's blood, that hurt!"

She crouched low, and for the first time he got a good look into her eyes. Whatever he thought of this, Fritha Kendrick was in earnest.

"Do you give up?"

"Never!" He sprang at her, catching hold of her skirt and pulling her to the ground, now as serious as she was. She hit him again with the ladle, but he grabbed her arms and twisted her wrist until the ladle fell from her hand. Then he got on top of her, holding her arms above her head with his hands. She squirmed, but he was too heavy for her to move. "I win."

She frowned sulkily. "I suppose. But I got in two good blows!"

"Can't you just admit that you were wrong? That it's dangerous for a woman to wander around the town at night, alone?"

She looked away, pouting. "I wasn't wandering. Maybe I shouldn't have gone down the alley, but I was not expecting anything to happen . . ."

As she spoke, Urien realized that he was lying on her prone body. Her full lips were enticing, her cheeks flushed, and her breathing came in soft pants.

When she stopped talking, he spoke quietly. "The victor usually gets a prize." She squirmed again, but this time it only made him more aware of her body beneath him.

"Very well. Name it."

"A kiss."

He waited for her to protest, but she didn't. "As you wish," she said. She lifted her head and pecked his lips like a chicken at corn. "There. Now let me up."

"That wasn't what I call a kiss."

Fritha blinked, then glanced away. "You're heavy," she said softly.

He put more of his weight on his elbows and let go of her arms, but didn't move off her.

"Aren't you going to let me up? You've won."

"Not till I get my prize."

"I kissed you."

"Not good enough."

She frowned, all too aware of his body on hers. But she wasn't frightened of him, even now.

He could be very dangerous, she thought as she looked up into his dark eyes, but not without good cause. She saw honesty there, and a sense of honor that would keep her safe whenever she was with him.

He was different from any man she had ever known, and she wanted to kiss him.

"I'm waiting," he said, his voice teasing but his eyes filled with passionate desire.

Chapter Five

Unable to deny the yearning in his eyes, or within her own heart, Fritha reached up and pulled Fitzroy's head down. Then she kissed him.

His lips were warm, soft and firm, and from the first touch, her body responded as if liquid flames were flowing through it, set into motion by his lips.

His hands traveled slowly, so slowly, over her arms, then entwined into the mass of her hair. She ran her hands over his muscular shoulders, aware of his body—and her own—as if they were newly made.

Then he opened his lips. His tongue brushed seductively over her mouth, sending a thrill beyond anything she had ever felt. Tentatively she responded, opening hers, feeling somehow bold and shy at the same moment.

The tip of his tongue touched hers, creating new waves of shock and delight. She clutched him tightly, not wanting this sensation to end.

Regrettably it did, when he pulled back and shifted his weight.

Fritha took a deep breath, and it wasn't because he

had been lying on top of her. It was because she had had no idea a kiss could be like that.

"Not bad," he said softly, "but I think you could do better." His smile was mocking, his eyes laughing.

Not bad? *Not bad?* She glared at him, seeing the smug, arrogant smile on his face.

She'd show him "not bad." Reaching up, she grabbed him by the neck and kissed him. She tried not to feel anything herself, but waited for his mouth to relax as she moved her lips across his.

That proved to be very difficult, for it was as if the first kiss had been but a forerunner of this one. Nonetheless, she managed to remember that she intended to pay him back for his insult.

So she bit him.

He rolled off her quickly. "God's *teeth!*"

She jumped up and snatched the ladle. "I suppose you've kissed a lot of women and I'm simply one of the multitude," she cried angrily as she swung her weapon and struck his foot as hard as she could.

"You damned devil!" he cried, standing up and stumbling. "I think you broke it!"

She dashed through the clearing. "You're not a bad fighter, Fitzroy," she called out as she ran into the woods, "but I think you could do better!"

"I don't know what's to be done with you," Adela said to Fritha the next morning as Fritha helped her dress. "The way you looked last night was a disgrace. You have a certain position to maintain. Despite your apparent affinity for the villeins, you are not one of them."

Fritha didn't respond. She wasn't about to tell Adela the reason for her rumpled and dirty garments last night. She didn't even want to be reminded of her stupid mistake. She should never have kissed that conceited, arrogant—

"I simply won't have you hanging about the town when Sir Giles arrives."

Fritha said the first thing that came into her mind, which was a decidedly unladylike curse. Sir Giles was a friend of Adela's who spent so much time traveling from one manor to another, staying at others' expense, that she doubted he had a home to go to. The last time he and his band of carousing drunkards had come to Bridgeford Wells, they'd eaten much of the stores meant for the winter months, ridden wherever they wanted without regard for the winter planting, and the girls of the town had wisely taken to staying indoors.

Adela turned to her and narrowed her eyes. "I suggest you stop talking like the peasants, too. I want everything made ready. Sir Giles should be here in about seven days' time."

"Certainly," Fritha replied, keeping her face and voice expressionless.

"He'll be staying here until after the tournament, and we'll be having a special feast on the day he arrives."

Why not, Fritha thought angrily. Adela wouldn't have to be concerned about the preparations a feast involved.

"You may go."

"Yes, my lady."

"Oh, I want some eels for supper. Make sure they're fresh."

"Yes, my lady."

Fritha hurried away, only too glad to be gone from Adela. She went out into the courtyard and hurried to the main road of the town.

Dunstan, the reeve, would probably be at mass in the town, and she could give him the news of Sir Giles' impending return. She was sure he would be just as pleased as she was.

Lord Gervais had listened with concern when Dunstan complained of the behavior of Sir Giles' men on behalf of the town last winter, but Adela had excused them all on the grounds that they were "young" and "full of spirit." The truth of the matter was, Adela enjoyed company, especially men's company. She didn't care how her guests' activities affected anybody else. Such a group was particularly unwelcome now, when the spring planting was coming on so well.

As Fritha drew near the small stone church presided over by Father John, she paused to look out over the common fields. The air was fresh with the morning dew, the birds sang from the nearby wood, and close by a few sheep munched the grass placidly. A short distance away she could see the smoke from the smithy. Somebody's baby—probably Lurilla's—cried loudly.

Fritha sighed softly. She loved this place, the only home she had ever known. Here she was a part of things, a necessary part.

She would hate to leave it. She couldn't imagine living like, well, like Fitzroy, always wandering from place to place like a stick floating down the river.

She entered the church and saw Dunstan's familiar shape. He was not tall, but stocky and cheerful for a reeve, who was responsible for making sure the villeins did their tasks quickly and properly. He had always lived in Bridgeford Wells and had married one of the prettiest girls in the town. The gossips said she was a terrible wife, however, given to making eyes at other men when Dunstan was out at the fields and—perhaps even worse—a wasteful cook. They all whispered it was a bit of a blessing that she died not long after the wedding.

Despite sundry attempts made by several of the local maidens—and their mothers—Dunstan had not married again.

"Good day," Dunstan said with a smile as she approached him after the mass.

She cleared her throat and decided not to beat about the bush. "Sir Giles is coming for another visit."

"God save us!" Dunstan muttered.

Fritha nodded sympathetically. "Perhaps you could suggest fences?" she offered weakly.

Dunstan scowled. "I'll *suggest* it, but no one's going to be pleased about this. And I think I'll warn the parents of girls." He grinned wryly. "Perhaps you should plan to stay out of sight."

Fritha shook her head. "It's tempting, but Sir Giles doesn't give me any trouble."

"Not after you blackened his eye, eh?"

"Oh," she demurred innocently, "he walked into a door in the middle of the night."

Dunstan chuckled. "The way I heard it, it was your door and your ewer. Either way, the blackguard was in the wrong place."

"I'll do my best to keep things from getting out of hand. Maybe it will rain and they'll have to stay inside the castle."

"Let's hope so."

"Is there any other news?"

"Well, we've had a few people complaining about the miller's weights again."

Fritha frowned. The old miller had died shortly after Adela's arrival, and the new one was reputed to be from her brother's estate. Since the mill was owned by Lord Gervais, he, or rather his new wife, had a say in who got the right to operate it.

Ever since Robert Purvis had come, there had been complaints that his weights were not right, but measured in his favor. However, this was a common cause of grumbling about any miller. Fritha looked at Dunstan.

"I suppose we'll leave that for now," he said after a moment. "We've no proof, and it could be people just wanting something to complain about."

"I don't think there's much else we can do," she replied. She bid him good-day and began walking back to the castle. She needed to see how the noon meal was progressing, and to tell Godwin, the cook, that Adela wanted eels. Fritha couldn't see the appeal of the things, but if Adela wanted them, they had better be on the table.

When she reached the inner ward, she heard the sound of several hoofbeats. The squires were practicing horsemanship, but something seemed rather peculiar. She looked closer. They had their hands tied behind their backs.

Sir Nevil, a plump, good-natured knight who always brought his squires to be trained by Lord Gervais' men and reciprocated by providing very fine wine for meals, was sitting in the sun watching. Fritha sidled over to him. "What are they doing?"

"That new fellow, he's a wonder. Never would have thought of that. Makes 'em use their knees, you see. Nothing else *to* use. Wonderful idea. But he's a bit of a cold pudding, eh?"

Fritha nodded, although she wouldn't ever have called Fitzroy a "cold pudding." A conceited, impudent scoundrel, perhaps, but not a cold pudding.

She could hear Fitzroy calling out directions, but couldn't see him. Then the horses and their riders moved to the right, and she saw him standing on the ground. He gestured and called out to one of the squires, but the poor lad's horse kept turning in confused circles. As Fitzroy approached the boy's horse, she realized he was limping. Not badly, but enough to tell her that he would not soon forget last night's encounter.

With a grin, she hurried off to the kitchen.

Urien caught sight of Fritha as she disappeared through one of the many doors in the main buildings of the castle. God, that vixen was everywhere, poking her nose into everything. He wouldn't be surprised if she even came into the squires' quarters.

He rubbed his leg, trying to ignore his throbbing ankle. It was swollen and painful, but he knew no serious injury had been done.

Perhaps he had made a mistake, teasing her about the kiss. In truth, although he had kissed, and been kissed by, many women, he had never experienced anything like it. It had felt as if they were melting into one another, the way two pieces of metal joined together in the heat of a furnace, bonded forever.

She had seemed as affected, too, returning the kiss fervently, and yet with an innocence that touched his heart.

If he wanted to kiss her again—and he most certainly did—he would have to let her know he repented teasing her.

One of the lads nearly slipped from his horse.

"Watch it!" Urien yelled at Donald, the thin squire whose intense gaze had gotten his attention that first day.

Enough thinking about kisses, he told himself. He would do better to watch the lads under his charge.

He began to concentrate on Donald, the youth he thought was the best of the bunch. The boy clearly came from one of the poorer noble families, judging by his garments, but the lad worked hard and had determination, which was much more important than fine clothes. "Let the horse know who's in command!" he called out.

Donald's lips pressed together and he finally got the horse to turn to the right.

One of the other lads, Seldon, sat watching with a smirk on his face. Seldon, a huge young man, obviously thought he was the next champion of tournaments. Urien had little use for vain louts who always seemed to think their brawn would stand them in better stead than skill. Men like that tended to die young and with an expression of surprise on their faces.

"You!" Urien shouted. Seldon started. "Come here."

The boy slipped off his horse with his wrists still bound and sauntered over.

"You find this amusing?"

"Well, it's not likely we'll be tied up in a battle, is it?"

"You think it's quite acceptable to smile at a fellow soldier's trouble?"

"He looks ridiculous, if you ask me."

Urien's voice went very quiet. "Do you think, Seldon, that Donald would wish to save your life after you've found him ridiculous?"

Seldon glanced over his shoulder at the other squires with another smirk. "I think it'd be more likely that I'd be saving him."

"I see. You have some skill at fortune-telling then?"

Seldon's smirk disappeared. "I'm a better fighter."

"And you don't believe you'll ever be wounded? Or your horse shot out from under you with an arrow?"

Seldon looked down at the ground.

"Now listen to me, every one of you," Urien said in a loud voice. "You have to understand that someday, the man next to you could be in a position to save your life. Or *not* save it. If you think you're invincible, go ahead. Make a jest of your fellows. But I've known of men who've been killed by their own allies in a tournament because they were fools and braggarts. And you'd best be prepared to fight all on your own, for nobody will come to such a man's aid." With a final withering look at the subdued youths, Urien turned his attention back to Seldon. "Now get back on your horse."

Seldon obeyed.

"There's one other thing I want to tell you this morning," Urien continued. "Lord Gervais has agreed to equip you all with new helms. Each one of you will report to the weapons store after the noon meal, to be measured. Now, ride one circuit around the ward and halt here, by me."

As the squires rode off, Urien saw Lord Gervais, Lady Gervais and Sir Ollerund come from the castle's chapel and walk toward him. Urien ran a hand through his hair, uncomfortably aware that he hadn't given much thought to the state of his garments that morning.

"Working them already, eh?" Lord Gervais said jovially.

"A month isn't much time, but I think they'll be ready for the tournament," he replied respectfully.

"You've hurt your ankle?" Sir Ollerund inquired.

Urien tried to suppress a blush, but he didn't think he succeeded. "Twisted it," he said brusquely. "It's nothing."

"You must be sure to take good care of yourself," Lady Gervais said. "My husband already feels you are indispensable."

She had the voice of an angel, too, soft and sweet— but perhaps too soft and too sweet, as if she were addressing a child.

"The material for the helms will be here in a few days. I think they can be ready in time for the tournament as well," Sir Ollerund said.

"Thank you," Urien replied.

"Well, don't let us stop you from your work," Lord Ollerund said as the squires approached.

"Good day, my lord. My lady. Sir Ollerund."

Lady Gervais smiled and watched as Fitzroy bowed and turned back to the squires.

He really was a handsome fellow. It would be a waste to let Fritha have him.

Perhaps she would have to reconsider that part of her plan.

Fritha watched the whole conversation from one of the kitchen windows. Fitzroy had seemed like a man with some sense, if no manners, but now she was sure he was as captivated as every other man by Adela. The way he ran his hand through his thick wavy hair as if he were a besotted youth! Of course Adela was adept at playing the helpless beauty, but it galled Fritha to know that no man seemed immune to her spell.

Well, it didn't matter. Not a bit. Fitzroy was only another soldier, albeit a very good one. He'd had a hard life, of course, but so had a lot of people. He wasn't deserving of any excuses on her part, especially when he thought her kisses worthy of improvement.

She watched him as he followed the squires. His limp was less noticeable. Maybe she should have hit him harder, she thought, her eyes narrowing.

The kitchen had grown very warm, from the baking surely. "I'd better see to the wood polishing," she said absently. "Oh, Lady Gervais wants eels for the evening meal."

"Eels!" Godwin cried.

Fritha turned to the middle-aged man who looked as if he had aged ten years since Adela had arrived with her culinary demands. She shrugged her shoulders. "Eels."

"I can't spare anybody to go running around the town asking if anybody's got any eels."

"I'll see to it then," Fritha said, going out into the cooler air of the courtyard.

For the rest of the day, Fritha supervised the various tasks necessary to the running of a large household. She checked the linens, then went to see Father John about the distribution of alms. On her way back to the castle she managed to find some eels at the fishmonger's stall.

Back at the castle she had to reprimand two maid servants for quarreling and throwing water at each other. Three of the pages came to her for new tunics, complaining that the ones they had were too small. She agreed and sent them to Sir Ollerund so that he could approve the expense.

Sir Nevil's steward arrived with two small kegs of wine and some very fine fish that would make a nice addition to the eels. Then she made sure the floors of the great hall were swept and new rushes laid down.

After that, she went to the mill to inquire about more flour for the additional baking that Sir Giles' arrival would mean. She lingered a little longer than necessary, watching Purvis measure. He glanced at her frequently, with his broad mouth stretched into a grin that made her wonder how many teeth he had. He seemed to have several more than most people. She couldn't tell if he was nervous with her watching, or trying to let her know that he liked her.

She didn't know if he was cheating or not. It was difficult to tell without getting a good look at his weights. Perhaps if she had asked him, he might have let her near them, but somehow the idea of asking him anything didn't appeal to her. She decided she would wait for another day, or a few more complaints.

The time was growing late. Adela would be looking for her to help dress for the evening meal, and she should make sure that the tables were prepared. She hurried back through the town, up the hill, through the first gate, through the second, and came to a halt as she went through the third.

Urien Fitzroy was striding across the yard directly in front of her, heading for the great hall. And to think she had managed to avoid him all day!

But she was late, and really, she shouldn't have to go through her days worrying about encountering him.

Trying not to pant like a horse that had just led a charge and to maintain a dignified posture, she began to walk toward him.

Chapter Six

As Fritha drew abreast of Fitzroy, he suddenly spoke. "I'm having a wooden ladle made for every squire," he said without turning to look at her. "A new surprise tactic, sure to astound our enemies."

His tone was perfectly serious, but Fritha thought she saw a hint of a smile.

She kept her own expression serious, even though she felt a strange mixture of relief and happiness. Ever since last night she had been telling herself that it wouldn't matter if he never spoke to her again. Now she knew she had been lying. "Be sure they're oak. It's the hardest."

"Thank you for the advice, my Lady of the Wondrous Kiss."

She glanced at him, wondering if she dare show him that she was no longer angry, and what would happen if she did. "I thought you said my kisses needed to be improved."

"My mind was momentarily addled. Or didn't you realize you had that effect on men?"

"I know nothing of the kind, sir, since I have not had your vast experience with kissing."

"That's a great pity. I shall, of course, be happy to help you gain more." He glanced at her, his enticing lips curving up ever so slightly.

"And I thought—" Holy Mother, she was squeaking! Fritha cleared her throat and forced herself to lower her voice. "And I thought you were only hired to train the squires!"

With that, Fritha hurried on her way. Either she would start giggling like the silliest servant in the hall or drag him someplace where they could be alone. Even now she felt curiously light-headed, like the time she had sampled a particularly strong wine Sir Nevil had sent.

If Fritha had not met Fitzroy in the courtyard that evening, it was very possible that she would have been able to ignore him for as long as he stayed in Bridgeford Wells. As it was, however, his unexpected comments about the kiss made her even more acutely aware of him.

She realized he had been teasing her in the clearing, which had annoyed her, but she simply had not been prepared for his sense of humor after she had nearly broken his foot. She had expected him to be rude, or sullen, or icily cool toward her, not that he would talk to her and make light of what might be viewed as something to keep silent about.

Now she felt silly for hitting him again. He probably thought her a completely foolish girl, or one with little experience of men, which was not far from the truth.

If only she knew what to do next without seeming brazenly bold! Maybe it would be best if she ignored him. Perhaps he was like this with all women. It would be humiliating to discover that this was his usual tactic when he wanted to seduce someone.

Over the next few days, however, Fritha found herself constantly watching him, or watching for him. She walked slowly through the courtyard if he was training the squires there. She always hoped he would be in the hall at the meals and was disappointed if he wasn't. If a morning or afternoon passed without a glimpse of him, she felt deprived.

She learned that Fitzroy's flashes of good humor were very rare indeed. She was most unaccountably pleased that she had been able to make him smile and knew that she wanted to make him smile again.

She discovered that while he was stern with the squires, he was just. He wasn't above demonstrating a fighting technique, even if it meant sweating like a workhorse and getting dirty, and the youths respected him for it.

She realized he admired Adela, but he never approached her and most of the time he didn't even look at her if she was near. That might mean he merely understood his place in Castle Gervais, but Fritha was pleased nonetheless.

She also paid attention to the town gossip about him. Bern had told everyone who would listen about his old friend, so the townspeople respected Fitzroy. Few ever said anything directly to him, however.

There was no gossip linking him with any women, although Bern made it clear that Fitzroy enjoyed the company of females. Fritha wasn't so foolish that she would even try to tell herself that she didn't care. She cared very much indeed.

Perhaps that was why she was so determined to have a new gown made for the feast when Sir Giles arrived. She couldn't hope to draw attention away from Adela, but everything she owned suddenly seemed old and worn and unattractive.

One day when she actually had a few minutes to spare, she went to the market and bought the finest piece of fabric she could find, with money Lord Gervais had given her the past Easter. It was a lovely blue wool, not thick, but close woven and very soft. She also bought some ribands to wear in her hair. Then she went to Meara, whose sewing skills were the best in Bridgeford Wells, and asked her to make the gown.

Meara smiled when she heard what Fritha wanted. "Who's attention might you be after?"

"No one in particular," she replied, but she blushed furiously.

"About time if you were," Meara said with a chuckle, measuring Fritha with a piece of thread. "Don't worry, this dress will make you the envy of every woman within ten miles. I've never seen a better piece of cloth."

"How's Tom?"

"Good, but he's got his head full of soldiering," Meara said with a sigh. "I'm hoping he'll see the foolishness of it and become an innkeeper like his father."

"I'm sure he will," Fritha said, and then the conversation turned to local gossip. Duff was recovering from his wound, and no sign had been seen of Covell. A merchant had sent all the way from London for Bern's ale. Everyone was dreading the arrival of Sir Giles and his men, and hoped they would keep to the castle. It also seemed most townspeople were convinced the miller was a cheat and a scoundrel.

That was the last chance Fritha had for a calm, quiet visit before the arrival of Sir Giles. Adela wanted every single garment she owned prepared, in case she wanted to wear it. She demanded that the storerooms be stocked with all manner of costly, unusual foods, and kept the cook and his helpers constantly at work. The tapestries had to be taken down and beaten, all the wood polished, and the floor rubbed with sand. Lord Gervais and the other knights went out hunting every day so that the cooks would have plenty of meat. Adela, meanwhile, stayed in her room and tried different ways of wearing her hair or her scarves or tying a belt.

To further complicate matters, Sir Ollerund fell ill. It was nothing serious, a mild stomach ailment, but Fritha couldn't help wishing he had gotten ill after the visit. No one liked to disturb him, but they needed to see him to get the money to buy what Adela demanded.

Sir Ollerund recovered in time for the day of Sir Giles' arrival, but he looked weak and old. Mercifully the day was warm and sunny, and the courtyard dry when Sir Giles and his entourage entered the castle. Fritha watched as the usual courtesies were exchanged. Sir Giles looked more dissipated than ever. He'd gotten fatter, and his drinking habits were taking their toll on his complexion.

She began to count the men in his retinue. There were ten more than they had planned for! All her calculations for food and drink were in jeopardy. With a muttered curse, she ran to the kitchen to tell the cook.

Godwin nearly had a fainting spell. "What! I don't have enough bread! There isn't time to bake more. This is terrible!"

Fritha thought a moment. "I'll go to the town and buy what I can."

"And ask Bern to send another keg. I think I can manage the meat, but I'd better make double that sauce..."

Fritha realized the cook was talking more to himself than to her and ran off to the town. It took some effort, but she finally managed to get enough bread for ten more hungry men. Then she dashed to the alehouse and got Bern to send another keg.

By this time she was hot and tired and in no mood for a feast, even with a pretty new dress. She decided to go to the woods, to a place she knew where the river flowed slowly and where a huge willow overhung the bank. A swim in the cool water would do her good, although she didn't have much time before she would have to help Adela.

She felt better the minute she reached the shade of the trees. It was good to be away from the castle and all the preparations. This would make her calmer, and less likely to say something to either Adela or Sir Giles that she might regret.

Soon she reached the familiar spot and bent down to push her way through the bushes.

Then she heard it. A low sound, deep and strange.

It was a man. Singing. Not very well, either.

Curious, she moved slowly forward, trying not to make a sound. She came upon some garments tossed on the narrow bank of the river. Someone else had discovered that the willow branches made an excellent screen for bathing. She listened more carefully.

Fitzroy. She was sure of it. She glanced at the clothes scattered around and gleefully reached for the shirt. She inched farther forward and grabbed his boots. She debated over his leggings, but decided not to embarrass him completely.

"Don't you have other tasks today, or are you intending to do my washing?"

With a gasp, Fritha looked up over her shoulder. Then down. Urien Fitzroy, as naked as a newborn babe, was standing right behind her.

She let go of his clothes and stood up, still not taking her eyes from the ground. "I...was...going to..."

"Make me the laughingstock of the town."

"No! I thought maybe someone had lost..."

"That's the most feeble excuse I've ever heard in my life."

"Good day," she said, trying to move around him.

"Did you follow me here?"

"No!"

He reached down and pulled on his leggings, to her infinite relief. "What are you doing here then?"

"I came to wash, the same as you."

"Go ahead."

She waited, but instead of leaving, he sat down.

"You're not planning on staying here?"

"You watched me. I think it's only fair that I watch you. Besides, I think the current's treacherous. I'd better stay here, in case you start to drown."

"I will not disrobe with you sitting there."

She tapped her foot impatiently, but he made no move to go. The water glistened on his bare chest, and his damp hair waved loosely about his face. She swallowed. "I see that *I* shall have to leave."

"Yielding?" He stood and pulled on his shirt. "I win."

When Urien finished tugging on his clothes, he glanced at her with a smile on his lips. Which vanished instantly. Fritha's mouth was a hard line, her eyes were flashing indignant fire and her hands were unlacing her gown. Before he could tell her to stop, she was stepping out of it.

Her body was as finely formed as he had guessed. Her breasts seemed made for a man's caress, her waist narrow, her hips slim, her legs long and shapely. He had only a moment before she turned and disappeared behind the willow branches, but that was enough.

Enough to make his blood throb with desire. Enough to make him forget Lady Gervais' beauty. Enough to make him want to stay and wait for her to come out.

He would have, too, except that she called out, "I win!"

As she waited for the feast to begin, Fritha smoothed her new gown nervously. She avoided looking at Urien Fitzroy, although she knew precisely where he was.

Whatever had possessed her! Letting him see her . . . like that! She must have been mad. Now she was too embarrassed to even look his way, let alone encounter his gaze. And tonight she had to sit at the high table, knowing that he could stare at her as much as he liked.

She didn't know what she would have done if he had been there when she'd gotten out of the water. She had waited as long as she dared as it was, and had to dress in a rush to avoid any complaints from Adela.

Finally, after what seemed an age, Adela entered, escorted by Sir Giles. Lord Gervais followed and took his seat with Adela on his left, giving Sir Giles the place of honor on the right. Beside the two men sat other visiting knights. Fritha sat at the far end of the table, where she had to endure the interminable talk of hunting.

At least the food was good, and there was plenty of everything. She would have to be sure to thank Godwin for his efforts.

When the meal finished, the tables were pushed back and the musicians came in with their tabors, flutes and flageolets.

Adela wanted to dance. It was all Fritha could do to stifle a heartfelt moan. She hated formal dances, because they felt stiff and unnatural. However, Adela loved them, especially the *estampie*. She and her partner would dance first by themselves, with everyone watching, then the couple next in rank would dance.

Fritha hoped she might be spared, but there were few ladies available. When Adela and Lord Gervais were finished, Sir Giles approached her, to her shock and dismay. She didn't dare refuse when he held out his hand, although she felt as awkward as a newborn calf when she stood up and walked with him to the space in the middle of the hall.

The worst was yet to come. When the dance was almost finished, she caught sight of Fitzroy, watching her with a knowing smile on his face.

How she wished she had never gone near the river that afternoon!

Contrary to Fritha's opinion, though, Urien wasn't trying to make her feel ashamed or embarrassed. He was thinking how pretty she looked in the blue dress and how she belonged with the knights and the ladies.

Since he had arrived at Bridgeford Wells he had become more and more aware of how popular Fritha was with the townsfolk. What he had taken for interference was, he realized, a concern for the people which should have been the model for most nobles. She listened to their problems and, together with Dunstan, who Bern said was the best reeve in the country, tried to solve them in a way that would please most everybody. She seemed capable of taking care of any and all problems that occurred in the castle, too.

Perhaps he'd been pigheaded down by the river, although he wasn't as remorseful as he might have been. He couldn't condemn himself, not when he'd gotten a glimpse of her naked body. She wasn't as beautiful as Lady Gervais, of course, but she was very pretty.

He sighed softly as Fritha danced with Sir Giles. He enjoyed their "battles," but he mustn't forget she was nobly born, if poor, whereas he was nothing but a bastard.

It would be better, he told himself, if he kept away from her.

After three days without leaving the castle, and trying to see that everything was done to Adela's satisfaction, Fritha felt even a visit from the king would not make much more trouble or work. She was thankful Sir Giles left her alone, but his men were making the servants' lives miserable. She had heard nothing but complaints from everyone.

The only good thing that had happened was that Urien Fitzroy didn't speak to her about her bath in the river. Of course she had been so busy he wouldn't have had the chance to talk to her at all. If he had been so inclined. Which, apparently, he wasn't. He hadn't so much as bid her good-day since Sir Giles had arrived.

She awoke early on the fourth day determined to get out of Castle Gervais, if only for part of a day. She dressed in her usual clothes, got her basket and went to the kitchen.

Poor Godwin, she thought when she saw the cook. This visit might be the death of him. The sweat was pouring off his face and he looked as worried as she had ever seen him.

"I'm taking some of the old bread to the widow down in the valley. Is that all right?" she asked cautiously.

"Fine, fine," Godwin muttered without looking at her.

Fritha gave a weak smile at the servants, who were also sweating and tense, and hurried out.

She glanced up the sky and frowned. There were masses of clouds on the horizon. It hadn't rained for a few days and the farmers were getting anxious, but she couldn't help hoping the clouds would stay where they were, at least until the afternoon.

She looked at them again. They were white, not dark. She would risk it. She simply had to get away for a while. She hurried out of the castle and along the road out of town. She kept looking at the horizon, and finally had to admit that the clouds were getting closer and darker.

Perhaps she should turn back, but by now she was closer to the widow's than the town, and at that moment a loud clap of thunder sounded in the sky. There was nothing to do except hurry on to the widow's.

She didn't get there before the rain started. It pelted down as if it held a grudge against the earth. A brisk wind whipped the trees until they looked like monks bending in prayer. Fritha was drenched and exhausted by the time she arrived.

The widow was glad to see her and fretted over her guest's wet state. She hurried about the small cottage, fetching dry linen and warming some ale on the tiny hearth.

She pressed Fritha to remain for the night. Fritha, knowing that Godwin could tell Lord Gervais where she had gone, felt she had little choice but to accept the widow's hospitality when the storm showed no sign of abating.

She hoped Hylda, one of the older maidservants, would be able to remember everything for the meals, and keep a stern eye on the pages. The boys could be so careless.

Despite the widow's efforts, and her own to make the best of the situation, Fritha did not sleep well. She kept worrying about things at the castle, and when she finally did doze off, she had a very vivid dream featuring a naked Urien Fitzroy pulling her into the river. She awoke with a start, unable to go back to sleep.

* * *

The next morning was damp and chill, but Fritha was ready to leave as soon as it was light. She thanked the widow and left, walking swiftly at first until she was warmed from the effort, then slowing her steps a little so that she could maintain a brisk pace without tiring herself.

She was still far from the town when she heard the sound of several riders. Not knowing who might be abroad at this hour, she ducked into the shelter of the trees lining the road.

It was Sir Giles and his men, mounted on their horses and with their huge hunting dogs on leads. Obviously a little wet weather wouldn't stop them from the pursuit of pleasure. She stepped back onto the drier road and waited for them to pass.

When Sir Giles saw her, he pulled his horse to a stop. His men, following behind, did the same. "Good day, my lady," he said with a smile. "We were beginning to be concerned for your safety."

"I stayed the night with the widow. I'm surprised you're out hunting, Sir Giles. The trees are very damp, and the ground, too. Your dogs will have trouble with the scent."

A strange expression passed over Sir Giles' face. Then he smiled and glanced at his men. "Oh, I think today we shall have a fine hunt."

"If you say so. Now, if you please, I must be on my way."

Sir Giles didn't move, nor did his men. "Would you care to join in our hunt, my lady?"

"No, thank you. I have many things that I must—"

"But Lady Gervais said you would ensure that our stay would be a pleasant one. I think, in the interest of courtesy, that you must join us."

"Perhaps some other time, Sir Giles, when I have a suitable mount."

"I had another task in mind for you," he said, making his horse move closer to her. He glanced back at his men. "We're tired of chasing after dumb beasts. I think we need a more intelligent quarry, don't you, gentlemen?"

They nodded and smiled—and suddenly Fritha was very frightened. "I really must be on my way, if you please."

"Indeed. By all means." He smiled, but he hesitated before making room for her to pass. She hurried away from the mounted men.

As she went down the road, she heard them dismount.

Then she heard Sir Giles say, "I don't think it would be fair for us to be on horses and our quarry on foot."

Fritha's heart began to pound. Surely he didn't mean to chase *her*. She quickened her pace. He wouldn't dare. She was the ward of Lord Gervais.

Now she was almost running, straining to hear if anyone was following her. She thought she heard something and dashed off the road into the trees. She ran as fast as she could, too frightened to think clearly. Sir Giles could be cruel, she knew. She didn't want to find out if he was making a joke at her expense or not.

She caught sight of a horse. Without stopping to see who it was, she turned and ran another way.

The man on the horse began to follow her. Terror, nameless, formless terror made her run as fast as she could until she tripped on a tree root and fell with a thud onto the soft earth of the woods.

"Don't touch me!" she cried as a hand reached down to pull her up.

Chapter Seven

"Fritha!"

One look at Fritha's pale, terrified face filled Urien with burning, intense anger. He knew that fear in a woman's eyes, and he would gladly kill the man who had put it in hers.

But that could wait. For now, he helped her to her feet. Her chest heaved as she drew in deep breaths. Obviously she had been running fast and for some distance.

"What happened?" he asked, taking off his cloak and putting it around her. He had to resist the urge to wrap her in the warmth of his arms, as well. If he had not been so recently reminded of the differences in their rank by the sight of her dancing with Sir Giles, he might have. But instead he stood an arm's length away.

He looked at her carefully. She had been badly frightened, but he didn't think she had been hurt, or worse. Nonetheless, he was very glad he had decided to go riding while the squires polished their armor.

"I was going home," she said. "I'm . . . I'll be all right."

He went to his horse and got a leather pouch containing a wineskin and a small loaf of brown bread.

She shook her head and glanced around nervously. "Please, take me home."

"If you like. But have some wine to warm you. I don't think anyone else is nearby."

Lowering her head, she took the wineskin without speaking and drank a small sip. Now she seemed very tired and lost and a little unsure of herself—different indeed from the confident, proud woman who seemed capable of making sure all went well in a large castle, and a town.

He wanted desperately to feel her body close against his, to hold her safe against the world, but now he was unsure of the way she would respond to such a gesture, and of his right to do it.

So he made no move toward her and instead tried to think of something to say to take the fear from her eyes. "I assume you didn't have a ladle about you."

She lifted the corners of her mouth in a wan smile. It was little better than a frown and he found himself wanting to kiss her apprehension away. He took one step closer to her.

"I'd like to go home now."

He ignored the pang of disappointment. "As you wish."

Before she could protest, he lifted her up and gently put her in the saddle. She was light in his arms, as if she belonged there.

He gathered up the reins and began to walk back toward the town.

He heard Fritha sigh and glanced up to see her wipe her eyes. She was trying not to cry, and somehow he found that more touching than weeping.

"What happened? Who frightened you?" he asked, hoping she would tell him.

"I was on my way home when Sir Giles and his men met me. They didn't do anything..."

He looked over his shoulder, but her gaze was fixed on his horse's mane.

"I don't know if he was merely jesting," she said softly. "He said that he was tired of chasing dumb beasts." Her voice sank to a whisper. "I thought he was going to chase *me*."

Again anger flared within Urien. If Sir Giles had appeared at that moment, he wouldn't have lived five minutes longer.

After a short pause, Urien said, "He wouldn't dare hurt somebody Lord Gervais cares about, and you're a—"

"A lady?" The bitterness in her voice surprised him. "I may have been born a lady, but I'm a poor one. It would be easy enough for him to make sport with me."

"Perhaps he was drunk." It would be a shoddy enough excuse, but it might be true. It didn't take a wise man to see that Sir Giles spent most of his waking hours the worse for wine.

"I don't know. But the look on his face..." She paused and gave a ragged sigh. "I suppose I was foolish."

"No, I think you were wise," Urien said, determined that she not blame herself for Giles' behavior.

In fact Urien was beginning to blame himself for arriving so late. If he had come upon Giles when he first encountered Fritha, the man wouldn't have had the opportunity to terrify her. "I wouldn't put it past a man like Giles to hurt you and then claim it was all a jest," he continued. "You'll tell Lord Gervais about this?"

"No! Lady Gervais will probably claim I'm trying to discredit her friends. I don't want Sir Giles to take offence, either. After all, I may have been wrong."

Urien was amazed at the intensity in her voice. Why should she try to excuse Giles? "I don't think any woman would be mistaken about something like that. Surely Lady Gervais would know you weren't simply trying to discredit the man." Why indeed, unless . . . "Or perhaps *you* don't want to see him disgraced."

"Huh!" she sniffed, and he was absurdly pleased— and not just because the sound told him she was over her fright. "Nothing would give me greater pleasure than seeing that man disgraced.

"Unfortunately, Lady Gervais likes him as much as she *hates* me, so she would no doubt think me capable of lying."

He looked back at her again, not prepared for the animosity in her tone, or her accusation. Lady Gervais certainly seemed a kind, demure gentlewoman, in every sense of the word.

"You think I'm wrong to dislike Lady Gervais?"

"I never said so."

"You don't have to. But you're forgetting I know her better than you do."

He shrugged his shoulders. He wasn't about to get into a discussion of Lady Gervais.

"I'm not jealous of her, if that's what you think."

He glanced back at her. He hadn't been thinking that, but it would explain the vehemence in her voice when she spoke of Lady Gervais.

"I'm not! As if I'd want to spend all my time thinking about my looks. She neglects everything except her clothes and her hair or her perfumes. She doesn't even bother about distributing the alms."

"Why should she?" he asked, voicing what he perceived as the truth. "You do everything, anyway."

"What do you mean?"

"I simply meant that there's no need for Lady Gervais to do anything, since you seem intent on running things yourself."

"Stop this animal," Fritha demanded. She slipped out of the saddle and walked toward him.

He saw her anger. That was better than fear, except that she was angry at him—when he had only said what was obvious to anyone who lived in Bridgeford Wells.

"So you think I enjoy having to make sure things go smoothly at the castle?" she demanded.

He shrugged and searched for an answer to her question. "I suppose it pleases you to think the whole place will fall into ruin without you."

Her eyes flashed with indignant fire and he thought she was going to protest, but instead she tore off his cloak, tossed it at him and began walking away.

He caught the cloak and hurried after her, grabbing her by the shoulders and turning her around to face him. She wiped her face, but not before he realized that she had started to cry. "If you don't mind," she said, her voice quavering a little, "I'd like to be on my way."

"I didn't mean to make you cry," he said softly. Her reaction to his words surprised and upset him. Apparently he had found the weakness in her armor.

"You didn't," she said with a trace of her fiery temper. "I . . . I'm just exhausted, that's all."

He put the cloak around her again, not moving away. Then he reached out and brushed a tear from her cheek. "I can understand how hard it might be to give up your command to somebody else," he said quietly.

Suddenly he was filled with a need that was more than simple desire, although desire was certainly a part of it. He wanted to protect her, and share her confidence as he was now, to experience an intimacy he had never known before.

It was a need so intense that it shocked him, and created a sense of undeniable dread. For so many years he had depended on no one but himself for everything except the most basic needs of his body.

He stepped back. Dependence was a weakness a man like him could not afford. He must never forget that he was forever alone in a world that had not wanted him from the day he was born.

And yet, as he looked down into her hazel eyes, he began to hope that he was wrong. That if he gave in to the overwhelming impulse to take her in his arms, she would respond with a willing heart.

Fritha looked into his eyes and saw that he meant what he said. His pity would have been easy to dismiss, but his understanding was not.

His gaze was so earnest she felt she had to be truthful with him. "I shouldn't angry with you. Perhaps you're right. It's just that . . . that I don't ever want to leave Bridgeford Wells." She tried to laugh a little, but it came out like a cross between a sniffle and a sigh.

"When you marry, you'll have to leave," he said.

"I shall never marry if I must leave my home."

"Does the town mean so much to you, then?"

"It's my home. And the people here are important to me."

"Oh."

She heard something almost wistful in his tone. She remembered the tale he had told Bern's boys and realized that Urien Fitzroy had probably never had a home, or anyplace remotely like one.

His gaze held hers so that she couldn't look away. Nor did she wish to. "Lord Gervais hasn't betrothed you yet, has he?"

"Not yet."

"Then you have no cause for fear. He'll choose someone you will come to care for."

That was not what she had expected—or hoped—he would say. Perhaps she had only been seeing what she wished to see in his eyes. "I'm afraid the choice will made by Adela," she answered. "And she won't care who it is or how they'll treat me, just so long as I'm gone."

"You must be mistaken." He turned and picked up his horse's reins.

Ignoring a pang of disappointment, she began to walk beside him as they went toward the main road. "At the moment, Adela seems to favor Sir Tallentine for my future husband."

Urien's steps hesitated for a moment, but when he looked at her, his expression was cool and sardonic. "Perhaps I should have killed Tallentine when I had the chance."

If he wanted to discuss her marriage as if it were of trivial importance, so could she. "You would have narrowed my choices, of course, but I would rather die than marry a fool like that."

"That shows you have some sense."

"I suppose I shall have to choose sometime, or go to a convent."

"Tell Lord Gervais how you feel. Tell him you don't want his wife to choose for you."

"Tell him that I don't trust her?"

"Are you sure you're not mistaken about Lady Gervais?"

She gave him a skeptical look. "I don't think so." She frowned, then decided to be honest with him. She wanted him to understand. "Lord Gervais' happiness is important to me, and he is happy with Adela. I won't spoil that by coming between them. I can only hope that he'll see that I'm needed in Bridgeford Wells."

"But then you may never have a husband."

"Perhaps that would be a small sacrifice."

"Would it?" He stopped and looked at her, and she knew she had not been mistaken before. If anything, she had underestimated the power of his emotions.

For the first time in her life, Fritha felt that not marrying might be a very great sacrifice indeed.

It also occurred to her that she had been speaking of things she had long kept to herself, not wishing to share them with anyone else. But today, here, telling her fears and hopes to Urien Fitzroy had seemed as natural as breathing.

When he bent down to kiss her, that seemed as natural as breathing, too. And as necessary. His lips touched hers gently and his arms moved slowly around her, enfolding her in an embrace of warmth and tenderness that was like coming home.

A crow flew up into the sky, its harsh call breaking the silence, and their kiss.

"We should go," he said softly.

"Yes," she agreed, but even as she said it, she was reaching up for another kiss. How else could she tell him how much she cared for him? How much she valued this time with him?

They were from two different worlds, but she knew that no longer mattered. All that mattered was that when she lifted her face for a kiss, she was reaching out of her lonely life of bustle and cares to touch his lonely life of weapons and battles.

There was nothing gentle or cool or calm in this second kiss. His lips burned upon hers, their movement filled with a passion that almost overwhelmed her as her body and heart responded like tinder to a spark.

This time she broke the kiss, almost frightened by the intensity of the feeling that had burst into being within her. But she did not want to stop holding him, so she laid her head on his chest.

"We should go," he whispered.

He was right. If they didn't leave now, she might be tempted to... Might be? She already was.

But it would be wrong to give in to the needs of her body. What she felt was glorious, without doubt, but it was too new and confusing. Urien Fitzroy had come into her life without warning, unsettling the routine of her days more thoroughly than Adela ever could.

Before, all she had known was the determination to stay in Bridgeford Wells and watch over Lord Gervais to see that his new wife didn't hurt him.

Now, she couldn't be sure what her life would hold.

She let go of him and moved away. He said nothing as they began to walk again, but he took her hand in his.

She knew, with quick, intense happiness, that she had never felt as loved as at that moment.

When they were close enough to see the town through the trees, she glanced at him. "I don't think we should go into the town together. It will only make gossip."

He let go of her hand. "As you wish."

She was surprised at the hard expression on his face. "I don't want people to talk about us."

He nodded without looking at her. "Oh, no, my lady. We mustn't have that."

She frowned. "No. I don't want anybody to know." She didn't want to be the subject of endless speculation. She smiled at him, but he moved away.

"Please, my lady. We mustn't give people any cause for gossip."

"Raymond, you don't understand—"

"Of course I do."

His expression was so cold and distant Fritha began to wonder if she had been mistaken about him, and about what he felt for her.

"For a while I allowed myself to forget what I am," he said. "But rest assured, *my lady,* I am well aware

that you are a lady—and I am nothing but a bastard.''

Quickly he mounted his horse and rode off through
the woods.

She stared after him, pulling his cloak around her.
She cared nothing for his past, but she realized that *he*
did.

Adela turned away from the window toward her
husband, who was sitting on the dais. Dunstan, the
troublesome reeve who was always bothering them
with some complaint or other, had just left, along with
Sir Ollerund.

"Sir Ollerund is still looking far from well," she
said sympathetically.

Gervais reached down and scratched the head of one
of his hounds. "Oh, he'll be well soon."

"I hope so."

Adela toyed with the dangling end of her gold link
belt. "Sir Giles tells me he's thinking of taking a
wife."

"Maybe that will keep him at home," Gervais
muttered.

His wife turned to him sharply. "I can see that the
reeve has upset you, my dear," she cooed as she went
to the table and poured him a goblet of wine. "If it
wasn't Sir Giles, they would be complaining about
something else. I think they spend their evenings
dreaming up grievances. I really do. And it isn't fair."
She put her hand on Gervais' arm. "After all, you're
the best lord in the whole country."

He smiled at her indulgently, then took a drink of
wine.

"I think Fritha could do a lot worse than Sir Giles."

"Fritha—and Sir Giles?"

"Yes." Adela stifled an impatient sigh. "She could do worse."

Gervais snorted. "She could find a lot better."

"Well, he wants a wife and Fritha needs a husband. Besides, I think Sir Giles would be willing to overlook her lack of dowry."

"I'll give her a fine one."

"You? That's very generous, my darling, but why should you? You didn't even like her father."

"That's true enough. But I care for Fritha as if she were my own. I can afford it."

"You are, without doubt, the most generous man I know. I believe I fall more in love with you every day." She kissed him lightly on the cheek. "However, if you don't favor Sir Giles, there is Sir Tallentine. He is still quite smitten with her."

"Is that why you were so insistent about inviting him back?"

Adela smiled and lowered her eyelids as if she were blushing. She could look as guilty as a maiden caught eyeing a man's body, and she knew that always had an effect on her husband. "You know me too well, Levander," she said. "I want everyone to be married, I suppose, since my husband makes me feel so happy."

"In that case, I'm glad I invited him." Her husband grinned like a boy. "But I don't think Fritha cares for him, and I still think he'll pay more attention to his garments than any wife."

"I'm sure Fritha can be made to see his merits—he is very clever with his money, my dear. Besides, she mustn't wait too long, or people will say she's getting *old.''* She made a little sigh. "She does deserve a household of her own, although I don't know how we'll manage without her. I shall be sorry to have her leave."

"We all will. But you're right."

"Then you'll think about Fritha's marriage?"

"I promise I'll give it some thought."

Adela wanted to stamp her feet with rage. He was always "thinking about" Fritha's marriage—and never deciding anything.

Gervais patted his wife's arm. "Maybe it's time something was decided. It seems like only yesterday she was running around here, getting into mischief."

Adela smiled, feeling the time had come. "Soon you shall have children of your own running about."

Gervais stared at her as she nodded slowly. "It is a bit too early to announce to everyone, but I believe I am with child."

He jumped to his feet and enveloped her in a crushing embrace.

"Be careful, my dear!" she cried, pushing him away gently. "The baby!"

Gervais smiled and loosened his hold as she submitted to his kiss.

Fritha came banging into the hall and stopped when she saw the tableau before her.

Adela moved away from Lord Gervais and smiled at her with all the warmth of a dead eel. "So, you've finally returned after leaving so unaccountably yesterday. We were beginning to fear that the wolves had gotten you."

For a moment Fritha was tempted to say that she had barely escaped from another kind of beast, but she held her tongue and looked at Lord Gervais. He was . . . beaming.

"Good morning, Lord Gervais," Fritha said, smiling sincerely and wondering what had happened during her absence. "You've had good news, my lord?"

She stopped smiling when she saw Adela's smug, self-satisfied expression.

Lord Gervais said, "It's early to tell, but we can let you in on the secret, Fritha. Adela is with child."

"I'm very happy for you, my lord," she said after a short pause. She *was* happy for him. But, oh, the look of triumph on Adela's face, as if she had conquered the world. "All my best wishes, my lady. Now, if you'll excuse me, I must change my clothes and be about my duties."

"Adela and I have been making plans for you, my dear."

Fritha tried to keep any expression at all from her face. "Oh?"

"We both feel we're being a little selfish keeping you here. It's time you had your own household, and perhaps even children of your own, eh?"

"Yes, yes, of course, my lord. But there isn't anyone I . . ." Her voice trailed off. There *was* someone, but he had left her angrily, apparently convinced that she was ashamed of their feelings for one another. Right now all she wanted to do was find him and try to make him understand that his past was surely unimportant to everyone who knew him, especially her.

"Sir Giles has expressed an interest," Adela said.

"Sir Giles!" Fritha pressed her lips together, determined not to say anything more, but she would die before she would marry him.

"Well, no need to be in a hurry," Lord Gervais said kindly. "There'll be many fine young men at the tournament, Fritha."

She nodded. "I really should get on with my duties now, my lord."

"Of course, my dear."

"Take care to keep our little secret," Adela said sweetly as Fritha hurried from the room.

Urien took his horse to the stable, removed his saddle and pack and began rubbing the animal down briskly.

He should have just brought Lady Fritha Kendrick home. He shouldn't have talked to her or listened to her troubles. It shouldn't have mattered that she seemed to want to talk to him.

And he certainly shouldn't have kissed her. For a moment he had allowed himself to forget who he was and who she was. Instead, his kiss had conveyed all the feelings he had tried so hard to hide. The tenderness she aroused in him, as well the passion. The joy he felt when he was with her, and the hope that there could be more for him than weapons and fighting and death.

He told himself he had simply fallen under the spell of an intimate conversation in the woods.

He wouldn't go near her again, not even to find out how she knew his name was really Raymond. Otherwise, she might be able to break his heart as surely as an opponent could shatter a shield if the lance struck at the right place.

He tossed the brush onto a bench and strode out the door. He heard loud, half-drunken voices and turned to see Sir Giles and his men come riding through the gate into the courtyard.

He waited.

When Sir Giles dismounted, almost stumbling, and obviously drunk, Urien walked up to him.

"If you ever frighten a woman like that again, I'll kill you," he said, his voice low and filled with cold calm.

Startled, Sir Giles drew himself up, his face reddening. "I don't know what you're talking about, you . . . you—"

"I will kill you."

"You bloody peasant, who do you think you are, to talk to me like that . . ."

Urien turned and walked toward the squires' quarters, ignoring Sir Giles. The man would bluster and rant, but Urien knew he need have no fear. Such men were bullies and cowards and Sir Giles would know that Urien meant exactly what he said.

Urien pushed open the door to the squires' quarters and stopped, crossing his arms. "What's going on?" he demanded, looking at the flushed, guilty faces of the lads.

When no one spoke, he stared at them one by one, his gaze finally coming to rest on Donald, whose cheek was swollen. The youth would also have a black eye before the night was over. "Well?"

Donald swallowed hard, but his gaze didn't waver. "I fell," he said.

Urien didn't believe it for an instant, especially when he saw Seldon hovering in the back, trying to avoid notice.

"Is that all you're going to say?" Urien asked, his voice as cold as a snow-covered rock.

"Yes," Donald said.

"Then to teach you not to be so clumsy, you will put on all your armor and run ten times around the courtyard. Do you understand?"

"Yes, sir."

"Now go."

"Yes, sir."

"Seldon!"

"Here."

"You're getting too thick about the stomach. I think you should do the same."

Seldon's face fell, but he didn't protest. "Yes, sir."

"In full mail, too."

"Yes, sir."

Then Fitzroy stalked out again.

"That bloody lout!" Seldon muttered as he drew on his mail. "Who does he think he is, to order noblemen about like that?"

"I suppose he thinks he's in charge of us," Donald answered, by now fully clothed in mail hauberk, boots, surcoat and cowl.

"Shut your mouth or I'll hit you again."

"Try it."

"I will!"

Donald stood and waited until Seldon was dressed. "Well, come on then. Hit me."

Seldon would have been an idiot not to realize that Donald, now dressed as if for battle and with a fierce, hungry expression on his face, would not be so easy to beat this time. "You're not worth the bother," Seldon said, pushing past the thin youth and going out the door.

Fitzroy, Seldon thought as he began running and the weight of his armor made him sweat and pant, Fitzroy was another matter. Perhaps the great warrior should heed his own advice and not make enemies before a tournament.

Chapter Eight

Fritha drew on her tunic, then glanced out the window as Seldon and Donald went running past for the third time. She knew this was one of Urien Fitzroy's methods of punishment, so he must have come back from his ride and found something amiss.

Then the door to the squires' quarters opened, and she watched as Urien stepped out the door.

Quickly she tied her belt and watched as he went toward the gate. Ignoring her nagging conscience, she picked up his cloak and hurried out of the room, determined to speak with him even though she hadn't yet gone to the kitchen to check on the progress of the evening meal. Nor had she seen to any other tasks. Right now it was more important to talk to Urien, wherever he had gone.

As she passed by the stable, she heard the unmistakable loud, slurred voice of Sir Giles. Her heart began to pound. Obviously he and his men had returned, as well. She began to walk quickly, but Sir Giles appeared at the door just as she went by.

She hoped she could ignore him. Instead, to her dismay, he called out to her. She considered pretending that she hadn't heard him, but decided that would look like weakness. "Yes, Sir Giles?"

"My lady, it seems that I made a terrible blunder this morning."

If she hadn't been so terrified by his "blunder," his contrite expression might have been amusing. But he had frightened her very much, making her feel as if she were of no more value than an animal.

With a sudden flash of insight, she knew that Urien must have been treated that way for most of his life—and she loved him even more.

"I didn't mean to frighten you. You must understand that."

She didn't say anything, wanting only to get away from him to find Urien.

"And I trust you'll tell that man Fitzroy that there's no need to get in such a muck sweat. I meant no harm."

So, Urien must have said something to Sir Giles. Her heart soared with the hope that she could make him see that all she cared about was *him,* not his parentage.

Filled with the confidence that feeling gave her, she smiled slowly. "Well, Sir Giles, I can only say that Urien Fitzroy's known to have a terrible temper. There's no telling what he might do if it were aroused. If I were you, I would keep well away from him. And me, too. He's not very clever, you know, and he might not understand that you were not serious."

Sir Giles nodded rapidly. Or as rapidly as a drunk man could. "Yes, yes. I'll do just that."

"Good day, then, Sir Giles."

"Good day."

She hurried across the courtyard, hoping Urien hadn't gotten too far ahead. She had even more reason to talk to him now. She wanted to thank him for making Sir Giles as frightened as she had been.

Urien was a far way down the main road of the town and Fritha had to suppress the urge to run after him. Fortunately people were used to seeing her walk at a brisk pace, and he didn't seem to be in much of a hurry.

When she was near enough to touch him, she glanced around. Nobody was watching.

She grabbed his arm and pulled him into the nearest alley.

He turned to her with a glare, lifting her hand from his arm as if it were poison. "What do you want, *my lady?*"

"I wanted to thank you—"

"Consider it done."

"And to explain about—"

"You don't have to. I'm no fool."

"It's just that—"

"That a lady shouldn't be linked to a bastard commoner, not even by gossip."

"That's not—"

"And even though I'm good enough to kiss, that's all I'm good enough for. Now, if you'll pardon me, *my lady.*" He snatched his cloak from her hands and began to walk away.

"Let me finish!"

He hesitated, turning toward her slowly, a cold expression on his face. "There is nothing more to say. You've had your fun with me."

She stared at him. Didn't he know what she felt? Couldn't he see it in her eyes? Feel it in her kiss? "I wasn't having *fun.*"

"No? I was simply a challenge then, I suppose? Well, I see through your little game now. You may consider your attempted seduction a failure."

"I wasn't trying to seduce you!" she protested, blushing.

"No? Then why did you take off all your clothes in front of me down by the river?"

His eyes were full of such scorn that it made her square her shoulders with defiant pride. "You wouldn't leave."

"And it was so very important that you bathe? Please, my lady, I'm not stupid."

"Perhaps you've been trying to seduce me," she said angrily. "Only I'm not such easy prey, not even for a great lover like you!"

"Perhaps you're so jealous of Lady Gervais that you'll do anything to attract a man."

That was the ultimate insult. That, after everything she had told him, he should still believe she was jealous of Adela! She drew back her hand, ready to slap his insolent face with all her might.

He saw her gesture and grabbed her arm, his grip as strong as steel, pushing her back until she was against the wall.

"What are you trying to do?" she said through clenched teeth. "Make me beg for mercy?"

Without a word, he dropped her arm as if it were molten metal and marched away, leaving her staring after him.

The look that had come to his face! Somehow, her words had wounded him far more than any weapon.

What was she to make of him? He had turned on her with such animosity, she could hardly believe he was the same man she had walked with this morning.

Apparently he was now determined to have nothing more to do with her—yet she had been able to hurt him with her impetuous accusation.

She frowned. She had spent the past year trying to avoid having someone control her life, and now she was letting Urien Fitzroy's puzzling emotions worry and influence her.

No more. She would concern herself only with the more important matter of protecting Lord Gervais and her friends from Adela's machinations.

She squared her shoulders and turned toward the castle. Urien Fitzroy could go to the devil.

"By Jove's jumping one, you look like you've been tortured by the infidels," Bern said, setting down a tankard of ale. "What's happened?"

"Nothing."

Bern leaned forward and whispered so that Lurilla, setting out the bowls of soup, wouldn't hear. "Then don't look like you've lost your balls, man."

Urien forced himself to smile, although he felt more like fighting ten men single-handedly.

He certainly didn't feel like returning to the castle. Not tonight. Not ever. If it wasn't for the fact that Lord Gervais paid ten times any wage he'd ever earned, he would have packed his few possessions and left Bridgeford Wells that very night.

He had let himself feel too much for Fritha Kendrick, allowed her inside the armor around his feelings he had carefully constructed over the years. She—or rather, the look in her lovely hazel eyes—had weakened him so that he could not resist the need to touch her, or kiss her.

Then she had forcefully reminded him of the great shame of his past. His bastardy was bad enough, even though that was not his own doing. But the other was worse, much worse.

He had hoped that if she was not ashamed of his lineage, she would forgive him the other, too. Only she had shown him that she was so conscious of his parentage that she didn't wish to be seen with him. It was better that he found out her true feelings before he was tempted to tell her all.

"So, how's the training going?" Bern asked.

"Fine."

"You'll be ready for the tournament?"

"Yes."

"Well, my lad, don't talk too much or you'll wear out your tongue."

Urien glanced at Bern. "I was thinking. Sorry."

"Wish Bern would think more," Lurilla said with a smile as she served them. "Talk less, think more."

"If I'd thought too much, maybe I wouldn't have married you," Bern said with mock gravity.

Lurilla hit him on the head with a handy loaf of bread.

Hale and Lud burst into giggles, then went back to playing with miniature versions of quarterstaves.

Urien eyed them, glad to have something to take his mind from Fritha, and women in general. "Bern," he said thoughtfully, "how would you like to show the squires a thing or two about fighting with a quarterstaff?"

Bern shook his head, giving Urien a lopsided grin. "I'm too old, and as rusty as a sword at the bottom of a pond."

"I'd be willing to wager you're still the best man with a quarterstaff within a hundred miles."

"But the squires don't fight with them." Bern took an enormous mouthful of bread.

"They should know how to, just in case. Sometimes that might be the only weapon they can find."

"You think they'd pay attention to me?"

"And why not?" Lurilla interrupted.

"I'm a brewster now, after all."

"They'd be fools not to," Urien said.

"Well, I'll give it some thought."

The serving girl came in from the alehouse, obviously flustered. "There's some men come in, Bern. They want a lot of ale, but they don't look like they can pay. And they're *Welshmen.*"

It was clear that Elva believed all Welshmen were thieves, which was a common enough prejudice.

Bern got up. "I'll take care of this."

"You'd better watch 'em," Elva cautioned as Bern went to the door. "The leader's a tough-looking fellow with the most terrible scar—and no *eye!*"

Urien jumped to his feet and followed Bern.

Sure enough, sitting in the alehouse as comfortable as you please, was the only man to ever beat Urien in a sword fight, Baron Emryss DeLanyea.

The baron's face broke into a grin when he saw Urien. "Fitzroy! Not expecting to find you here, me!"

"Nor I you, my lord."

"Sit down, man. Have some ale. I'll buy."

"This is *Baron* DeLanyea," Urien announced.

When Bern still looked worried, Urien went to him and pulled him over to the ale kegs. "This isn't Cynric DeLanyea. This is his *brother*—and a very fine man."

"He'll pay?" Bern asked dubiously.

Urien couldn't quite blame his friend. Baron DeLanyea and the men who were obviously with him were not dressed in very fine garments.

When Urien assured Bern he would be paid, Bern grinned and began pouring mugs of ale.

"Now, how did you come to be here?" Baron DeLanyea said when Urien sat down beside him.

"Looking for work."

"You're still welcome at Craig Fawr."

"No!" The vehemence of Urien's response shocked himself as much as Baron DeLanyea. "No, thank you, my lord," he said quickly, not comfortable under the baron's shrewd one-eyed gaze. He had no reason to be so discomfited. After all, Lord Gervais was paying him more than the baron could ever hope to afford.

On the other hand, there would be no hazel-eyed vixen to trouble him in Wales.

God's blood! Was he letting this woman—any woman—determine the course of his life?

"Wales is too cold," he said when he realized the baron was still watching him. "I don't think I ever felt warm, or dry, the whole time I was there."

Baron DeLanyea laughed. "I suppose so."

"I'm with Lord Gervais now."

"A good man, I hear."

"Are you in Bridgeford Wells for the tournament?"

To Urien's surprise, Baron DeLanyea smiled sheepishly. "Yes, but on our way to Lord Trevelyan's." Baron DeLanyea nodded at a boy about the same age as Donald. "Hu's horse threw a shoe, so we stopped here."

"Then we'll be on opposing sides."

"Perhaps getting to finish that fight properly, eh?"

Urien nodded. Five years ago Baron DeLanyea, not understanding that Urien was bringing him information, had set upon Urien and knocked him out cold.

"How's Lady Roanna?" Urien asked, remembering well her beautiful face, and the way she had looked at him before he left, her green eyes filled with concern and an understanding that had moved him beyond words. She had said then that she hoped he would find love one day.

She might just as well have cursed him.

"Never been better."

"She's not with you?"

"No, my old nurse wouldn't let her stir out of the castle. The baby's not coming for another two months, but no arguing with Mamaeth. And it would have been a slower journey, with Roanna and the children."

"Children?"

Baron DeLanyea grinned. "A boy and a girl. The boy's just like his mother, quiet but sharp as a sword point."

"And the girl?"

"Mamaeth claims she's just like me, but she looks like Roanna."

Urien thought he had never seen a happier man and he tried not to feel envious. He knew that DeLanyea's life had not always been easy, but at least he was a nobleman and now master of a large estate. Besides, the baron's troubles were all in the past, and his wife rivaled Lady Gervais for beauty and grace—although Lady Roanna's eyes, he realized suddenly, were more like Fritha's, displaying her feelings like windows opening on her soul when she chose to show them.

He would not think of Fritha now.

When they finished their ale, Baron DeLanyea stood up. "Time for seeing how that smith is coming along."

"I'm sure Lord Gervais would like to meet you. He's a great admirer of fighting men."

Baron DeLanyea shrugged and stood up. "It's getting late, but we'll stop by in the morning."

Urien halted on the way to the door, an idea forming in his mind. "I don't suppose you'd care to fight me tomorrow?"

"Before the tournament? Not wanting to exhaust you, man."

"I'm training Lord Gervais' squires and it occurs to me that a little demonstration would be beneficial."

"Well, might get rid of some of the stiffness from the riding. Why not?" Baron DeLanyea signaled to the boy, Hu. He spoke to the youth in Welsh, then turned to Urien. "I've sent him to an inn to see if there's room."

Then Baron DeLanyea turned to Elva, bowed very low and spoke a long string of Welsh. The serving wench smiled, obviously flattered now that she knew she was being addressed by a nobleman.

As they went out, however, Baron DeLanyea leaned close to Urien and said, "I told her that she should be ashamed of herself for even thinking we might be thieves and lucky she'd be if any Welshman ever gave her a second look."

The next morning Fritha was in the kitchen helping the cook before first light.

She had awakened early, before dawn, and been unable to get back to sleep, despite her resolve not to think about Urien Fitzroy.

Obviously she was a weak, stupid fool, at least where Urien Fitzroy was concerned. She kept telling herself that the look on his face the last time she had seen him was merely anger, nothing more. Not horror and shame and pain all mixed into one terrible expression that made her want to take him in her arms and hold him tight.

She wouldn't think of him anymore, she vowed for the hundredth time.

When she went to the kitchen, her frowns were as dark as her mood, but the other servants were all in fine humors. It appeared that Sir Giles had suddenly received news that his presence was required on his estate far to the north. He would be leaving before the tournament, and so would his men.

"Samuel!" Fritha snapped at one of the cook's boys. "For the tenth time, come away from that window."

Wiping her hands on her apron aggressively, she strode to the window to close the shutters. "I don't know what's so fascinating—"

She stopped when she looked out. The squires had formed a ring around two men circling each other, swords drawn. One of them was Urien, the other a broad-shouldered stranger. Both of them wore only chausses and boots.

Over to one side of the courtyard sat a group of strangers, including one very handsome youth about the age of a squire. They all leaned against the wall almost negligently, yet she realized they were watching the men with the swords despite their pretence otherwise.

Bern leaned on a quarterstaff and watched with frank interest. Sir Nevil, Sir Giles and some of the other knights also lounged nearby and they, too, were trying to look rather unconcerned, although their heads kept turning in the direction of the fighting men.

She banged the shutters closed. What did it matter?

Nevertheless, a short while later, when Godwin wanted more flour from the storage rooms, Fritha was the first to volunteer to fetch it.

The storage rooms were close to where the men were fighting, and there was a cart near the door. When she was sure no one was paying attention to her, Fritha sidled behind the cart, out of sight. Godwin didn't need the flour immediately. She could watch for a moment. She told herself it would serve Fitzroy right if he got wounded. Not seriously, of course. Not before the tournament. Just enough to bleed.

The man circling Urien was tall and very muscular. Shoulder-length brown hair brushed his broad shoulders. His back and chest were crisscrossed with several scars, and he seemed to favor one leg. When he turned, she saw with some surprise that he was half-blind, his right eye gone.

"He won't take Fitzroy," one of the squires whispered to the boy beside him. "He limps and he surely can't see properly."

Fritha agreed, until the man swung his sword. He did so with amazing swiftness and ease. The stranger was obviously a match for the strength and skill of Urien.

Urien dodged, but their swords connected with a loud clang. Now Fritha realized that both men were sweating and taking deep breaths. How long had they been at this?

Urien lifted his sword, but the other man moved quickly, then spun around. Urien's sword swooshed through empty air. As he tried to recover, the man knocked him backward and Urien's sword skidded along the ground.

Fritha gave a little cry of alarm. The other man glanced at her, giving Urien time to run and pick up his sword.

Blushing with embarrassment, Fritha hurried into the storage rooms as the fight resumed. It took only a minute to get a small bag of finely ground flour. When she came out, the two men were still fighting and nobody looked her way. Quickly she ducked back behind the wagon.

The fight went on for several more minutes, and several times Fritha found herself holding her breath.

Then Lord Gervais and Adela came out of the great hall. The squires seemed to sense their presence and turned toward them. Urien and the stranger, however, continued to fight until Lord Gervais caught sight of them and hurried over.

"What's this?" he asked warily.

Urien stopped, panting. His opponent stopped, too, putting his hands on his knees and drawing great breaths. Fritha saw Lady Gervais' lips curl in disgust at the other man's disfigurement.

"Lord Gervais, may I present Baron DeLanyea," Urien said when he'd caught his breath. "He's been helping me illustrate some of the finer points of sword fighting to the squires."

Fritha's mouth fell open in surprise. This man covered in sweat and dust was noble?

"Quite a fine display of swordsmanship," Lord Gervais said.

"Yes, indeed," Lady Gervais said. Fritha noted that Lady Gervais seemed less disgusted by the stranger now that she knew he was a nobleman.

"You'll stay for the evening meal, I trust," Lord Gervais insisted.

"I would be honored," Baron DeLanyea said, his mouth twisting into an attractive grin that made Fritha forget all about the scars.

Lord Gervais smiled and moved off toward the stable, followed by Adela.

Fritha suddenly remembered that she was supposed to be taking the flour to Godwin, and that she was determined to ignore Urien Fitzroy.

Later, seated in the squires' chamber, DeLanyea rubbed his aching leg and made a face. "God's wounds, Fitzroy, I didn't realize you'd be going at it quite so hard."

Urien looked up from wiping his sword. "Nor I you, Baron."

Baron DeLanyea chuckled softly. "Once a soldier, always a soldier, I expect. Who was that girl?"

"What girl?"

"God's teeth, I'm the half-blind one, man. That girl who was watching us. I'd have had you if she hadn't distracted me."

"Oh, Fritha. I mean, Lady Fritha Kendrick."

Baron DeLanyea raised his eyebrow. "I thought she was a serving maid."

"She's Lord Gervais' foster daughter."

"Really? Married?"

Urien was shocked. He had thought Emryss DeLanyea the most fortunate of married men.

DeLanyea looked at him, then burst out laughing. "God's blood! Not interested in her that way, man! But you should be."

"She's a noble. I'm not."

"She looks like a fine young woman."

"I'm not interested."

"Pity." He stretched. "Lady Gervais didn't think much of my fine face."

Urien glanced at him. He had seen Lady Gervais' revulsion, and it had made him feel ashamed, somehow. Apparently, however, her reaction seemed to amuse rather than insult Baron DeLanyea.

"She is very beautiful, but your own wife is even more lovely."

"I thank you, and of course, I agree completely," Baron DeLanyea said with a laugh. "Still, Lady Gervais is quite beautiful, in a cold-blooded Norman way."

"Cold-blooded?"

"Aye. Don't you see it, in her eyes?"

"No."

"But that other girl—her blood's plenty warm, or I'm in my dotage."

"It doesn't matter to me what her blood's like."

"God, Fitzroy, I gave you credit for brains. Must have been wrong."

"I'm not a nobleman."

DeLanyea shrugged his shoulders. "If that's the way you think, that's it then. Now, I'd best find the rest of my men and get ready for dinner. You'll be there?"

Urien nodded.

DeLanyea sniffed and made a face. "God, I stink! Needing a bath, and no mistake." He took a step, cursed softly and limped out of the room.

Urien watched him go, convinced that there were some things a nobleman could never understand.

Chapter Nine

Fritha waited near the end of the high table, absently tying the fine leather belt she wore into knots. Sir Tallentine, standing to her left, smiled at her.

She had been in the kitchen shortly before she had to dress for the evening meal when she had heard of Tallentine's arrival for the tournament. The news had not pleased her, but she told herself she shouldn't make her dislike so obvious. It was clear that Adela had persuaded Lord Gervais at last that it was time she married, and at least Tallentine's estate was close by. That might be all she could ask for in a husband, that he wouldn't take her far away.

She let go of her belt and attempted to smile back, uncomfortably aware that Urien Fitzroy was standing at a table near the center of the hall. He wore a new black tunic that emphasized his lean, muscular body and his handsome face.

She noted with some satisfaction that Sir Giles was to sit at the opposite end of the high table from her, and that he refused to meet her eye.

Lord and Lady Gervais were, as always, to be seated at the middle of the long trestle table on the dais. Sir

Nevil and his equally plump, good-natured wife would sit beside Lord Gervais on his left. Lady Gervais would be on her husband's right. Fritha wondered where Baron DeLanyea would be seated, but supposed that Tallentine would move over to the chair on the other side of her, so that the baron would have a place of honor beside Lady Gervais.

Baron DeLanyea and his men arrived. The pages showed the baron's men to seats near Fitzroy's table, then escorted Baron DeLanyea to the high table.

To Fritha's dismay, the baron was led to the chair on her right, farthest away from Lord and Lady Gervais. Tallentine would have the more honored place. Placing a baron so far from the host, especially when there were other lesser nobles in between, was an insult.

Mercifully, after one swift glance that told Fritha he knew that he was being snubbed, Baron DeLanyea apparently decided not to be offended.

Lord and Lady Gervais arrived soon after. Fritha saw at once that Lord Gervais realized the insult, his eyebrows lifting in surprise. Lady Gervais acted as if nothing were amiss at all, so it seemed nothing was to be done.

The meal began and as it progressed, Fritha tried to enjoy herself. Although Baron DeLanyea was one of the most entertaining men she had ever met and he told amusing stories about Wales and his tenants that made her feel she would know them all by sight, she found the evening rather tedious.

Fritha decided she was too tired to truly appreciate the stories Baron DeLanyea told. Or perhaps it was because he also made it very clear that he adored his wife. It was only natural that she should envy a woman who could inspire such love in a man and feel somewhat impatient as she listened. She would be very lucky if she were able to even tolerate her husband, whoever he might be.

Tallentine, mercifully, said little to her, but when he did, she sensed a certain triumph in his voice and manner. He occasionally cast looks at Baron De-Lanyea that told her he thought sitting in the more honored place was like winning a great prize. Trust Tallentine to think so!

She also had to endure Tallentine's laugh, even when he wasn't conversing with her. It was, after his beady little eyes, the most unattractive thing about him—and it was *very* unattractive. She couldn't imagine hearing it daily.

As the meal continued, however, Tallentine's laugh grew rarer, and his glances in her direction more and more proprietary.

Anger began to build inside her. It was her privilege to enjoy Baron DeLanyea's conversation as long as she chose to, at least for the present. Tallentine had no right to presume to have any say in the matter.

She glanced at Fitzroy's table. The Welshmen seemed to be having a good time, and they certainly relished the food.

She tried not to look again at Fitzroy, telling herself she didn't care whether he was enjoying the company or not.

Tallentine was talking to her again. When she turned to him, she found his gaze fastened on her gown. Or rather, the tops of her breasts.

How dare he peruse her body as if she belonged to him already! To make the situation even worse, he then had the effrontery to regard her with such a smug, self-satisfied smile that it was all she could do to keep from slapping him across the face.

Instead, she tipped her goblet, sending wine spilling all over Tallentine's fine white tunic. He stared at her as if she had tried to decapitate him.

"Oh, I'm so sorry!" she said, dragging her napkin through the wine—and incidentally sending more over the edge of the table onto his lap. "Please forgive me."

When his face turned angry, she wondered if she had gone too far. Her first flush of pleasure at her revenge gave way to doubt. If she did have to marry Tallentine, she would be wise not to show her disgust for him so openly.

She gave him a contrite smile, attempting to look the way Adela did when she seemed particularly interested in a man.

Apparently that worked. Tallentine never said a word as a page hurried over with another larger cloth, and he mutely submitted to the boy's efforts to blot up the wine.

It took a major effort, but she managed not to see if Urien Fitzroy had noticed what had happened.

She apologized to Tallentine again and, before he could reply, turned away.

Baron DeLanyea was giving her a most speculative look. Somehow, she thought he knew exactly why she had spilled her wine. He leaned toward her conspiratorially. "A pity it is, his fine tunic ruined. But I'd pay him a little more attention, my lady, unless you're *trying* to make him jealous and angry. I've a notion that fellow could be rather a nuisance otherwise."

Out of the corner of her eye, Fritha saw Tallentine jab a small chicken with his knife and realized that Baron DeLanyea was a perceptive man. She made an effort to talk more to Tallentine, and while he made no remarks about her clumsiness, he did sulk.

After the fruit was served, Tallentine leaned forward, looked at Baron DeLanyea and smiled coldly. "You're a long way from home, my lord. What brings you to Castle Gervais?"

"I'm going to visit a friend. By chance, one of my men's horses threw a shoe. It was mere coincidence that Fitzroy met me in the alehouse."

"You've known Fitzroy a long time?"

Fritha tried not to betray any interest, telling herself it was only natural that she should be curious to know how a man like Baron DeLanyea came to know Fitzroy. She also told herself there was no reason she should feel personally insulted at the contempt in Tallentine's voice when he said Urien's name.

"He was employed by my brother briefly. Unfortunately, Wales didn't agree with him. I would have liked him to stay."

"May I ask whom you're planning to visit?"

Fritha didn't know whether she was more surprised by the barely polite way Tallentine asked his question or the look that came on the baron's face as he paused before answering. Tallentine was not an overly intelligent man, but surely anyone could see it would not be wise to insult a man like Baron DeLanyea.

The baron grinned slowly, and Fritha thought that perhaps with the baron, a grin was not necessarily a pleasant thing. "Lord Trevelyan, I must confess."

As Tallentine stared, the baron winked at Fritha, and for a moment she wondered if the baron had simply been baiting Tallentine, something she could easily understand.

"Trevelyan?" Gervais' voice boomed out in the hall as he leaned over the table to stare at his guest. "You're going to Trevelyan?"

Baron DeLanyea shrugged his shoulders, his face so pleasantly contrite that Fritha would have forgiven him almost anything. "Trevelyan is an old friend of mine. I was given to understand that your tournament was a friendly competition, but I fear I've made myself most unwelcome now. If you like, I'll go this very moment."

"Stay," Lord Gervais said, his smile telling Fritha that although Lord Gervais liked to act as if the tournament were based on some kind of ancient grudge, the baron knew the truth of things. "How do you know Trevelyan?"

"I met Lord Trevelyan many years ago in the Holy Land."

"You were in the Holy Land?" Lady Gervais asked.

Fritha stared down at the tablecloth. So much for *her* evening. Lady Gervais would dominate the conversation now, with her soft, demure voice and flirtatious looks.

"Yes, my lady."

Lord Gervais leaned forward eagerly. "Where exactly did you meet Trevelyan?"

Baron DeLanyea smiled broadly. "Did he tell you about the ambush in the hills, the one where he got wounded in the..."

"Yes, he did. The way he tells it, some foolhardy fellow yanked the arrow right out, killed one of the attackers, put some stinking stuff he carried with him on the wound, then killed another fellow, wrapped some linen around it and took on six more before the sun set. Come to think of it, he did say the man was Welsh. It was you?"

The baron nodded. "That was quite a day."

"I thought you died. Trevelyan thought you did."

The baron looked down at the table. "I was badly wounded and it took me several years to get back home."

"Oh, how terrible! I've heard Lord Trevelyan talk about this many times. It is an honor to meet you, Baron." Lady Gervais smiled graciously.

The baron returned her smile, but again Fritha had the distinct impression that the baron knew exactly the kind of woman he was facing. And once again, Fritha was filled with envy for the baron's wife.

"We've heard this story so many times, and yet Lord Trevelyan has never said where he was wounded," Lady Gervais said coyly. "My husband also refuses to tell me the location. Since you were the physician, perhaps you'll reveal this great secret."

The baron feigned horror. "Oh, my lady, I don't think I should tell such a thing." He paused. "But I will say it was several days before he was able to sit upon his horse."

Sir Nevil began chortling, and Sir Giles, now clearly feeling the effects of wine, laughed loudly. Even Lord Gervais seemed to be trying to decide whether it would be too undignified to laugh out loud.

"Perhaps you found that particular part of the man's body most interesting," Tallentine muttered, but loud enough for all the high table to hear.

Fritha stared in horror as the baron's face hardened and he pushed back his chair, rising slowly to his feet. Lady Gervais looked scandalized, Lord Gervais frowned, Sir Nevil gasped and even Tallentine shifted uncomfortably in his chair, obviously regretting his hasty, petulant words. The hall fell silent.

Urien knew something terrible had happened. He had flushed with shame when he saw where Baron DeLanyea was to sit, but apparently Baron DeLanyea was too polite to act as if he were offended. But now something infinitely more serious must have happened, judging by the hard, cold expression on DeLanyea's face. He looked as if he would dearly like to dismember Tallentine. Tallentine looked as though he were about to be sick. Perhaps the pretty boy had been too busy leering at Fritha to think clearly and had said something he shouldn't.

Lord Gervais stood up quickly. "I apologize for this insult, Baron DeLanyea. You have my permission to satisfy your honor."

"Is this person going to take part in the tournament?" Baron DeLanyea asked, his voice quiet but hard and unfeeling as granite.

"Not anymore," Gervais said.

"Let him," Baron DeLanyea said, grinning in a way that made even Urien's blood run cold. "Honor can be satisfied on that day. Good evening, Lord Gervais." He bowed. "Lady Gervais." Baron DeLanyea strode from the hall, his men rising hastily and following him.

Urien glanced at Fritha and saw, when their gaze met for a moment, that she was as appalled by this turn of events as he was. Quickly he got up and followed Baron DeLanyea out the door.

He hurried after the baron, catching up to him near the gate. "I'm sorry. I should have warned you about Tallentine. He's a dolt."

Baron DeLanyea paused and frowned. "A dolt he may be, but to imply that I was a sodomite—" He didn't finish, but he didn't have to. Urien knew that Tallentine had made a very serious error, one that might cost him his life.

Baron DeLanyea's expression also made Urien very glad he had never had to fight him in a real battle. The baron spoke to his men. "You go ahead to the inn. I'll come slower."

As the Welshman's companions walked on down the road, Urien said, "I would have killed the man."

DeLanyea sighed and looked at him with a hint of a grin. "In front of the ladies?"

The baron began walking toward the town and Urien went with him. "At one time I would have, also," the baron said. "But I've learned to take the time to calm myself. I'm glad my men didn't hear, or I wouldn't give Tallentine any odds on lasting the night."

"But to let the insult pass..."

Baron DeLanyea halted. "What pass? There's the tournament. I'm for letting the man suffer, me. Do him good."

"You'll fight him in the tournament?"

"Maybe. But I don't think he'll be a worthy opponent. Still, if there's nobody else at the time..."

Urien shook his head. "I wouldn't find it at all amusing, my lord."

"The man's clearly stupid. He won't be much of a challenge." The baron gave Urien a sidelong glance. "For all that, he's got good taste in women."

Urien flushed hotly but said nothing.

"Thought Tallentine's eyes would drop out of his head, staring at her. Can't say I blame the man."

"So what's it to me?"

"You think she deserves to be chased after by that fool?"

"He's a nobleman."

"To the nobility's shame. Besides, she kept looking at *you*, despite my best stories."

"She never did."

"How do you know?"

There was no way, short of torture, that Urien was going to admit that he'd been keeping his attention on Fritha throughout the entire meal. She glanced at him occasionally, but he always looked away. She had no need to remind him that she was now with men of her own class. "I can see she's very pleasant, if one's a baron."

"You mean she didn't really enjoy my company. Now I *am* insulted."

"I didn't mean..."

DeLanyea punched his arm. "I know what you meant. God's blood, Fitzroy, a serious man you are. You really think she just pays attention to a man's rank?"

"Isn't it obvious?"

"No. She kept looking at *you*."

"Maybe she wanted to make sure I saw that I wasn't sufficiently . . . interesting."

"Why would you think that?"

This was the last kind of discussion Urien wanted to have, ever. He wondered how far they were from the inn. "My feelings for her, or hers for me, are not important. If she has any. Which I doubt."

DeLanyea smiled. "Despite what you both think the other one thinks, you're *very* interested in each other, only neither one of you wants to show it." He paused and when he spoke, his voice was low. "I know all about trying to pretend you don't care for someone. Waste of time, that. Besides, I think she's too good for a lesser man."

"She's a noblewoman."

"She's a *woman*, you dolt."

Urien halted. "I don't care if you are a baron, you've no right to call me . . ."

DeLanyea also stopped and held out his hands in a mock gesture of submission. "Very well, Fitzroy, I'm wrong. I didn't see anything. I didn't see that the beautiful, intelligent young woman beside me could hardly pay a jot of attention despite my best efforts to be charming—and I've been told I'm very charming. I didn't see that you could hardly keep from staring at her all night, and I expected to see you drooling every time I glanced your way. She's worth drooling over, too. But I admit, I've only one eye, so my sight's not what it was."

Urien was ashamed he'd lost his temper. Nevertheless, he *did* think DeLanyea was seeing more than actually existed, at least as far as Fritha was concerned.

They walked on in silence until they reached the gate of the inn. "Well, good evening, Fitzroy. I'm looking forward to seeing you again at the tournament."

Urien smiled. "Yes, good evening, Baron."

Then, as the baron walked away, Urien heard him say, "Just because she's nobly born is no reason to make her miserable, Fitzroy." He glanced at Urien over his shoulder, flashed a grin and disappeared inside the door.

Urien turned on his heel and marched away. God's blood, everyone seemed to have advice on the way he should feel. Wasn't it enough that he knew she was beyond him? *She* certainly seemed aware of that.

He made his way to Bern's alehouse. He needed a mug of ale. A big mug of good ale. A huge mug of the best ale.

Bern took one look at Urien's face and wisely said nothing, just served.

Urien took a gulp. It was true that he had had to struggle not to stare at Fritha all night. That new gown was a masterpiece of fit, the way it emphasized her perfect figure and rounded breasts. When she laughed, her eyes glowed and her cheeks flushed and it was all a man could do to sit still.

She belonged at the high table, beside the baron, whereas he didn't deserve to belong anywhere.

In the alley, Fritha had asked if he wanted her to beg for mercy.

He closed his eyes, trying not to remember that other girl's cries, pleading for mercy. How she begged for help, staring at him with terrified eyes before she died.

After three mugs, Urien got up and walked out. He couldn't get good and drunk, not when he had the squires to deal with in the morning.

He heard a small sound and paused, looking about. He wasn't far from where he had rescued Fritha that night. He listened and heard it again. He didn't know what it was, but he didn't like it. Moving cautiously, he kept listening, heading for the sound. Then he rounded a corner and stared, shock and pure rage boiling up inside him like steam in a pot.

Donald and the Welsh boy Hu were standing on either side of a young girl. Her back was up against the wall and they blocked her way. She was clearly terrified, and they were clearly drunk.

"God's teeth, what is this?" Urien demanded, his voice full of anger.

The boys lurched around and tried to focus their bleary eyes on him.

"Let her go this instant or I'll make you sorry you were ever born," he said slowly.

Donald appeared to recognize the speaker, for he moved away quickly. The other boy, the Welsh lad, stood as defiantly as a drunk boy of thirteen could. "I don't take orders from you," he slurred.

The girl, seeing that the boys were immobilized, darted past, crying softly.

Urien let her go, then walked up to Donald. He punched him in the stomach. Not hard, but enough to achieve the desired results. Donald's eyes widened for an instant before he was quickly, violently ill.

Urien turned toward the other boy, but he was too late. Hu was already losing most of whatever he'd imbibed that night.

After several minutes, Urien managed to steer both boys toward a nearby trough, where he submerged their heads several times, despite their efforts to escape.

At last, sick and soaking, they slumped on the ground. Urien towered over them, his feet planted wide apart, his hands on his hips. But when he saw how completely wretched they were, he crouched down beside them.

"Listen to me, both of you," he said, the anger disappearing in the memory of his own youth. "I want you to promise me that you'll never do that again."

Donald looked up at him, his eyes like a puppy's. "Get drunk?"

"No, accost a woman that way. Or worse. It's wrong, and it certainly doesn't prove your manliness. All it proves is that you're bigger and stronger than one woman. It's the way a bully and a coward acts, going for the weakest opponent."

Hu started to protest. "We weren't going to hurt her. Just wanting to have some fun, is all."

At that moment, Urien had the sensation that he was addressing a potential Sir Giles. That made him speak firmly and frankly. "*She* didn't know what you were going to do, and your idea of fun is amusing to no one but yourselves. If it's the pleasures of a woman you want, pay for it honestly."

Whether it was his words or his sincerity, they now looked a little sober and a lot contrite. Urien hauled them to their feet.

"I want you both to give me your word that you'll never do such a thing again," he said.

"I swear," Donald said at once.

Hu nodded, his handsome features flushing with shame. He said something in Welsh.

Urien eyed him, uncertain if the lad had given his word or not.

Hu shook off Urien's hand and faced him squarely. "I, Hu ap Morgan ap Ianto, swear by the blood of my people that I will never accost or take a woman against her will."

Urien had to admire the boy's determination to make his pledge so thoroughly. "Come on, then," he said. "I'll help you both get to where you can sleep this off."

Hu drew himself upright. "I don't need any help." He tried to turn and promptly fell over.

As Urien pulled the boy up, assisted—or, more precisely, hindered—by Donald, he reflected that boys of that age all seemed to have much in common, especially a rather odd sense of pride.

There was no great shame in getting drunk, as long as the only person who suffered for it was the drinker. After all, he himself had been in this condition several times, especially when he was traveling with Bern. But this time the boys had come perilously close to hurting that girl, or doing something even worse. Hopefully, they would remember the promise they had made.

Supporting them, Urien first took Hu to the inn, letting the boy stagger in alone to save him from the embarrassment of being seen carried in. Then he took Donald back to the barracks.

Fritha stared at the ceiling of the chamber she shared with the other maidservants.

How could Tallentine have said that... that awful thing to Baron DeLanyea? How could he have been so absolutely stupid? The insult was truly unforgivable.

A part of her would enjoy seeing Tallentine defeated in the tournament because of the possessive way he had looked at her tonight. Nonetheless, he had only *looked*. She wouldn't want him to be seriously injured.

She had to pity Tallentine, too. He would live through hours of torment before the tournament, knowing that Baron DeLanyea would be waiting for him if he had the courage to partake.

She wondered what Urien Fitzroy would think when he heard the whole story. Tallentine would probably be lucky if Urien left the matter alone until the tournament.

Not that she really cared what Fitzroy thought or did.

She decided she had had enough of lying unsleeping in her bed. Ignoring the coldness of the stone floor, she got up quietly so she wouldn't disturb the other maidservants, wrapped her covering about herself and went toward the narrow window.

Emryss DeLanyea was, after Lord Gervais, the most charming, amiable nobleman she had ever met.

Whatever Urien Fitzroy was, he couldn't be called charming. Aggravating, arrogant and mocking, perhaps, but not charming.

Nonetheless, here, now, in the dark quiet room, she knew she found him exciting, interesting and the most compelling man she had ever met. She was certain he was capable of deep feelings, but she had only had a fleeting glimpse of the true emotions that stirred within him.

She sighed softly. She wanted to reach his heart, just as he had touched hers, try as she might to deny.

Something moved in the shadow of the gate. She listened carefully and thought she could hear the sound of muffled voices. There was no urgency to the talk, so it must not be anything alarming. She waited a little longer, and saw two men come into the courtyard and head for the squires' quarters.

It was easy to tell that the man supporting his limp companion was Urien Fitzroy.

It looked as if one of the squires had been hurt. She quickly went to the door and slipped out, then hurried into the courtyard, catching up with the two slow-moving figures when they had nearly reached the squires' quarters.

"Who is it? Is he hurt?" she asked softly.

The boy lifted his head and gave her a weak, drunken smile.

"Oh, Donald! Not you!"

"I'm sho...shew...sorry..." he mumbled.

Urien glanced at her. "Open the door, will you?"

She did as he asked and followed them inside.

Urien practically dragged the boy to his cot and threw him onto it, although he was very quiet about it.

"Is he going to be all right?"

Urien put his finger to his lips and nodded toward the door.

Fritha just looked at him. Did he think he was going to make her leave? She wouldn't, not until she knew what had happened to Donald—and if Urien had somehow been responsible.

Urien pulled off the boy's boots and tossed a blanket over him. He looked at her again, one eyebrow raised quizzically, but this time she put her finger to her lips and nodded at the door.

He followed her out. The moon was only partly full, so the courtyard was dim and full of shadows. She pulled him into a corner.

"What happened? How did he get so drunk?" she whispered.

Urien shrugged, his face hard to see. "I don't know. He'll be fine once he sleeps it off. But I might have known you would appear like some magician. Don't you ever sleep?"

Fritha decided not to let him anger her. "What will you do? Will you tell Lord Gervais?"

"Are you asking me to keep this a secret?"

"He's just a boy—and if he's disgraced it will break his mother's heart. She's a widow and the family doesn't have much money. All she has left is her pride in her son."

They were standing very close together in the shadows, very close. She could feel his breath on her cheek.

"Since you asked me so nicely, I will."

She wished she could see his face. It might have made up for the flash of annoyance she felt at his condescending tone. "Thank you."

She was ready to walk away when he spoke again. "Baron DeLanyea has a fine way with words." His tone was defiant, but she heard a faint trace of wistfulness that made her hesitate.

She pulled her covering more tightly around her shoulders. "I've heard it said that Welshmen are like that. But it was your words, I think, that sent Sir Giles away."

He came a step closer, but she still couldn't see his face clearly in the shadows. "I wish, sometimes, that I had some of Baron DeLanyea's skill."

"Some men have little need for words, and in other things I believe you are a match for him."

Urien didn't speak, but he didn't move away. Unsure what to do or say, but not willing to leave, she took refuge in a question. "Will he try to kill Sir Tallentine?"

"Would you be sorry if he did?"

"No...yes! Of course I would. It would be a terrible thing if anyone were badly hurt in the tournament."

"And if he were only slightly wounded, would you be very sorry?"

"Perhaps a little."

"If I were wounded, would you be a little sorry, too?"

"I would be...very sorry." She hesitated, knowing that she might say too much. Then decided in an instant that she would take that risk. "But I would make it my duty to see that you got well again."

"Duty?"

"Sometimes duty can be a pleasure." She dared to touch his hand. "Your past doesn't matter to me, Urien, or your ancestry. I truly didn't want the townspeople to gossip about us, because I...care for you very much." She thought she heard him take a deep breath.

He stepped away. "My past should matter to you, Fritha." He paused and then continued slowly, "I wouldn't have told Lord Gervais about Donald, because I was a young and foolish lad once myself. Only I did something much more foolish and cowardly and shameful than these boys ever could."

There was anguish in his voice, and such remorse that she ached to embrace him.

"Good night, Fritha," he said softly. "It would be better if you found another man to care about."

She watched him walk away, knowing he had just shared something far more intimate and precious than a kiss.

Another man to care about?

She knew, as surely as she drew breath, there would never be another man she could care about half so much.

Chapter Ten

Adela sat in the great hall, working on a large tapestry. Hylda, who seemed to hold her mistress in appropriate awe, sat beside her, helping to thread needles and tie knots.

Adela was proud of her skills with a needle and spent many hours sewing, either on fine trims for her gowns or ornate tapestries. It was also rather amazing what men would discuss while she sat working only a few feet away. It was as if they could not comprehend that a woman could work with her hands and listen at the same time.

Sitting near the kitchen corridor, they could hear the muffled sounds of the kitchen servants as they went about their tasks. Adela glanced up and noticed a beam of sunlight coming in through one of the narrow windows on the other side of the room. "Let us move to the brighter light," she said, getting up from the ornately carved ebony chair.

Hylda nodded and followed, carrying Adela's chair. She set it down beside the window, then went back to fetch the stand, basket of wool and needles and her stool.

As Adela began to sew on a rather simple part of the tapestry, she turned her attention to the sounds in the courtyard outside.

The squires were marshaled there and the man Fitzroy was telling them something about jousting.

Fitzroy really was a handsome fellow, Adela thought as she wet the end of a piece of wool with her lips before threading it through her needle. She was more sure than ever that it would be a waste to set him to seducing Fritha.

Her mind toyed with the idea of attempting to seduce him herself, and she spent several minutes smiling as she envisioned it.

Then two other voices broke the spell of her thoughts.

"Let's rest here a moment."

It was her husband, obviously sitting upon a bench in the courtyard on the other side of the wall.

"It is a beautiful morning."

Ollerund was with him.

"It's nothing short of a miracle what Fitzroy's done with them, eh?"

"You can't make me forget what we were discussing so easily as that. I still think you're spending too much for one meal."

"They'll deserve it, if what I've seen so far is any indication. Fitzroy's proving to be worth every penny I'm paying."

"Which is a good thing. It's rather much."

"Pity he's not a knight. He'd be a fine husband for Fritha, eh?"

Adela pushed a piece of light blue wool down to the bottom of her basket. "Hylda, go to my room and see if I've left a skein of blue wool, a pale one,'' she ordered quietly.

"Yes, my lady."

As the girl hurried away, Adela wound some wool into a tight little ball as she continued to listen.

"As you said, it's a pity he's not a knight."

"Maybe I'll change that."

"The others won't like it."

"If he does well in the tournament, I'll think about it."

"There'll be complaints."

"I've seen many men knighted who deserved it less. It's nothing short of miraculous how he's gotten the squires ready."

"I think you're jesting with me, Levander. And I *still* say you're spending too much on the feast."

Adela frowned. Despite his words, surely Gervais would be too wise to knight a man like Fitzroy. The other nobles would not tolerate such an action. After all, what did anybody know about the man?

And as for the feast, Ollerund was like an old widow woman with only one penny to her name. Gervais would spend the necessary money, which was only right. It was well to let others be impressed by his wealth.

"Ah, Fritha, my dear. Good morning to you," Gervais greeted jovially.

Adela pulled the wool in her hands even tighter.

"Good morning, my lord."

"Perhaps you can convince Lord Gervais not to spend a small fortune on the feast after the tournament," Ollerund said.

"God's blood, it's my money." When Gervais spoke again, his voice was full of fatherly concern. "You seem tired, my dear."

"I've ... I've not been sleeping well."

"You take on too much, Fritha. You should rest and enjoy things more."

While you can, Adela thought, her hand resting for a moment on her rounded stomach. In a few months Gervais would surely be willing to do whatever the mother of his child should suggest, especially if the child were a son.

"I will, my lord."

"Good."

Fitzroy shouted a command.

"Tell me, my dear, what do you think of Fitzroy?" Gervais asked.

Adela slowly threaded another needle.

"He's a good fighter, my lord. You said you saw him at another tournament once. Was it long ago?"

"A few years. Sit down here and I'll tell you about it."

Adela's hand moved rhythmically through the taut fabric as she resumed sewing.

"He would probably be embarrassed if he knew I'd spoken of it, so keep this to yourself. There was a young lord there, Baldric, with very fine weapons and the best horse I'd ever seen. Fitzroy went right at him—after all, the ransom would have been incredible—and no doubt he could have made fast work of the man, but another fellow, a ruffian named Audwin, got to Baldric first. Well, that would have been it for poor old Baldric, except that Fitzroy took on Audwin. They were going at it pretty hard, and it was difficult to tell who was beating who. Then Fitzroy managed to get in a good, solid blow and Audwin was carried off the field. It would have been a simple matter for Fitzroy to still take on Baldric, because by this time the poor fellow was absolutely terrified.

"Anyway, instead of going for Baldric, Fitzroy took on everybody who came after the green fool. Sort of protected him, in a way. Fitzroy got some ransoms, of course, but nothing to what he might have made defeating Baldric."

"Is that all you know of him, my lord?"

"Isn't that enough?"

"I agree it's admirable, but I'm sure Baldric rewarded him suitably."

"Well, my dear, this is the really incredible part. I truly think Baldric would have knighted Fitzroy, except that after the ransoms had been collected and paid, nobody could find him. Gone, just like that."

There was a short pause before Fritha spoke again. "I, too, must go, my lord. Sir Nevil's men just brought some more wine. I want to see how many bottles."

"Do you think we should try and persuade Fitzroy to stay a little longer?"

"Does he plan to leave?"

"No, not that I've heard of. But you know men like him. They're liable to pick up and go at a moment's notice."

"Yes, my lord."

"But you agree we should convince him to stay?"

"The squires like him, my lord."

"As you say, the squires like him. Well, I'll see what I can do, then."

"Yes, my lord."

Adela drew a piece of green wool through her needle. She knew when a woman was interested in a man, however much she might try to hide it. It was easy enough to surmise that Fritha was very interested in the handsome, muscular Fitzroy.

She was a little surprised, she had to admit. She never thought Fritha would be swayed by good looks, although Fitzroy was extremely attractive. Perhaps it was because he seemed so aloof. A challenge. Yes, now that she could understand.

In some things Fritha was like a man: incapable of the necessary devious skill to achieve a goal, loyal to the point of imbecility, and liking to think she could win. At anything.

It wouldn't do, of course, for Fitzroy to ever be knighted, so there was no possibility that Gervais would allow a marriage between Fitzroy and Fritha, should Fritha ever actually manage to bring things to such a pass. Of course, a man like Fitzroy would probably be all too eager to agree to a marriage. He had everything to gain and nothing to lose.

But it would not happen. Gervais would not allow it, nor would she. She would make very sure that Fritha would never be able to marry a man of her own choosing. There was no reason for that chit to have a privilege denied to other noblewomen.

There was, Adela realized with a slow smile, a possibility that Urien Fitzroy would see that the girl liked him. If he was the shrewd man she believed him to be—and she had never been wrong in her estimation of a man yet—he might very well wind up in Fritha's bed with no suggestion from her.

"Fritha doesn't look well. Has she said anything?" Ollerund said after a few moments' silence.

"No, you know she never complains."

"Perhaps she merely needs rest. She works too hard sometimes."

"Yes, but I don't think I could make her do less. She seems to like being busy."

Interfering, Adela thought.

"I know you would miss her, but have you given any more thought to the matter of her marriage?"

"You sound like Adela. If only I could be sure of finding a man that would please Fritha!"

"I assume Tallentine is no longer a consideration?"

"He would make her miserable."

"Or vice versa."

"Whatever. He's got powerful friends, unfortunately. I can't afford to offend him, but no, I don't think he's the man for Fritha."

Well, Adela thought, so much for Tallentine. He would be of little use to her unless she could get him the steward's place. If not, she would do well to put some distance between herself and the man.

"Giles is obviously out of contention."

"Drunken sot!"

"It's a pity Baron DeLanyea's married."

"He lives in the north of godforsaken Wales anyway. I wouldn't want her to go so far away."

"What about Sir George de Gramercie? He's coming to the tournament."

Adela leaned a little closer to the window. She had never met *this* nobleman.

"There's an interesting suggestion, although he'll be with Trevelyan. He's seems a bit of a fool, but I think that's just the way he talks."

"What about Trevelyan himself?" Ollerund suggested.

Adela suppressed a gasp of surprise.

"Don't look so shocked, Levander."

"His wife's only been dead a year," Lord Gervais protested.

"He's powerful, wealthy, and—"

"He's too old."

"He's younger than you."

"Yes, well…"

"And his estate's not far."

"I don't think he'd suit Fritha, somehow." The bench banged up against the wall, telling Adela that the two men had gotten up. "I'm thirsty. What do you say to some wine? Something cheap, to keep you happy, eh?"

Adela's mind worked as quickly as her hands.

Trevelyan! He was at least as rich as Gervais, and just as powerful. His only child was a girl about ten years old, so she would be easily dealt with.

It would be too good a match for Fritha. She didn't deserve it. She hadn't worked for it, studied for it, sacrificed for it or earned it in any way.

Trevelyan. Adela leaned back in her chair. If she were widowed and then married Trevelyan, the wealth and power would be incredible.

All that stood in her way was Gervais.

"You look sicker than a plague-ridden corpse," Urien said to Donald as the boy stood in the courtyard trying to prepare himself to practice jousting. He leaned against his lance as if he could barely stand up, which Urien suspected was the case.

"I'll manage," the boy muttered, shuffling his feet.

"No, you won't. Get back to bed."

"I'll do it," Donald insisted, straightening a little.

Urien saw the unbending stubbornness in the boy's pale face and heard the stifled snickers of the other squires. He knew Donald would sooner lop off a finger than be excused for being ill, so Urien shrugged his shoulders. "As you wish. All of you, get your horses. We're going to a pasture outside the village." He paused. "The castle has no space large enough for what I intend to teach you."

He turned and headed for his quarters to get his helm. Regrettably he wouldn't have time to see Baron DeLanyea before he left for Lord Trevelyan's estate, but he did have a job to do, and the tournament was less than a week away.

Spending a sleepless night wondering what had possessed him to confess to the shame of his past hadn't put him in a good humor, either.

He had tried to tell himself it was the masking darkness of the shadows and not the quiet concern in Fritha's voice. Or perhaps it was the result of a need to speak of it too long suppressed, not her touch on his arm, which felt like a saving hand being held out to a drowning man.

He hoped she would forget what he had said and hinted at. He was beginning to enjoy life in Castle Gervais. He didn't want to see the disrespect that would appear on people's faces if they found out what he had done. Or rather, not done. He didn't want to see it on Fritha's face.

To his surprise, Fritha was waiting inside the squires' quarters. It struck him that she didn't seem out of place in the rather bare room. It suited her, somehow, more than the luxury of the great hall. Nonetheless, he spoke brusquely. "You don't belong in here."

"I wanted to thank you again, for Donald's sake."

"There's no need. I have no time to talk now."

"There's something else I wanted to tell you."

"Yes?"

She stood looking at him the way he supposed she looked at young children, with a sort of kind, maternal smile. He didn't like it.

"Seldon—I'd be careful of him."

He reached into a small chest and pulled out his helm. "Why? He's a boy."

"He's a young man. I don't know what you've said to him, but I saw the way he watched you this morning. He doesn't like you."

Urien straightened and crossed his arms, his helm dangling loosely from his hand. "I don't want him to *like* me."

"I'm merely offering you some advice," she said firmly. "You may think you're the best fighter in the country, but Seldon is young and strong and apparently has some kind of grudge."

"I've got years more experience, so you need not think any boy as green as Seldon will trouble me."

"I know you've been fighting ever since you ran away from home, Raymond, but don't underestimate Seldon."

He regarded her steadily, but his thoughts were churning. How had she found out his real name? Who had told her?

"Why do you think my name is Raymond?" he asked, surprised that he could sound so unconcerned.

She blushed, suddenly awkward. "I . . . I overheard you telling Bern's boys about your childhood."

So, she already knew that he had been no more than a common, laboring peasant boy. Could he truly believe that it made no difference to her, or her feelings for him?

As she stood there, he began to believe it might be so. Still, the caution of a lifetime made him keep his voice calm as he spoke. "Perhaps that was only a story."

"No, it wasn't."

He raised one eyebrow at the complete certainty of her tone, still unwilling to believe that his childhood didn't degrade him in her eyes. "Then it wasn't very honest of you to listen."

She gave him a small, guilty smile. "No, I suppose not. I was . . . interested, that's all."

"I would appreciate it if you didn't tell anyone," he said, but not as coldly as he might have.

She sat down. On *his* bed. "Why did you change your name?"

He shrugged his shoulders. "I didn't want to be found."

"And Fitzroy? Is that your name?"

"A bastard has no name," he replied. "I made it up."

"Is that the shameful thing you did, run away and give yourself a false name?"

He turned away. "No. That was the best thing I ever did."

How could she understand what his early years had been like? She couldn't possibly know what he had survived, thank the Lord. He didn't want to try to tell her.

Because he was suddenly afraid. He knew, deep in his heart, that if he did try to make her understand, he wouldn't be able to keep anything from her. Not even what had happened to that girl. And then she would be lost to him forever.

"Raymond—"

He whirled around to face her. *"Don't call me that!"*

She looked shocked. That was good. Perhaps she would leave him alone and let him keep his secrets.

"I'm only trying to help."

"I don't need your help. I can handle boys like Seldon."

God's blood, why didn't she leave? She stood up and came to him, looking at him with concern and...and something that made his heart beat strangely and a lump come to his throat.

"I don't want any harm to come to you."

He looked away. He was not worthy of her love. Not worthy of any woman's. "I can take care of myself," he repeated harshly. "I don't need you to tell me how to do that."

Still she didn't leave. Why wouldn't she see that he didn't want her? That he couldn't? What would it take to make her understand?

He faced her squarely, looking down into her beautiful trusting eyes and dreading the way they would change. "Do you want to love a coward? A man who would stand by and do nothing while a girl was raped and murdered, even as she pleaded with him to save her?"

A horrified look appeared on Fritha's face. He waited for her to speak. To condemn him with her musical voice. To show him that she could never care for him now.

"Tell me what happened," she said quietly.

He had expected many things, but not the respect and trust that still shone in her eyes.

For that alone, he would love her until he died.

He reached out to touch her cheek, but in the stillness he heard the jingle of harness and the voices of the squires as they waited for him in the courtyard. "I must go now," he whispered, "but I . . . I want to tell you. Will you meet me tonight, at Bern's?"

"Of course."

He picked up his helmet and walked away.

She watched him go, a man filled with anguish and silent suffering, needing love in a world that had only been cold and merciless to him.

Whatever had happened, she was sure it had been long ago and it was obvious he still regretted it.

If she could do anything to remove that anguish from his eyes, she would. And she knew, with complete certainty, that she would love him until the day she died.

Chapter Eleven

Urien watched as the squires returned to the starting place. Their handling of their mounts had improved considerably, he was pleased to note, but their skills had yet to be tested in a hastilude. Some who were doing well now might panic when confronted by a line of armed and mounted men bearing down on them.

He hoped not. This tournament would not be just a test of their abilities, but a test of *his*.

Bern had told him that Gervais and Trevelyan had argued for years over the best methods for training squires. Gervais felt that it was best accomplished at one location, with experienced men and good weapons. Trevelyan favored the more usual approach, that squires be trained by the individual knights they served, and those knights should be responsible for arming their squires.

If Gervais' squires did well, that would give credence to Gervais' opinion. Urien wanted to prove his master correct, and not just because Gervais was a generous man who treated him with respect.

If things went well at the tournament, Urien felt that perhaps all those years spent fighting would not have been wasted.

He wondered, and not for the first time that morning, if Fritha would still feel as she did after he told her about the girl. Now that he seemed to be making a place for himself at Bridgeford Wells, it would be painful to have to move on.

And even more painful to leave Fritha.

One of the squires' horses whinnied, bringing his attention back to the training. He scanned the sky. It was clear now, but the air was chill for a summer's morn, and the dew heavy. It would be best, perhaps, to keep the squires on their horses.

He reached for his lance. Donald, who was still unsteady on his feet, had been designated to take care of Urien's weapons. It kept the boy off his horse, for one thing. He was swaying so much on the unmoving ground, it was easy to believe he would tumble from his mount.

Urien spent the better part of an hour discussing jousting with a lance: the proper way to carry it; how to aim; how to keep it straight; how to hold it loosely at the moment of contact so the force of the hit wouldn't break your arm or ribs. The squires listened obediently, watching open mouthed when he held his lance out straight above the ground with one hand, not supporting the heavy weapon with any other part of his body.

He had to suppress a satisfied smile as Seldon stared, his eyes wide and obviously impressed. Only a very strong man could hold a lance like that.

As Urien had told Fritha, he could take care of himself, and one of the best ways was to make sure your opponent had a very good idea of the man he was contemplating fighting.

Toward the later part of the morning, Urien walked to the end of the meadow where he had had a groom put a bale of hay. Beside it on the ground was a white linen sheet. Urien asked Donald to fasten it onto the bale.

Donald took hold of the sheet and shook it open, then paused with an uncertain expression. Urien looked at it.

There was a simple outline of a man done in charcoal to make a target for the squires' lances, as he expected, but someone had drawn a monstrous face on it. There was a word, too, and an arrow pointing at the figure. Urien didn't know how to read, but he knew "Fitzroy" when he saw it.

Slowly he turned back toward the waiting squires.

Seldon and his few friends glanced at each other and smiled. Urien resisted the urge to smile back. To think they would believe that he would find such a childish prank cause for animosity! He had seen provocations that would freeze the blood in their veins.

Nonetheless he fixed his gaze on Seldon. "Seldon!" he called out, not moving from beside the target. "You first."

Seldon stopped smiling as he put on his helm, lifted his lance and steadied it against his body. He kicked his heels against the sides of his horse, which broke into a lumbering canter.

The tip of Seldon's lance was pointed right at Urien's chest. Urien waited, his arms crossed and a small, cold smile on his lips.

At the last moment, Seldon did not have the nerve to keep his aim on an unarmed, unmoving, unimpressed man. His lance turned away and his eyes closed before he struck the target.

Urien had spent days watching Seldon and knew he would do so. The boy was proud and had a grudge because he had not been deferred to; however, Urien felt the boy was honorable at heart. He simply had to learn that fighting skills were not determined by rank or wealth and that a man like Fitzroy was very hard to frighten.

"If you must close your eyes," Urien said quietly as Seldon wheeled his horse around, "aim first and keep the lance steady."

Seldon looked his way and Urien saw anger and hatred in his glance. Obviously he had not learned his lesson yet.

The boy said nothing, but rode back to the line.

The squires spent the rest of the day practicing with their lances. By midday Donald was recovered enough to participate, and by late afternoon Urien could tell the lads' arms were beginning to ache. He decided to be merciful and let them finish a little early, with a warning that their weapons and mail had better be well polished in the morning.

He rode back to his quarters to wash. He was glad the day was nearly over, but at the same time he was beginning to dread the evening to come, just as part of him wanted to tell Fritha about that terrible night so long ago and another part urged him to stay in the castle.

His heart won. He decided he couldn't ignore his feelings for Fritha any longer, and by telling her everything, he would discover the true depth of her feelings for him.

He washed, put away his helmet and went out. As he hurried across the courtyard, he heard the light sound of female laughter and looked up.

Lady Gervais stood at her window for a moment, then pulled the shutter closed. After she had smiled at him.

He hesitated before moving on, not quite sure what to make of that smile. It was more than mere politeness, if his experience was any guide.

And yet, what was his experience, really? Mostly whores, who, if their smiles didn't get his attention, soon made their desires clear with words.

Surely Lady Gervais could mean no such thing.

He quickened his pace and was soon at Bern's. Lurilla and his friend greeted him warmly and asked him to join them for supper. He agreed, but insisted on paying for some very fine wine.

Throughout the whole meal he was jumpy and uncertain, wondering when Fritha would come and what he would say to her when she did.

Finally she arrived. "May I have some ale for Peter?" she asked, the only sign that anything unusual might be happening evidenced by the way she twisted the corner of her tunic in her hands.

"Of course, Fritha," Bern replied, stepping out and coming back shortly with a mug full of his best.

"I'll go with you," Urien said, standing abruptly and going to the door.

"Thank you," Fritha returned stiffly, and together they went out.

Bern looked at his wife. "What do you make of that?" he asked softly.

"I make a marriage before the summer's over," she said with a grin.

"What are you taking about, woman? She's nobility."

"He's a fine man, Bern, and Fritha's no fool. Anybody can see she likes him."

Bern could not disagree, but he still gave Lurilla a skeptical frown. "Do you think Lord Gervais will agree to such a match for her?"

"He'd be stupid not to. Everybody knows Fritha won't take anybody but a man she chooses, and I'm certain she's chosen *him*. Besides, Lord Gervais likes him, too."

Bern let out a low whistle. "Who'd have thought it, eh?"

"He's your friend. Don't you think they're well matched?"

Bern grinned. "Aye, and that's a fact."

"Did I tell you about the time my dog caught the horse thieves?"

"Yes, Peter," Fritha said, nodding with a patient smile. She felt anything but patient, however. She had waited all day to hear Urien's explanation; she could hardly stand to wait another minute. Still, Peter had no one else to tell his stories to.

"What about the time the pigs got out? I ain't told that."

Fritha glanced at Urien, who stood by the door of the inn, obviously anxious to leave. "No," she said. "You haven't." She couldn't hurt Peter's feelings and hoped Urien would understand. "But I haven't much time this evening. The tournament's soon, you know."

"Oh, aye. Well, it's a short story. Edgar Thomas had this fat old sow..."

Fritha looked at Urien over Peter's head as he began telling about his dog and the fat old sow. She gave a barely perceptible shrug of her shoulders. To her relief, he gave a shrug back and sat down.

Fortunately, Peter was true to his word and his story was short. When he was finished, he thanked them kindly for the ale.

"It's no trouble, really," Fritha said as she went out. "Good night, Peter."

"Good night, lass. May God bless and reward you."

Urien nodded his good-night.

Without speaking, they walked toward the river. After a few minutes, Urien sighed. "I thought he would keep us there for hours."

"He wasn't very well this past winter. I'm afraid he won't last through another."

"You worry about them all, don't you?"

She gave him a sidelong glance. "Somebody should. Actually, I think of Peter as a kind of grandfather, in a way."

"His story was rather funny."

"Yes, his tales usually are. And he was the one that taught me...well, that day in the stable. That was thanks to Peter."

"You mean he's the one who taught you to render men eunuchs?"

"It wasn't as bad as that."

"How would you know?"

By now they were close to the woods, and she led him toward the willow on the riverbank. The moon was low in the sky, but provided enough light for them to see their way.

She went beneath the willow and leaned against its broad trunk. He joined her there, standing an arm's length away.

A slight breeze moved the slender branches of the tree, sending shadows dancing over his lean, handsome face.

"Are you sure you want to know about me?" he asked, his voice quiet and tentative.

"Absolutely," she replied firmly.

Urien sighed and walked a little distance away so that his back was to her, as if he couldn't bear that she should see his face. "I was...fourteen. I had run away from that damned farmer nearly a year before," he began haltingly, and she knew this was painful for him. She would not make it any harder by interrupting or even moving.

"I had no money and no hope of earning any. I didn't know how to do anything except farm, and I had vowed that I would never work like that again.

"One day I came to a small tavern. There was a group of soldiers there. Mercenaries, I found out. They were going to find service with a lord in the north. They bought me some food and told me that they thought I had the makings of a soldier, too.

"They seemed so... bold. Courageous. Rich." He laughed, but it was a hollow, empty sound. "They asked me to join them.

"Why they offered, I don't know. Perhaps because they thought I could fight. Perhaps because they were half-drunk. I didn't wonder then. All I knew was that they were letting me go with them. They were even going to lend me a horse."

How easy it was in her mind to see him as he must have been then! Young and strong, but filled with uncertainty and fear, and alone. It was easy to understand how pride must have filled him when those men apparently saw merit in him.

"Later that night, we were riding down a road. It was late summer and the sky was clear. Somewhere close by, a field of hay had been cut. I remember the smell of it, damp and strong. I was thirsty, so when we drew close to a stream, I got down from the horse to drink.

"The others stopped, too." His voice dropped to a whisper. "That's when they saw her."

Fritha shivered. She could imagine that, too. The girl, unprotected, unsuspecting. The men, drunk, cruel, uncaring. And the boy.

"She was no older than me and had come to the stream to fetch water. The others caught her and dragged her into some bushes. They tied her hands. They pulled her skirt up. And then, one by one, they..." He paused, and a ragged sigh broke from his lips. "I knew what they were doing, and I knew it was wrong. She cried and begged them to stop, to let her go. I didn't try to help her. Even when she looked right at me, pleading with me..."

His shoulders began to shake as he put his face in his hands. "And then they killed her."

She ran to him, putting her arms around him and holding him tenderly.

In a moment he took a deep breath and pulled away from her, swiping at his eyes almost angrily.

Fritha touched his arm, searching for words to comfort him. "You couldn't have stopped them. Not men like that. They would have done it anyway."

He turned to look at her, his expression once more the cold and merciless warrior. "I could have stopped them from murdering her."

"They outnumbered you, and you were only a boy."

"They were *drunk*—I could have beaten them."

"Perhaps, but they might have killed you, too."

"Or I might have saved her life. Don't you see? *I didn't even try.*" His voice sank to a whisper. "Don't you see that I am not worthy of your love?"

She took his face gently in her hands, looking at him intently. "You were little more than a child, alone and afraid. And for telling me this, I love you all the more."

In his dark eyes she saw everything she had ever hoped to see in a man's eyes. Love. Trust. Desire.

"Fritha!" He pulled her close, taking her in his strong arms and kissing her. Fires of passion and longing soared through her body. "I love you, Fritha Kendrick," he whispered, his lips against her cheek.

"Just as you are, you are all I could ever want," she said, kissing him.

Hungrily, his kiss deepened as his arms tightened about her. She ran her hands through his hair and down to the muscled hardness of his shoulders and chest. Boldly she opened her mouth, her tongue reaching out to touch his. Soon he broke the kiss and her head went back as his lips and tongue trailed across her burning flesh, traveling slowly down her neck to the soft skin of her breasts. He turned, pulling her with him, and lowered her onto the dry ground beneath the canopy of the willow branches.

His lips returned to hers as he joined her, covering her with his body. He moved his hips against her, their motion enticing and exciting.

Slowly he moved away from her. "Fritha, perhaps..."

She wanted to feel him become a part of her. To show him that she was his completely and forever. He was everything she had ever wanted or needed a man to be, and even more. This passionate, loving closeness was the way it should be between a man and a woman. There was no sin in the way she felt and what they were doing. "I love you." She pulled him toward her. "I want you. I need you."

"I love you." He had no other words. Had never needed even those. But now, here, he wished he knew the way to say what he felt, about love and joy and happiness.

He kissed her, slowly, with great tenderness. He wanted more, much more, but he wouldn't take it unless she offered.

She did. In the next kiss she gave him. And when she began to undo his tunic.

He took her hand in his. "Are you sure?" he asked, holding his breath, scarcely daring to believe it.

She smiled at him, her eyes telling him everything as she nodded.

In the past, his lovemaking had been swift, sure and silent. With her, he was as cautious as a boy, learning what pleased her, enjoying the learning. As if they had been made to please the other, they instinctively moved together, their hands exploring, demanding, their lips tasting, touching.

She felt so good in his arms, so right. He lay beside her, and for the first time in his life he whispered soft words of endearment as he caressed her.

At least at the beginning, until he could restrain his desire no longer.

She responded in kind, surprising him with her fervor.

When his lips touched her breast, she sighed with the pleasure he was giving her, then arched against him, clutching his hair, burning with need. Her hands moved inside his loosened tunic, her fingers touching and teasing as the tension became almost unbearable.

Now there were no more words, and no more thoughts. Everything became sensation and desire and love.

When he moved his body against hers, she smiled into his eyes and parted for him, gasping when he entered her.

"Am I hurting you?" he asked softly, his brows furrowed with concern.

She ran her fingers over his eyebrows, smoothing out his worry. "It's all right..."

In the next moment, nothing mattered but him and the sensation of completion she felt when his body joined with hers.

His sinuous movements increased in speed. His kisses, demanding, hungry kisses that she returned with equal measure, only fed another hunger. He whispered her name, and she whispered his, wrapping her legs around him, pulling him closer. Deeper.

She clutched his arms and cried out, the tension released in one glorious moment of pure sensation.

He held her tightly, the cords in his neck taut, his face strained as he thrust inside her once more. He gave a low, ardent moan, then relaxed his grip slowly.

He smiled at her tenderly, brushing her lips with a kiss, then moved off and lay beside her.

Contented beyond anything she had known, Fritha sighed in the darkness.

He raised himself on one arm to look at her, a smile on his lips. "Be my wife."

"With the greatest pleasure," she answered. Then practicality, the thing that had ruled her life for so long, reasserted itself. "Can we stay in Bridgeford Wells?"

"Wherever you like, as long as we have a bed."

She smiled, then frowned a little. "I mean it, Urien. Will we live here in Bridgeford Wells?"

He grinned, looking boyish and handsome and altogether too wonderful. "Wherever you wish, my love. I'd gladly chain myself to a wall if you promised to stay with me. I'm done with wandering." He bent down and kissed her. "I've found what I wanted."

She sighed happily. "Adela will not be pleased."

"Why not? I plan to keep you too busy to bother anyone."

"How, may I ask?"

"Babies."

Blushing, she laughed softly. Babies! His babies! It would be wonderful . . . and yet . . . "I don't intend to stay inside nursing babies and cooking your meals for the rest of my life."

He chuckled. "No, I didn't think so. I can see you now, charging through Bridgeford Wells like a knight in a tournament, one babe on each hip."

"Probably."

"As long as they're my children and you can spare a moment for me, Fritha."

"I don't want to have anyone else's children and I'll happily spend hours with you."

He frowned. "Do you think Lord Gervais will give his consent to our marriage?"

"I'm sure he will. He likes you."

"But I'm a bastard, with little money—"

She stopped him with a long, lingering kiss. "That's what I think about those fears, Urien Fitzroy. I don't want you to mention them again." She grinned devilishly. "Leave Lord Gervais to me."

"I don't know how the man survives, with all you women maneuvering him."

"Well, if you have your way, he'll have one less. I suppose Hylda will be able to see to—"

This time *he* stopped *her* with a kiss. When he pulled away, he looked at her with mock severity. "Promise me you'll try to stop worrying about everything and everybody."

"But—"

"Promise me! You've been looking very tired lately."

"I didn't think you were even looking at me."

"I confess, I tried not to."

"Very well, I shall promise—after the tournament."

"Is that the best you'll offer me?"

She nodded her head solemnly.

"Very well, my lady. I know there's no point arguing."

"No, there isn't. I also think that perhaps you shouldn't speak to Lord Gervais about our marriage until after the tournament. He'll be very busy with that for now."

"I don't want to wait."

"Will you never admit that I have a better knowledge of the people here than you? *I* think it would be best to wait."

He sighed and rolled over onto his back. "Very well, I yield."

She kissed him quickly on the cheek and stood up. "Good. We really should go back. The maidservants may wonder where I am. And it occurs to me, sir, that there may be those who wonder what mischief you're about."

"They would know better than to ask."

He got up and took her in his arms. "Just promise me you'll spend some time with me."

"As much as I can," she answered, taking his hand in hers.

Together they walked back to the castle.

The next two days were filled with activity. Fritha had never been busier, or happier.

While she saw little of Urien as he worked the squires harder and harder trying to get them as prepared as possible for the *béhourd,* they shared secret smiles whenever they did meet and even his slightest glance filled her with fire. Unfortunately, they had no opportunity to be alone, for as the time for the tournament grew near, many people needed Fritha's advice.

The castle was too crowded with guests and their servants for them to leave together unnoticed. Several times Fritha found herself wishing that she didn't have to share sleeping quarters with the maidservants, or that Urien didn't have to sleep in the same quarters as the squires.

The day before the tournament, it began to rain. It wasn't a heavy downpour, but Lord Gervais paced the hall, concerned that the tournament would have to be delayed. Since Lord Gervais' accommodations were lavish, however, the rest of the knights only worried about fighting in the mud, which would be slippery. To pass the time, they played chess and dice and talked to Lady Gervais. There were some other ladies present, but Adela was always at the center of the conversation.

Fritha had to admit that as a hostess, Adela was a marvel. She never seemed to say the wrong thing and could be a most masterful diplomat, diffusing quarrels before they progressed to impromptu fights.

The servants had to take turns eating in the kitchen and mumbled a few complaints, but since Fritha, who was doing as much work as any of them, was also eating there and seemed so happy, they generally kept quiet.

Fortunately, the day of the tournament dawned as fine as an English summer's day could. There were a few scattered puddles, but these would be dry before the day was over. Fritha scanned the cloudless sky as the sun began to rise in the east. She had been too excited to sleep any longer and had much to do. Nonetheless, she waited a while at the window, drinking in the beauty of the rosy flush of dawn and watching the door of the squires' quarters.

She was rewarded by the sight of the man she loved stepping out and looking up, no doubt wondering what the day's weather would be. Fritha softly called his name.

He turned and smiled as she waved.

Already dressed in a simple gown, she hurried to the courtyard. No one stirred, but the guards were still on duty, so she made sure she walked slowly, as if she had no great business with Fitzroy.

"A fine day," he said when she drew nearer.

Simple words, but, oh! the look in his eyes. She wanted to kiss him.

"Yes," she replied. "Do you think the squires will do well?"

He nodded, moving off toward a still-shadowed corner of the yard. "They're a good bunch, all things considered. As long as they don't forget what they're doing, they shouldn't shame me."

She followed him, looking at the ground and hoping the guards would think they were talking about a problem with the squires until they reached a nook between two buildings. She led him into the shadows. "What about you? Do you think you will win some rewards?"

"I won't be in the tournament."

She stopped and looked at him wonderingly. "Why not?"

He reached out and pulled her closer. She tilted her face expecting a kiss, but it didn't come. "Because, my lady, I am not a knight."

She gave him a skeptical frown. "What of that?"

"Somehow I don't think Sir Tallentine and most of the other knights will take kindly to a landless bastard involving himself in their sport."

"Lord Gervais won't feel that way."

"You're certain of that, are you?"

"Absolutely."

"I wish I could be as sure."

Fritha stepped closer and ran her hands up his muscular forearms. "Lord Gervais couldn't care for you the way I do, but he hates to lose, especially to Lord Trevelyan. He'll want you to fight."

He tugged her gently toward him. "Then I shall be *your* champion, my lady." He kissed her, his lips gentle and tender.

She wanted very much to stay in the cool, dim shadows, but she heard the sounds of other servants stirring. Today, of all days, the castle would be a hive of activity. With a sigh, she stepped back, grinning. "I only wish I could watch you, my champion. I would enjoy seeing you knocked to the ground."

He frowned, but his eyes were laughing. "I'm sure you would—*if* I got knocked down. Then I would expect you to visit me. On my sickbed, of course."

The heat of a blush blossomed on her face. This conversation was leading her thoughts—and her body—in a direction she couldn't go. At least not now. She had too much to do.

"I understand some ladies in Europe have been known to watch," he said.

"That may be, but Lord Gervais feels it's too upsetting for women."

"Obviously Lord Gervais hasn't seen you wield a ladle."

Fritha laughed and curtsied. "Farewell, my champion. I look forward to the evening meal, when the prizes will be awarded."

Urien grinned. "I have a wonderful prize in mind, my lady, but it's not something Lord Gervais could give me."

"You have already won my heart. I await the day I give you my hand." She smiled at him, then hurried away. He began to chuckle as he watched her go, no doubt to supervise everything except the actual tournament itself—and he wouldn't be surprised if he found her overseeing that as well. He walked back to his quarters, letting the joy he felt flow over him.

He wanted to shout for joy. She would marry him! A landless, titleless bastard who didn't even have a second name. A man who had spent his whole life fighting, living among things designed to maim and kill. Who had never known what it was to be loved, or to love in return.

Dear sweet Lord, she would marry him!

He paused as he opened the door and heard Seldon's muttering voice. "The other knights'll soon put that blackguard in his place. He won't be allowed to be in the tournament, I tell you."

Reality came crashing down on Urien's pleasant dream. No matter how she felt, Fritha was used to a fine home. What did he have to offer her?

Only himself.

And his skills. He straightened, suddenly determined. If he was allowed to fight today, he could win some fine ransoms, or at least enough to show Lord Gervais that he could earn enough money to keep a wife.

Before, he had had no purpose to joining in tournaments, beyond obtaining money to live. Now, he had a better one.

It was true that the number of tournaments he might enter would be limited because he wasn't a knight, but he would simply fight harder when he could participate. That would mean asking Fritha to wait, but he was certain she would.

He pushed open the door, planted his feet wide apart, crossed his arms and surveyed the excited group of youths standing beside their cots, clothed in their hauberks and surcoats and clutching their helmets nervously. "So, are you ready to do battle?"

Chapter Twelve

Fritha entered the courtyard of the inn with her basket over her arm. Although she had to return to the castle soon, she had decided to make a short visit to the inn. She hadn't had much of a chance to see Meara lately.

She had also gone to the village to buy from some of the new merchants who had arrived in Bridgeford Wells. Whenever Lord Gervais hosted a tournament, it attracted peddlers from far and near.

When she called out a greeting, Tom's voice came from somewhere nearby, and she looked around. She gasped when she saw him. He was perched rather precariously on the stable roof with a sheaf of thatch in his hand, all his attention on the meadow on the other side of the inn's wall.

"Tom! What are you doing?"

He grinned sheepishly. "Thatchin' the roof."

That, and watching the knights as they waited, she thought. She nodded. "Of course. Have Lord Trevelyan and his men arrived yet?"

Tom shook his head after another glance over the

roof. "Not yet. Lord Gervais and the others are all just sittin' there."

"Stay where you are. I'm coming up."

Fritha tucked her skirt into her belt and began climbing the ladder. When she reached Tom, she saw that he had chosen an excellent viewing place.

Below them, Lord Gervais sat in the middle of a line of the mounted knights and squires facing the road down which Lord Trevelyan and his men would come. Urien, holding his helmet under his arm, sat on his horse at the end of the line. His hair ruffled in the slight breeze, but otherwise he didn't move a muscle.

The rest of the men chatted among themselves, but she could see that Lord Gervais was getting impatient.

She smiled. He was always ready early, and Lord Trevelyan was always prompt to the point of obsession.

"Wish I was there! I'd give 'em a fight!"

She looked at Tom's eager face. "Why? That wouldn't be a very wise thing for an innkeeper to do."

The boy gave her a sour look. "Innkeeper! I don't want to be an innkeeper."

"It's not easy being a soldier."

"I don't want an easy life—and I don't want to be stuck in Bridgeford Wells forever. I want to see the world and be in great battles and win honor and money—"

"And perhaps die?"

"I might die anyway."

Fritha nodded reluctantly. "True. But don't say such things in front of your mother, at least not for a while. All right?"

"All right," the boy agreed sullenly.

They heard the sound of hoofbeats and the jingling of harness in the distance. Fritha knew she should go, but she delayed another minute as the sun glinted off mail and the wind fluttered the plainly colored banners of Trevelyan's men as they rode toward the meadow.

Lord Gervais nudged his horse to a walk, meeting Lord Trevelyan halfway between the two groups. "I was beginning to think you had decided to quit the field before the battle commenced," he said loudly.

"Against you? Never!" Lord Trevelyan's reply was loud with bravado.

Fritha had to smile. As always, the two lords' voices increased in volume the more excited they were. Lord Trevelyan scrutinized Lord Gervais' men. "Still spending too much money, I see."

"I can afford it."

"The same boundaries for the squires as for the knights?" he asked.

Lord Gervais nodded. "The river on the south, the London road on the west, the hill to the east and the convent on the north."

"You don't think that's too large a field for the squires?"

"Not for mine."

"Nor mine."

"Good."

The two men began riding toward the castle, followed by Lord Trevelyan's men and then Lord Gervais'.

Fritha waited to catch a glimpse of Urien.

As the two lords rode close to the inn, Lord Gervais jerked his head over his shoulder. "I see you've got some Welshmen."

"I hear you've met them."

"Yes, indeed I have."

"DeLanyea told me he's particularly hoping to meet one of your men again. Tallentine. They've fought in a tournament before?"

"Didn't he tell you?"

"No."

"They have a score to settle."

Lord Trevelyan's eyes widened. "God's wounds, I wouldn't want to have DeLanyea wishing to settle a score with me! He fights like a fiend when he's angered."

"Tallentine's a fool, but I wouldn't want him killed."

Lord Trevelyan nodded. "Don't worry, DeLanyea can control himself." He nodded back toward Lord Gervais' men. "I see you've got a new man, too."

"You remember Fitzroy?"

"Who could forget? You'd think a sword was a twig, the way he swings it."

"He's been training my squires."

Lord Trevelyan's expression almost made Fritha laugh out loud, and when he spoke, she noticed that his bantering tone had completely disappeared. "The squires' *béhourd* will begin after some refreshment?"

"Of course."

As they rode on, Fritha skittered down the roof and hurried nimbly down the ladder. She really had little time.

Dunstan came striding into the courtyard. "Meara!" he called out.

"She's inside," Tom shouted.

Startled, Dunstan looked up at him, then smiled at Fritha. "Good day, my lady," he said.

"Good day. I see we've got even more merchants than usual this time."

"Yes, but we'll be watching out for any other strangers, too," he said, and she knew he meant thieves and cutpurses.

Meara came bustling out of the inn. Then, to Fritha's surprise, she began to blush. Fritha exchanged a brief greeting with Meara and left quickly, feeling that her presence was no longer very necessary.

She smiled to herself as she hurried down the main street of the village, weaving through the wagons and handcarts.

Meara and Dunstan. Could it be that Dunstan hadn't married again because he wanted Meara? Could it be that Meara, slowly ending her grieving, was thinking of Dunstan in a new way? That would be wonderful, Fritha thought. They would make a fine couple.

Of course, she could be only imagining things, since so many thoughts in her head these days had to do with men and women and love, but she hoped it was so.

Urien was glad Lord Gervais had made the women keep to the castle. He was having one of the most tense, exciting, despairing mornings of his life watching the boys he had trained as they participated in their first tournament. His horse pranced nervously beneath him, reacting to his master's shifts and sudden movements in the saddle. Urien would have preferred being in the battle itself, and probably so would his horse.

Urien tried to ignore the assembled knights. Their hastilude would be the next day, but they amused themselves by watching the squires. A pavilion had been erected, and Lord Gervais and Lord Trevelyan watched from seats that afforded a fine view of the melee.

Fritha would also have been even more of a distraction, which he didn't need.

The opening charge, with raised lances, had gone well. Donald, Seldon and a few others had managed to unseat some of Trevelyan's squires. They had also been able to draw back and charge once more, again proving more often victorious than not. No doubt hoping to have another chance with their lances, Donald and Seldon had ridden off after their opponents. Others had dismounted and now fought with swords. Several of Trevelyan's squires were much better with swords than they had been with lances, especially the ones in Baron DeLanyea's retinue, who were also the only group to have consistently good equipment. Many of the other squires had swords that were poorly made and improperly weighted, which made sword fighting more difficult. Trevelyan's men also had all kinds and conditions of mail and other armor. Those with finer equipment were obviously more confident, but they were not necessarily the more skilled. Such differences made Urien appreciate Lord Gervais' generosity even more.

The fighting went on for hours, as one by one the individual battles ended in victory or defeat. As they neared the conclusion, Donald came back, covered in mud, but leading his opponent's horse. His opponent, walking beside him, was even muddier. It was easy to see from Donald's broad smile and the opponent's slumping shoulders who had had the victory.

It was several more minutes before Seldon returned, horseless and on foot. He had made the mistake of taking on one of the Welsh squires. Urien had to wait until the other lad doffed his helm before seeing that Seldon had been beaten by the boy Hu. Baron DeLanyea was off his horse in a minute, offering congratulations to the lad, who beamed with undisguised pride.

For a moment Urien envied DeLanyea the easy rapport he had with his men. Always feeling different from his fellows, Urien had little idea how to joke and take his ease with other soldiers.

In the main, though, Urien was delighted. His squires had won most of the battles. He could easily imagine Fritha's happy smile when she heard.

Suddenly Lord Gervais signaled to him. Wondering what was about to happen, Urien approached. Lord Trevelyan, looking disgruntled, nodded briefly.

"It would appear, Fitzroy, that your methods of training my men are most effective," Lord Gervais said.

Urien had the distinct impression that Lord Gervais' words were intended more for Lord Trevelyan than him, but he answered anyway. "Yes, my lord."

"Baron DeLanyea was speaking of you," Lord Trevelyan said. "He thinks most highly of your skills, as do I. I look forward to seeing you fight in the tournament tomorrow."

"My lord, surely you don't intend to let this landless *peasant* fight in the tournament."

Urien turned around very slowly. Tallentine, who had been conspicuously absent earlier, sauntered closer. Behind him Urien saw a band of unfamiliar, rough-looking men.

"Ah, Sir Tallentine," Lord Gervais said politely. "I was afraid you were not going to be joining us."

"Naturally I had planned on participating, my lord, but tournaments should only be for knights."

Lord Trevelyan spoke. "In my younger days, whoever had the arms and the mail was welcome in a tournament."

Tallentine glanced around at the assembled knights. Urien did, too, as did Gervais. It was clear most of them agreed with Tallentine.

"So be it," Lord Gervais said, with a shrug of his shoulders.

Urien wished Fritha had never given him the hope of fighting in this tournament. It made it even more galling to be disqualified by a fool like Tallentine.

"Dismount, Fitzroy."

For a moment Urien wanted to refuse, but he decided it was more prudent to obey. After all, he could find other tournaments than this one.

"Kneel and draw your sword."

Urien stared at Lord Gervais as he came forward, pulling his sword from his scabbard. Disbelieving, he knelt in the mud, placing the tip of his sword in the ground so that the hilt made a cross.

"Do you swear by our Savior and his Blessed Mother to be loyal to the king, to me, and to my household, to uphold the laws of the land and the church, and to do all with honor?"

"I swear."

Lord Gervais struck his shoulders with his sword. "Then, rise, Sir Urien Fitzroy, newly made knight."

Urien got to his feet. Of all things he had hoped for in his life, being made a knight was not one of them. And yet in his joy he thought not only of himself, but of Fritha. How pleased she would be for him—and how much sooner they would be able to marry!

Lord Gervais ignored the shocked expressions of the other knights, saying only, "It's time to rejoin the ladies and have our meal. You must join us at the high table today, Sir Fitzroy. Come."

Urien wanted to rush ahead to tell Fritha, but for now he knew he would be expected to ride with Lord Gervais' retinue.

Coolly he walked back to his horse, gazing stonily at the other knights, except for Baron DeLanyea. When he caught the baron's eye, he grinned.

Tallentine did not follow Lord Gervais and the rest of the knights to the castle. He stomped back to the motley group of ruffians he had hired, ignoring the mud spattering all over his cloak. Fitzroy was going to be the bane of his life! That no good, impudent wolf's head who surely deserved to be hung...

"Excuse me, my lord?"

Tallentine halted and scowled at the brawny youth blocking his way. "What do you want?"

"I want to kill Urien Fitzroy."

Tallentine's eyes widened. "What?"

The young man took him by the arm and drew him away from the waiting men. "I want to kill Urien Fitzroy, and I think you want him dead as well."

"You mean *Sir* Fitzroy?" Tallentine asked sarcastically. This boy hadn't a hope in the world of defeating a man like Fitzroy.

"Yes."

"How do you intend to do that? Magic?"

"I'll kill him in the tournament."

"Oh, as easy as that, eh?"

"Yes."

"But you're not going to be in the tournament. You're a squire, aren't you?"

"That's where I need your help—and where I can help you."

"Go on."

"We are almost the same size, my lord. Your armor would fit me, I think."

Tallentine's mind worked quickly. This boy wanted to take his place in the tournament, with the intention of harming Fitzroy? Tempting idea, especially as it would also mean that Baron DeLanyea would be aiming for the wrong target. "Even if I agreed to this, how could I be sure you would succeed?"

"Because I will."

The boy was certainly confident, as well as arrogant. Still, if he failed, one could always claim the lad had stolen his armor. After all, Fitzroy had humiliated him and made Lord Gervais send him to his estate like a chastised child. The knighting of the fellow was the final insult. "Come to my tent in the morning at first light."

Seldon nodded as Tallentine walked away.

Adela sat at the high table after the feast, listening to a minstrel sing a song about unrequited love.

Tallentine, the bumbler, had made an idiot of himself once again. She would do well to leave him to his own foolish ways.

Who would have guessed her husband would have knighted Fitzroy? She would have liked to have been there, to see the other knights' faces. Not that she agreed with her husband's actions. It would be unwise to knight every man who was simply skilled with a sword or a lance, or soon the nobility would be completely degenerated.

Her hand paused as she reached for her wine. Surely Gervais had no other plan. She took a sip. No, his mind was not made for complicated schemes.

Still, there may have been more in his thinking than a simple reward. She glanced toward the end of the table, where Fitzroy sat next to Fritha. The girl couldn't hide her pleasure at his company.

Did Gervais have plans for *those two?* She gazed over the assembled people in the hall. Fritha and Fitzroy? Well, that would be better than Fritha and Trevelyan.

But the girl didn't deserve Fitzroy, either. His other skills—the skills of a lover—which Adela didn't doubt were considerable, too, would be wasted on some virginal creature incapable of appreciating them.

The man beside her shifted slightly, and she turned to smile at Lord Trevelyan. He was only slightly younger than her husband, but quite handsome in a majestic way. He also seemed more aware of his position in society, as well as being rich and powerful, whereas her husband was much too generous and softhearted, like her weak, pitiful father.

Perhaps she had been hasty marrying Lord Gervais, but who could have guessed that Trevelyan's wife would die so soon?

"A fine meal, my lady," Trevelyan said when he caught her glance.

"Thank you, my lord. I'm happy we can please such a discerning man as yourself." She used her most flirtatious tone, testing her powers with him.

"Your hospitality is always most impressive, my lady."

He gave no sign that he heard anything other than a genuine compliment in her voice, and she suppressed a frown. Was she losing her talents to arouse and entice men, or was he too stupid to sense her meaning?

With a graceful gesture, she brushed back the silken cloth covering her hair and reached for a piece of fruit on the platter before her, letting her other arm lean against his in, perhaps, a careless manner.

She felt him stiffen slightly and was very pleased. Wisely she made no other innuendos, now that she was sure Trevelyan was not immune to her.

Baron DeLanyea, who had been seated at the other end of the table, rose and signaled to his men, who also got to their feet. "I must bid you good-night, Lord and Lady Gervais, and thank you for a fine meal. I intend that my men be at their best tomorrow, and that means well rested."

Trevelyan chuckled. "He means, Gervais, that they're going back to their camp to sing battle songs so they're ready to fight like barbarians tomorrow."

DeLanyea didn't deny it, but shrugged his shoulders. "To a Welshman, my lord, singing *is* rest. As for battle songs, some are—and some aren't."

Lord Gervais nodded, smiling. "Whatever you intend to do, Baron, I must agree that the hour is getting late. We should all retire."

Wiping her fingers delicately with her napkin, Adela looked at Trevelyan. "I hope your bed will be to your liking," she said softly. A brief flicker of emotion crossed his face, but he said nothing.

Fitzroy also rose. "If you will excuse me, as well, my lords. I should ensure that the squires you have so kindly rewarded by allowing them to participate tomorrow are also getting their sleep."

Fritha tried not to sigh or smile like a lovesick maid as Urien bowed and went out of the hall.

But she and Urien had made good use of the opportunity of sitting together. She had never been more anxious for a meal to end!

After a few long minutes, she also stood up and excused herself, saying she had much to do before the morning.

And she did—with Urien.

Chapter Thirteen

Fritha made sure no one was watching, then, keeping to the shadows around the walls of the courtyard, she hurried to the stable. She slipped inside and heard Urien's voice as he spoke softly to his horse. With a devilish grin, she crept toward the huge animal's stall.

"Do well tomorrow, and I'll see you're rewarded properly," he crooned, stroking the horse's neck.

"Who could resist such an entreaty?" she said, using the same words he had said the first time they had met in the stable.

Startled, he turned to her. Then he smiled. Slowly. Enticingly. "I was speaking to my horse," he replied, his eyes mocking as he walked toward her.

"A pity."

"If I do well tomorrow, my lady, will you reward me, too?" His gaze locked onto hers.

She smiled innocently. "Lord Gervais has already given you a fine reward. What could I offer?"

By now he had reached her, standing only inches away. "Only *you* can offer what I want most, my lady."

She put her hands on his shoulders and reached up for a kiss, letting her action tell him that he could have whatever he wanted of her.

He gathered her into his arms. His kiss deepened, his tongue probing tenderly until she yielded him entrance into the soft, moist warmth of her mouth.

He ran his hands through the mass of her hair and down her slender back. ''I have never been happier,'' he whispered as his lips trailed slowly down toward the silken flesh of her neck, lingering on the throbbing pulse he found there.

Fritha moaned softly, her skin tingling where he pressed his mouth. She wanted to touch him. Reaching inside his tunic, she caressed his chest.

She heard his sharp intake of breath, pleased that she was returning some of the pleasure he was giving her.

Behind them, the horse moved. Without a word Urien swept her up in his arms and carried her toward a dark empty stall at the back of the stable. Easing her onto a pile of fresh hay, he lay beside her, pulling her toward him, his need and hers joining in a new sense of urgency.

Impatient, she tugged at his tunic while they kissed. When it was off she ran her fingers along his smooth, hard muscles, touching a nipple. The increased passion of his kisses told her he enjoyed it. His hands moving quickly, he untied the knot in the laces of her gown and she felt his hot, confident hands against her naked back.

She burned for him, arching herself against him, trying to get even closer. He pressed fervent kisses to her neck, going lower and lower until he captured the hardened peak of her breast in his mouth.

His touch was ecstasy, and exasperation when he slowed, caressing her as he removed her gown and shift.

They came together with whispered pleas and demands, each one seeking to satisfy the other in fervent haste.

This time they spent their passion quickly, like a brief summer storm of lightning and thunder. After the storm had passed, they lay still in each other's arms.

Until Fritha sneezed. She looked at Urien, gloriously naked beside her, and laughed. Somehow, when she was with him like this, even a sneeze was delightfully intimate.

He grinned at her and kissed the tip of her nose.

"It's the hay," she said, plucking a piece of it from his hair.

"I don't want to move."

"I hope this... activity... won't affect your accomplishments in the tournament tomorrow."

He ran his hand over her round breast. "I don't think so."

She sat up. "I should get back to my quarters. Adela may want me."

"Stay. *I* want you."

"Are you asking or demanding, Sir Knight of the Naked Body?"

"Which would you prefer, my Lady of the Luscious Flesh?"

"Well, if you *ask*, it proves you're a gentleman. On the other hand—"

"I'm very good with my hands."

"I've discovered that. On the other hand—" she leaned toward him "—I've also discovered that I like your demands." She kissed him. "However, Sir Knight, if you make demands of me, I shall insist upon the right to make demands of you."

He smiled. "As you wish, my lady. Make your demands."

"First, kiss me."

He complied at once, moving his mouth and tongue in such a way that she forgot everything except the kiss—until he drew back and raised his eyebrow. "What else, my lady?"

She knew exactly what else she wanted him to do. As he looked at her, his body barely visible in the dimness, she suddenly felt bold and wanton. "I want you to touch me."

"Any particular place, my lady?"

"I leave that to your imagination, Sir Knight."

His imagination was very...imaginative. He started at her shoulders, moving with frustrating, exciting slowness lower and lower, teasing her at her most vulnerable points until she wanted to scream.

Then he stopped. "What else, my lady?"

It was all she could do to speak. "Make love with me again."

"Most willingly, my lady."

So he did, in the truest, best meaning of the words.

Adela sat alone in her bedchamber, frowning as she removed the silken scarf from her hair.

Hylda had not yet arrived to help her disrobe, and Adela doubted Fritha would be in the castle yet.

She was probably still in the stables. With *him*.

Adela's long, slender fingers bunched her scarf until it was a shapeless mass in her hand. She was glad she had happened to look out her bedchamber window, to see that little whore sneaking off like a thief to share a tryst with Fitzroy. In the castle stables, of all places.

She was also glad, too, that her husband had elected to remain behind with his fellow noblemen when she retired. She had been able to leave the bedchamber, slip outside unnoticed and go to the stables.

Adela threw her scarf on the finely carved table beside her ornate chair. She closed her eyes, remembering what she had seen.

The fiery, passionate kiss. Urien Fitzroy's bold, strong hands traveling down Fritha's body. And, worst of all, his look when he picked her up and carried her off into the dark shadows.

Adela covered her face. He had looked at Fritha like a lover should. Like no man had ever truly looked at *her*.

Many men were devoted to her—they said. Many claimed they would die for her love. Many perhaps thought they meant the words.

But not one man had ever looked at her with such love and passion in his eyes.

Adela took her tear-dampened hands from her face.

Fritha Kendrick didn't deserve such a love. She had a father's love in Gervais, a father's love denied *her*. Fritha had the love of the townspeople, which, although worth about as much as the love of a dumb beast, was love nonetheless. That she should inspire such passion in a man was... was unfair.

With angry motions Adela wiped her palms on her fine gown, then made them into fists. She would not let Fritha Kendrick have what she did not.

The next morning the town buzzed with gossip and excitement.

Lord Gervais' squires had soundly defeated those of Lord Trevelyan. If his knights did the same, there would surely be a fine celebration afterward. Dunstan was a little concerned about the number of people who would probably be fined for being drunk and unruly, but was somewhat mollified by the prospect of dancing a *carole* with Meara.

Bern was so pleased with the knighting of his friend that he tapped a keg of his very finest ale, complaining loudly and laughingly that if he hadn't been tempted by bright eyes and a fine figure, he too would be a knight by now.

Lurilla replied, just as often and just as loudly, that he'd more likely be lying drunk in some London gutter.

Tom entertained himself with visions of the day he would be knighted, and practiced kneeling with a great flourish until his knees ached.

Some of the townspeople made wagers that Tallentine wouldn't dare come to the tournament to face Baron DeLanyea. They speculated that he had brought the motley band of protectors—who would never be allowed to be involved in the tournament—as guards against the rough and uncouth Welshmen, but no one expected the Welshmen to actually attack Tallentine in the street.

Adela said very little to Fritha, which filled Fritha with relief. She had stayed nearly the whole night in the stables. Even thinking of the things she had done there with Urien made her blush when she recalled them. Then she blushed even more when she realized she wanted to do them all again.

In the squires' quarters Urien was hard-pressed to keep a smile off his face as he donned his armor. The night had surpassed his wildest dreams as he held Fritha in his arms.

She was all he would ever want, and more. More than he deserved.

But today he stood a good chance of earning some rewards. Now he had a goal beyond food and clothing, and he enjoyed the sense of purpose it gave him. How much better to be working toward a life of happiness with Fritha than simply running away from a painful, empty past!

When he was ready, he waited in the courtyard with the other knights and the squires who were going to be in the main tournament. There was a sprinkling of clouds in the sky, but it was hard to tell if rain would come before the day was out or not.

He glanced about. Sir Nevil was there, looking rather like a large turnip on a horse. Donald, excited but calm, waited patiently, as a well-trained knight should. Tallentine had not yet come.

Lord Gervais came out of the door of the hall. Urien had hoped to see Fritha before the tournament began, but none of the ladies appeared.

Perhaps she was too tired, he thought to himself, a secretive smile crossing his lips. They had parted only an hour before the rooster crowed.

Nonetheless, he had never felt less tired in his life.

"Gentlemen," Lord Gervais began. "We meet Lord Trevelyan and his men at the meadow. The boundaries you know. The retreats are the inn outside the village, the mill and the convent. Sir Ollerund and Lord Trevelyan's steward will act as *diseurs* in case of dispute and will give the signal to begin. Good luck to you all, and may you win many ransoms!"

The knights cheered and began riding out of the castle.

Trevelyan's men were waiting, a long line of mail-clad, mounted warriors. Like his squires, Urien noticed, Trevelyan's men had all sorts and conditions of weapons and armor.

Urien adjusted his helm, holding his lance easily in his right hand, and surveyed his opponents, deciding which ones would yield the higher ransom. He caught sight of Baron DeLanyea and nodded briefly.

Donald, beside him, flexed his shield arm as Lord Trevelyan and Lord Gervais met in the center of the field, bowing slightly. Together, they recited a vow of honorable fighting, which all the men repeated. Then they returned to their sides.

Urien picked his first man. The knight's mail was in excellent condition, his surcoat richly embroidered and his helm finely polished, but he shifted awkwardly in his saddle and had trouble balancing his lance.

Sir Ollerund sat at the side of the assembly in the pavilion accompanied by another, older knight. Together they raised their arms and brought them down in a signal to begin.

Urien kicked his heels against his horse's sides and the animal began a lumbering canter toward the opposite line of men. Despite the beast's seeming uncontrollable weight and speed, it responded immediately to the slightest direction from Urien.

He raised his lance, holding it against his body as he took his aim, adjusting it easily to the jolting strides of his horse. He clenched his jaw as he moved the weapon slightly away from his body, so that when it hit, there would be some space to absorb the blow.

He adjusted his lance a little higher, for the man coming toward him was tall. The fellow also held his shield badly, low and turned too far out. It would be a simple matter to push his lance under the shield, not only knocking the man from his horse, but piercing his mail as well.

But this was not a battle, merely a tournament. At the last moment before impact, Urien turned his lance slightly. It struck the shield dead on, the force of the weight and speed of Urien and his horse sending the other knight tumbling into the dirt while his lance swung high in the air.

Urien dismounted quickly, leaving his horse to find its own way from the field. His sword was in his hand before the other knight rose to his feet, but the fellow was not to be underestimated. He stood and drew his sword in one fluid motion. Urien quickly realized that while the knight was a poor aim with his lance, he knew what he was doing with a sword. And he had managed to keep hold of his shield.

Urien crouched low, wary and watchful, waiting for the other knight to swing first. It was a test, of sorts, of nerve and patience. Urien usually won such tests. This man, however, seemed to possess great patience, too, so they circled each other like dogs.

Finally, the man lifted his sword to strike. Urien was ready, parrying the blow easily, and happy that he had shown the greater patience. Half the battle was already over.

Nevertheless, it wasn't easy to defeat the knight. He was a good, well-trained swordsman, and against a man with less experience he would have had a good chance of winning. Unfortunately, the knight had the ill luck to meet a man who had spent the past ten years of life fighting, and who was determined to win.

After nearly two hours of trading blows, Urien finally felt his opponent was beginning to weaken—as he was. Now he had to keep his wits about him and hope that his strength would outlast the other man's.

It did, and one last blow sent the knight's sword spinning out of his hand. "I yield," he said, his breathing labored as he stood with his hands on his knees.

"Accepted," Urien replied, panting and putting his sword in his scabbard. He drew off his helm.

Around them, most of the other knights were still involved in sword fights. Over by the mill he saw others sitting on the ground, drinking and laughing. He didn't see anyone who looked injured.

"I am Sir George de Gramercie," his opponent said affably, doffing his helmet to reveal a pleasant, friendly face.

"I am Urien Fitzroy. Sir Urien Fitzroy."

"I'd say it was a pleasure, sir, if I wasn't nearly dead of thirst. Shall we discuss the terms of my ransom over some wine?"

"With the greatest pleasure."

Urien bent down to pick up his shield as Sir George began walking toward the mill.

Later Urien realized that had he not taken off his helmet only moments before, he would never have heard the sound of the sword being drawn behind him or caught the brief, unusual movement out of the corner of his eye.

Fortunately, he did, wheeling around just as a man behind him swung his sword. The blow glanced off Urien's mail harmlessly, but if he hadn't moved, it would have split his head.

Quickly Urien drew his sword, realizing that his attacker had been thrown off balance by his defensive movement.

This was no mock battle, no tournament for ransom and glory. The man had struck to kill, and Urien instinctively did the same, using all that remained of his strength.

Fortunately the fellow's mail had been made more for the way it looked than the way it protected the wearer, and Urien's blow pierced it, causing his opponent to cry out and sink to his knees, his hand to his side. Blood oozed out slowly between his gloved fingers.

Urien held his sword at the man's throat, well aware that he had every right to execute him.

"God's wounds, trying to kill you, he was."

Urien turned his shoulders and saw Baron DeLanyea standing with his arms crossed, surveying the scene casually. "Going to kill him or not?" the Welshman asked.

Urien stared down at the person who had attacked his back when he was unarmed and unprepared. "Maybe."

Sir George and some of the other knights who realized something unforeseen had occurred hurried toward them, including Sir Ollerund. "What happened?" the steward asked.

"He came at Fitzroy shamefully," Baron DeLanyea said. "Not even on the field for the lance charge, I don't think."

Sir George nodded in agreement. "I've never seen that armor before."

Sir Ollerund hoisted the wounded man to his feet. "Take off your helmet, sir."

Fitzroy's attacker lifted his helmet gingerly, to reveal the terrified, pale and pain-racked face of Seldon.

Everyone gasped, except Urien. He had recognized Seldon's particular grip of a sword, the way he moved always to the left, even the hunch of his shoulders. The boy licked his dry lips and his gaze flicked from knight to knight before coming to rest on Urien.

"Go to the mill and wait," Sir Ollerund said coldly, since it was clear by now that Seldon's wound was not mortal.

The boy trudged off the field, still clutching his side.

"Dishonorable, cowardly thing to do, I must say," Sir George said. Several other of the knights nodded their agreement. "What do you intend to do to the fellow?"

Urien shrugged. Now that the fight was over, he felt exhausted. But he was not too exhausted to realize that

these knights, every one of them born noble, were reacting as if one of their own had been the victim of the
cowardly strike. As if he, Urien Fitzroy, was one of
them. He grinned suddenly. "Demand a huge ransom, of course."

Sir Ollerund nodded and returned to the pavilion.

"Plucking two chickens at the same time?" Baron
DeLanyea said with a laugh as the other knights began to move off.

"I must protest being called a chicken, even if I *am*
going to be stuffed," Sir George said. "I understand
Lord Gervais' cook is something of a marvel."

"If Lord Gervais' chickens are as tough as you, he
would have to be," Urien replied. "Or perhaps it
would be wiser to have venison."

Together the three men walked off the field toward
the castle.

Fritha stared in dismay at her blue gown. Something—or someone—had spilled red wine down the
length of the front. It was completely ruined.

As she surveyed the damage, she didn't know
whether to scream in anger or cry in despair. Tonight
she wanted to look her very best. For Urien.

"A pity, my dear, but I've warned you that the
maidservants can be very careless."

Fritha wheeled around. Adela, most uncharacter-
istically, had come to the maids' quarters. "Have you
nothing else to wear tonight?"

"Nothing as nice, my lady."

"As I said, a pity. I would be happy to lend you one
of my old gowns."

"No, thank you, my lady."

"Lord Gervais particularly wishes that you make a fine impression tonight. There will be so many young knights. And it is high time you were wed, you know. People are beginning to talk."

Fritha looked at Adela's lovely, cold face and kept the smile from her lips. Adela's words meant nothing now. But that didn't prevent a devilish impulse from putting words in her mouth. "Do you think Lord Trevelyan might find me pleasing?"

She had said it as a jest, but Adela's mouth narrowed and her nostrils flared. A cold, angry look came to her eyes.

Suddenly Fritha was afraid. Adela didn't find her remark at all funny—she was upset by it.

"I wouldn't aim too high, my dear," Adela said mildly as her expression became more placid. "Nor would I be so unwise as to do anything that might sully my reputation—if I were you."

With that Adela smiled and left the room.

Fritha stared after her, all thoughts of gowns and feasts gone. What had just happened?

It could be that she had been too obvious in her affection for Urien, but that wouldn't matter after the tournament. Urien would ask for her in marriage, and Lord Gervais would agree. It was clear that Lord Gervais thought highly of Urien, so surely he would not refuse.

No, what was more confusing was Adela's reaction when she had mentioned Lord Trevelyan.

But Adela had been trying to have her betrothed for a long time. She could understand that Adela wouldn't want any hint of scandal around a woman she was hoping to get rid of, but why be upset about Lord Trevelyan?

She thought back over the times she had seen Adela with Lord Trevelyan, especially the previous evening. She remembered the little flirtations, which had seemed harmless enough, since flirting came as easily as breathing to Adela.

Could it be that Adela didn't like the idea of Fritha marrying someone even wealthier and more powerful than Lord Gervais? Was Adela *jealous?* Of her?

For a moment Fritha smiled at the idea. It would be worth something to make Adela suffer a little, although Adela had nothing to be jealous about, after all. She was happily married. . . .

Wasn't she?

What if she were not so happily married?

Fritha shivered. What if Adela's ambitions had not yet been achieved? What if she required another richer, more powerful man?

Surely Adela wouldn't go that far. Dear God, surely not!

Fritha ran to the window. She wanted to tell Urien of her fear.

Most of the knights and squires were milling about the courtyard, talking about the hastilude before retiring to prepare for the evening's feast.

There he was, standing beside Baron DeLanyea and another knight. Quickly she hurried outside and walked toward the men.

"I beg your pardon, gentlemen," she said, trying not to sound panicked. Urien smiled at her, a warm, secret smile that nevertheless could not lessen her dread.

"Lady Fritha, a pleasure to see you again," Baron DeLanyea said with a grin.

"I must speak with Sir Fitzroy on a matter of business, if you please."

"Ah, but then we'll be deprived of your charming company," said an unfamiliar voice.

Fritha turned toward the knight who had just spoken. She didn't recognize him. He was about Urien's age or a little younger. He smiled in an attractive, friendly way, and his clothes were very fine. She nodded back with a brief smile.

"Since none of these louts will introduce me," he said, "I shall be forced to do it myself. I am Sir George de Gramercie, my most charming and lovely lady."

"This is Lady Fritha Kendrick," Urien said brusquely.

Fritha nodded impatiently. "If you please, gentlemen, I must speak with Sir Fitzroy."

When Urien moved away from the others, she hurried toward the hall, trying hard not to glance back over her shoulder to make sure he was following.

"A most beautiful woman," Sir George said speculatively to the baron as they watched her walk away with Fitzroy sauntering behind. "It's a pity you're leaving without sharing another meal in such fine company."

"I've been too long from home already," Baron DeLanyea said. "I'm missing my wife. And about Lady Fritha—keeping your opinions about her to yourself, I'd be. Unless you want to find Fitzroy's fist in your face.''

Sir George chuckled. "Oh, it's like that, eh?"

"Yes, it's like that."

"Thanks for the warning."

Chapter Fourteen

Fritha led Urien into the kitchen corridor and upstairs to the maidservants' quarters. Fortunately, the maids were all occupied, and they managed to get upstairs without being seen.

As she hurried along, she tried to convince herself that she had let her imagination get carried away. After all, it *was* Adela's nature to flirt. Perhaps she had been too quick to see an intrigue that didn't exist.

They reached the long upper room. Quickly she pulled Urien inside and closed the door after him. She opened her mouth to tell him she had probably made a stupid mistake, but before she could say anything, he took her in his arms and kissed her passionately.

"Urien!" she managed to gasp after a moment.

He gave her a wicked, roguish look. "I thought you couldn't wait. I don't want to."

He bent his head to kiss her again, but she put her fingers on his lips and wiggled out of his arms. "No, please. I ... I have to talk to you."

"So you've heard all about it."

"About what?"

"The tournament."

"I haven't had time to hear anything but—"

He frowned with mock displeasure. "And I thought you were concerned because that fool tried to kill me."

She stared at him, everything else momentarily forgotten. "What fool? What happened? Are you hurt?"

He pulled her into his arms. "Now that's better. Don't worry, though, it was nothing serious."

"Who attacked you? In the melee? Are you injured anywhere?"

"I've had closer brushes with death before. It was after the melee, when I had captured Sir George, who, I should mention, is quite rich. I should be able to get a fine ransom—"

"What about the attack?"

He looked down at her, truly serious this time. "It seems, my love, that your warning about Seldon had merit after all."

"*He* attacked you? But he wasn't one of the squires chosen to be in the tournament."

Urien shook his head. "No. He had on Tallentine's armor."

"Tallentine!"

"Who now claims that his armor was stolen from his tent."

"Did Seldon take it?"

"He's not saying anything."

"What's going to happen to Seldon?"

"I'm going to make him pay rather dearly for his little escapade."

She leaned back and looked at him with slight dread. "How?"

He smiled at her. "Money. For my wedding. Now, what was so urgent that you practically dragged me from the courtyard?"

"It's Adela." She clasped her hands together and shrugged. "Maybe it's nothing, but I said something about marrying Lord Trevelyan—"

"Trevelyan!"

"It was just a jest, Urien. She was talking again about betrothing me, and I suppose I wanted to make her stop."

"Did it?"

"No. Then she said I shouldn't do anything that would ruin my reputation. I think she knows about us."

"I'm going to talk to Lord Gervais first thing tomorrow. Perhaps, in the meantime, we should keep our distance," he said, reaching out and running his hand along her arm.

She smiled, then frowned. "I wish we could get married today."

"I do, as well. But you're still worried about something. Or someone."

"It was the way Adela looked when I mentioned Lord Trevelyan. She looked...upset. I'm...I'm afraid she has plans, plans that don't include Lord Gervais but that do include Lord Trevelyan now that his wife is dead. I'm afraid that Lord Gervais is in danger."

Urien stared at her, understanding dawning on his face. "You can't mean that. Why would she do such a thing? Lord Gervais is a fine man. I can't believe she would do anything to harm him."

Fritha went to him, putting her arms around him. "I hope I'm wrong. I know she's ambitious—"

"No woman is *that* ambitious."

Fritha held him tight, wanting to believe his words.

Urien returned Fritha's embrace with equal force, trying to make himself believe his own words. Surely no woman would ever contemplate ridding herself of a fine husband like Lord Gervais on the chance of marrying another, even if the other was richer and more powerful.

It was absurd, truly absurd. Fritha had to be wrong.

Nonetheless, he decided he would watch Lady Gervais very carefully tonight as she sat beside Lord Trevelyan, just to reassure himself.

Fritha sighed. "I feel better for having talked to you, Urien. I hope I'm imagining plots that don't exist."

He kissed her forehead. "You can't worry about Lord Gervais all your life. He can take care of himself, you know. Besides, when you're my wife, I'll expect you to be thinking of other things."

Her smile was devastatingly enticing. "Such as, Sir Knight?"

"Such as pleasing me." He ran his hands up her arms and took her face between his palms, pressing a kiss to her warm, willing lips. She seemed to melt into his arms, molding her curves into his body, causing heat to course through every fiber. He stepped back. "If there's a temptress in Bridgeford Wells, it's you. I should be preparing for the feast. And shouldn't you?"

Fritha gave a guilty little start and a quick glance over her shoulder. He saw the stained dress on a bed. It must be her bed, he realized, and he was hard-pressed to keep from picking her up and throwing her onto it, then kissing her, pulling her bodice down slowly...

He cleared his throat, but his voice was a rather strained when he spoke. "What did you do to it?"

"*I* didn't do anything," she said ruefully, "but I won't make any unfounded accusations. However, I won't be wearing that to the feast."

"You know what I'd like you to wear?"

"No."

"Nothing."

She slapped his arm. "You are a very wicked man, Urien Fitzroy, knight or no."

"Merely a suggestion."

She looked at him boldly. "I will...if you will."

This time *he* looked scandalized, and she laughed gaily. "Very well. We shall both be properly covered. Since that is the case, you'd best go get ready, and I should be making sure everything is going well in the kitchen."

She went to the door and opened it, peering down the corridor. She saw no one and wiggled her finger for him to follow. He came to the door, but before following her, he pulled her to him for one quick, ardent kiss.

"Remember," she whispered with a grin, "we must keep our distance."

Urien could hardly stand the wait. Would she wear his gift, or not?

After he had left Fritha, he had gone to his quarters, washed quickly, and then found Baron DeLanyea and Sir George in the courtyard.

Baron DeLanyea was about to leave, so Urien and Sir George went with him to Bern's for a final drink. After several final drinks, DeLanyea had departed with a hearty farewell.

Alone with Sir George, Urien finally managed to announce that he wanted to buy a present for a lady and needed some help.

Apparently Sir George didn't think it at all unusual for a knight to buy a lady a gown, but he said, "I don't believe you have enough time, now, if the lady's to wear it this night."

Urien couldn't keep the disappointment off his face.

"Is it for Lady Fritha, by any chance?"

Urien nodded, frowning.

"Just a simple question, sir. I have other interests at home, I assure you. It just so happens I may be able to help."

"How?"

"Well, my 'other interest'... she's not my wife, but very accommodating. I bought a gown for her the other day. I've plenty of time to get another before I go back home. It's a very lovely shade of red and would suit the lady to perfection—if you don't mind me saying. Would you accept it as part of my ransom?"

Urien had quickly agreed, and then got one of the maids to take the wrapped parcel to Fritha.

Just when he was beginning to think Lord and Lady Gervais and the other important guests were never going to enter the great hall, a herald blew a blast on a trumpet.

And then he saw her.

Her smile was as glorious as dawn, her eyes as bright as a new moon. The gown, a deep, rich red embroidered with gold, hugged every delicious curve of her body as if it had grown there. The merest swell of her breasts showed above the bodice, just enough to remind him of what lay beneath. Her slender, wondrous hands peeked out of the voluminous sleeves. And she was looking at him. Only at him.

Fritha tried not to stare, but Urien looked so marvelous that she couldn't take her gaze from him—nor did she truly want to. He looked like some dark, mysterious animal, his vitality masked only by the fine clothes.

He wore a new black tunic that hung below his knees. The sleeves were cut wide, but that only seemed to emphasize the breadth of his chest. His muscular calves, encased in black *chausses,* showed beneath. But most wondrous of all was the look in his eyes as he stared back. As if she were the most beautiful woman on earth, and the love of his heart.

Unfortunately, tonight Urien was not to sit at the high table. He was below the dais, at another table. Sir George de Gramercie was seated beside her instead. Tallentine was not in the hall, and it appeared that Hylda's gossip—that Tallentine had ridden home in disgrace—was well founded.

Sir Ollerund sat with Lord Trevelyan's steward and some of the squires who had taken part in the tournament, and Fritha watched him for a little while. He looked tired. Perhaps after the tournament he would get some much-needed rest.

Godwin had prepared an astounding variety of dishes, each with its own particular sauce. There were several kinds of fish, venison, mutton, a whole boar and several chickens. During the meal, a minstrel sang, accompanied by two men playing harp and tabor.

Adela had wanted the finest linen spread on the tables and had ordered them strewn with fresh flower petals. Expensive candles lit the hall rather than rush torches, even near the kitchen corridor.

Although Sir George was polite and even rather amusing, Fritha thought the meal was never going to end. The pages, who had been allowed to watch much of the tournament, were in such a state of excitement that Fritha feared for wine stains, but they behaved themselves admirably.

As the pages brought clean trenchers and set out platters of fresh fruit, more musicians entered the hall.

Fritha sighed softly. Of course there would be dancing. She glanced down at Urien again and frowned slightly. He shrugged his shoulders.

As always, Adela began the *estampie*. Tonight Lord Trevelyan was her partner, and as Fritha watched them dance, she reflected that she had probably been mistaken about Adela's intrigues. Adela smiled at her partner, but Fritha could detect nothing more than friendliness in her eyes—and she was watching very carefully. For the first time since that afternoon, she truly felt that her fears had been the stuff of dreams and old worries.

Sir George commandeered Fritha when it was his turn for the dance, and Fritha complied, although she still didn't enjoy dancing in the middle of the room and being stared at.

At least there was one compensation. After the *estampie* Sir George led her to Urien, and together they watched the rest of the dance.

Then Sir Nevil, obviously bored by the formality of the *estampie,* demanded a *carole*.

Sir George smiled. "I must insist upon dancing this," he said to Urien. "But I don't see any reason you shouldn't take the other side of the charming Lady Fritha in the circle, my friend."

To Fritha's surprise—and delight—Urien actually began to blush. "I don't know how to dance," he said coldly.

"It's much easier than a lance charge. Really. Just watch me." So saying, Sir George practically dragged Urien into the circle.

Once the dance began, however, Fritha could only marvel at how quickly Urien learned the simple steps. The music went faster and faster and they moved more quickly in the circle, hands held fast. When it was finished, she could scarcely breathe.

Sir George wandered off toward Sir Nevil, leaving Urien and Fritha standing at the side of the hall.

"You dance very well," she said, laughing and trying to catch her breath.

"So do you."

His arm brushed against hers, sending her pulse racing for another reason. He looked out over the floor. "Come to the riverbank tonight," he whispered.

"Why?"

He cleared his throat. "I'm not going to say right here."

Another *carole* began, and she pulled him into the circle. "Tell me, or I won't come."

The dance began, the circle moving to the right. He tried to concentrate on the steps, but it was very difficult with Fritha smiling and looking so delectable he wanted to carry her to the stables or her bedchamber above and make love with her all night long.

They moved close together in the circle. "I need you," he managed to whisper before they moved apart again.

The next time she came close, she batted her eyes innocently at him. "For what, Sir Knight?"

"For—" The circle moved faster. It seemed like an hour before she was near enough for him to risk speaking. "Will you come?"

She moved away, laughing gaily as Sir George uttered some nonsense about the music. At last the music ended, and Urien marched off to lean against the wall. He wasn't going to beg. That was a certainty.

If she found Sir George so vastly amusing, perhaps she would rather *dance* than come to the river.

Fritha sauntered up to him. "Good night, Sir Urien Fitzroy," she said solemnly. "I'm very tired and must beg to be excused further dancing."

He scowled at her. He wasn't going to utter some polite meaningless words. He'd done enough trying to master those silly dances. And he'd had enough of her teasing, too.

"I believe the moon will be full," she said softly. "A perfect night for a walk by the river." Then she winked at him and moved away.

* * *

Fritha waited in the shadows by the gate in the courtyard until the guard turned away to talk to his fellow. Feeling like a child sneaking off to steal apples, she quickly and quietly hurried under the portcullis and into the town.

Keeping to lesser known ways, and in shadows, she was soon in the woods.

A sound made her halt, but it was an owl hooting nearby. She listened carefully, but heard only the small scuffling sounds of forest animals.

It was a rather dangerous thing to do, going off into the woods in the middle of the night. But it was also exciting, especially when she was going to meet Urien.

She didn't dally, but hurried onward to the river, hoping he would already be there.

No one was on the riverbank. She tried to subdue her disappointment. Then she heard splashes.

Ducking under the huge willow tree branches, she moved forward. Urien was in the water, floating on his back under the canopy of the willow's overhanging leaves.

He was completely naked. She glanced about and smiled to herself when she saw the neat pile of clothing beside the tree. And the cloak spread out beside it.

She was going to let herself enjoy watching him, but he saw her and stood up.

"I didn't expect to find you bathing," she said as he stood motionless in the waist-deep water.

"You surely didn't expect to find me washing my clothes."

She grinned. "No."

"Join me."

"It's too cold."

"I'll keep you warm."

"You come *here*."

He shook his head, a wonderfully seductive expression on his shadowed face.

A warm fragrant breeze stirred the lacy branches of the tree. He looked like some ancient god of the stream, rising up to take a human woman for a lover. "Come here," he whispered.

He *was* a god. The god of her heart, her life. And yet he was a man, with needs and wants like hers. A home. A place to belong, secure and happy.

He was irresistible. Fritha wanted nothing more than to be in his arms. Slowly she untied her gown, letting it slip from her body. Her toes tingled when she stepped into the river.

Then he had her in his warm, strong embrace. His lips turned hers to molten fire, his hands caressed her as only he could.

She felt wild and pagan and free here under the branches, the water of the stream slipping past them. With a low moan, she trailed her lips across his cheek, down his neck and down again. His hands pressed on her back as he arched, groaning as her mouth toyed with his nipples. She felt the muscles in his back tense and dragged her lips back to his.

His strong, firm hands cupped her buttocks, lifting her. Wrapping her legs about him, buoyed by the water, she clutched his shoulders. And gasped when he entered her, surprised for only an instant. He began to move, his hands gripping tighter and tighter as she clung to him, moving rhythmically, passionately attuned to the surge of his body within and without. Then he groaned and shuddered, and his hands relaxed their grip.

She slipped slowly down, letting her breasts brush against him. He picked her up and carried her from the water, laying her on the cloak and pulling it around them so they were like a caterpillar in a cocoon.

"That was wonderful," she said quietly.

He toyed with a lock of her damp hair. "For me, certainly." His hand journeyed toward her neck, and one finger traced a path to the tops of her breasts. "Not so much for you, I think."

His finger continued downward, making her squirm with delight and impatience. Then he bent down and with his tongue he teased her hardened nipples until she wanted to pull him inside. "Please, Urien!" she gasped.

He chuckled softly, not stopping, although she thought she would die if he didn't take her soon. His mouth left her breasts, but before she could protest, she felt it elsewhere. Her eyes widened, but a moment later she closed them, the sensations of his touch and his tongue altogether too new and powerful for her to do anything except experience and enjoy.

Tension, delightful and excruciating, built inside her. He cupped her breasts in his hands, his thumbs brushing softly. And then, in one glorious moment, the tension burst. Wave after wave of release flooded through her.

"Was that 'wonderful'?"

She opened her eyes, to find Urien leaning over her, a wide smile on his handsome face. "You know it was.

Better than wonderful." She gave him a sidelong glance. "I think I have a lot to learn."

"And I shall be delighted to teach you."

Chapter Fifteen

Beneath the cloak Fritha cuddled closer to Urien's naked body. "Cold?" he whispered.

"A little. The dew is heavy. It must be nearly morning."

"Nearly."

She made no effort to leave the warm cocoon of his arms. "I wish we could stay here forever."

"It would get rather uncomfortable after a while," he said solemnly. "I've slept on the ground many times, but you're not used to sleeping in anything but a bed."

"There was the stable."

"There was straw to cushion you. And me."

"Ah, yes. And you..."

He shifted slightly after their kiss. "I'm going to ask Lord Gervais for your hand tomorrow—I mean today. Or do you want me to wait any longer? Obviously we're not very successful at keeping a distance from one another."

She smiled at him. "No, we're not. And no, I don't want you to wait any longer before asking for my hand. Or any other part of my body." She gave him a smug, knowing look. "Much as I know you *can* wait for certain pleasures..."

"It isn't good to rush instruction," he said, just as smug and knowing.

She reached up and tweaked his nose. He grabbed her hand in his and held her other arm, but then pressed a kiss to her palm.

"You are a wonderful teacher, Urien."

"And you sleep very nicely, even if I have to be the bed."

"Did I sleep?"

"Yes. I obviously exhausted you."

"You *are* rather exhausting. Still, that's something I've never been told before, that I sleep well."

"I should hope not."

"I'm sure the maids would have said if I snored or spoke aloud."

"You didn't snore, but you did say things."

"Such as?"

He bent closer and whispered words that made her flush with embarrassment. Then she looked at his face and saw the laughter in his eyes.

"I never said those things! I don't even know what some of them *mean*."

Desire flashed in his dark eyes as he leaned closer. "I plan to show you each and every one."

He started by caressing her thigh, his touch making her feel warm and soft—until he encountered a ticklish spot that made her squirm.

"Ah, now I find that most interesting," he murmured, his lips against her cheek. "Even if you weren't speaking out loud in your sleep, I'm sure you were dreaming such things."

She laughed softly and drew back—but not too far. "Urien Fitzroy, I believe you are an arrogant, conceited lover."

"And you're a hot-tempered vixen who doesn't listen to anybody. But I'm willing to forgive you."

"If you feel that way about me, perhaps I should leave."

He sighed. "I suppose we should get back to the castle."

"Soon," Fritha assured him. "Are you going to the fair? I saw that the jugglers who came for the last tournament have come back, and there are many merchants."

"No," Urien said.

"Why not?"

"I don't like crowds much. Too many cutpurses. And don't you have things to attend to?"

"You were the one who told me I was always doing too much. Besides, Hylda should be able to manage for a part of the morning."

"I'm very tired. I didn't get much sleep last night."

She gave him a sidelong glance. "A lot of young men take their sweethearts to the fair."

"You're not my sweetheart."

She frowned and pulled away, now able to see his face clearer in the brightening morning. "I'm not?"

He smiled, his eyes full of love. "You're certainly more than a sweetheart. I suppose." He sighed and assumed a virtuous expression. "I should be prepared to make sacrifices to prove my feelings. I'll go with you. But only for a little while in the morning. Remember, I have something very important to discuss with Lord Gervais—our marriage."

Fritha leaned forward and rewarded him with a passionate kiss. "I'll meet you at Meara's as soon as I can."

"So Lady Gervais has no opportunity to see us together?"

"So she can't spoil our happiness."

Despite some minor problems that needed Fritha's attention at the castle, she was soon able to leave. Hylda seemed only too happy to take charge of the morning duties and also put Fritha's mind at rest about the previous night. Apparently all the maidservants assumed Fritha had simply gone to bed late and risen early, as she had been known to do before when there were several guests staying at the castle.

Fritha had a wonderful time at the fair, seeing a carefree side of Urien she now knew existed, but had never seen when others were present.

As they wandered from stall to stall examining the wares the peddlers and other merchants had brought to Bridgeford Wells, Urien often made straight-faced remarks that either made her giggle or blush. He laughed out loud at the antics of the jugglers and tumblers and watched a group of traveling players perform a mock battle.

Fritha was waylaid and greeted by almost everyone they passed. Urien realized she wasn't spoken to with the kind of deferential treatment that met the progress of Lady Gervais when she appeared in the hall. No, this was more like people greeting a member of their family.

He had never seen anything quite like it.

They finally reached the alehouse, but one look at the crowd around it made Urien decide he could do without ale at the moment. As Fritha paused to speak to some of the women whose husbands were dallying over their mugs, he wandered over to a peddler's cart. The shrewd, wizened old man had quite an interesting collection of jewelry. One piece, a silver pin in the shape of a snake, caught his eye.

The peddler grinned like a gargoyle. "That's a very fine piece, sir. Made by a Northman."

Urien gave the man a skeptical look. "I didn't realize the Vikings were known for their jewelry."

"Ah, but they could do most wonderful things. Just look at the workmanship in that, and it's more than fifty years old, sir."

"It is very finely wrought."

"I could let you have it for, oh, say fifty pence, and that's just giving it to you, 'cause you're such a fine gentleman."

"I am no gentleman."

The old man backed up a bit. "Well, you *look* like one. No harm meant, sir."

"Oh, Urien, isn't that beautiful?"

He turned to find Fritha at his elbow, eyeing the brooch in his hand. "Do you like it?"

"It's very pretty. And it seems almost alive."

He turned it over in his hand to check the clasp for wear.

"Good day, Mistress Fritha!" the old man said with a huge smile. "I tell you what, seein's as you're so taken with it, I'll let you have it for, say, oh, twenty pence."

Urien glared at the old man. "You told me fifty."

"I don't have twenty pence, Derrin."

"This gent . . . man does, though, I think."

"I'll take it."

"Oh, Urien, you don't have to—"

"I want to."

Fritha laughed gaily. "Very well—because I know Derrin's given you a more than fair price."

"Huh." Urien took his purse and counted out twenty pence.

"I have some other fine things—" the peddler began.

"No." Urien gave the peddler the money and took the brooch. "Here," he said, handing it to Fritha.

"Oh, Urien, it's lovely!"

"I'm glad you like it. Now, I want to see Lord Gervais. I should think you'd want me to talk to him, too, instead of wandering around all these carts."

At that moment Hylda ran up to them. She was close to tears and winded.

"What is it?" Fritha asked.

The girl began to cry and Fritha suddenly found it difficult to breathe. "Hylda, what is it?"

"Oh, my lady! It's Sir Ollerund. He's taken sick. He's very bad. Come with me, quick!"

Fritha didn't wait to question Hylda, but took off at a run with Hylda and Urien following behind. When they reached the castle, several servants were standing in the courtyard talking in hushed voices. Fritha ignored them, running as fast as she could to the great hall.

The knights who had not left yet after the tournament were speaking together in small huddled groups, their faces grave.

Her heart began pounding with a horrible dread. Sir Ollerund had not been well, and last night he had looked so tired! She should have done something. Said something.

She hurried on toward the small room that Sir Ollerund used as both place of business and bed-chamber when he stayed at the castle.

Sir Ollerund lay on his narrow bed, and Lord Gervais sat beside him, holding his friend's hand. Two pages, their faces unnaturally solemn, stood silently by the wall.

Her foster father looked up at her with sorrowful eyes.

"What happened?" she asked softly, kneeling down beside the bed.

"I was talking to him and suddenly he fainted. The apothecary's gone to the kitchen to make a draft. He looked unwell this morning, but he said he was merely tired."

Fritha heard a sound at the door. It was Urien. She looked up at him, too filled with anxiety and worry to speak.

"I should have made him rest," Lord Gervais whispered. "I should have told him not to trouble himself with anything. I should have..." He sighed raggedly.

Fritha reached out to take Lord Gervais' hand in hers, squeezing it tightly as tears welled in her eyes.

She waited with Lord Gervais for the rest of the day.

Lady Gervais came once and stayed for only a moment, claiming she was too distraught to remain.

Fritha was relieved when she left. This was not her sorrow. She had no place here.

But then she realized that Urien was no longer in the room, either. His absence puzzled and hurt her. She wanted him there, even if he said nothing. She needed to feel his presence, his strength, his love.

He never came back.

Sir Ollerund revived a little to drink some of the apothecary's strong-smelling draft, but he slumped back afterward, unconscious. As the day passed, the apothecary's expression grew graver and graver.

"How long before the medicine works?" Fritha asked when she could no longer stand the silence broken only by Sir Ollerund's labored breathing.

The apothecary shrugged apologetically and whispered, "It should have roused him by now."

She glanced at Lord Gervais, his face drawn with sorrow. She went to him and gently laid her hand on his shoulder. He looked at her, his eyes shining with unshed tears, and patted her hand gently, saying nothing. There was nothing to say.

Toward nightfall, Sir Ollerund suddenly stirred and opened his eyes. He looked first at Lord Gervais, then Fritha.

"Fritha," he said quietly, his voice calm.

She wiped the tears from her eyes and managed to smile. She took the older man's hand in hers. "I'm here."

Sir Ollerund smiled at Lord Gervais. "My friend," he whispered.

He turned back to Fritha, a trace of his gentle smile on his lips. "Take care of him. Don't let him spend too much money."

And then he died.

* * *

With a heavy sigh Urien busied himself in the weapons store, checking lances and swords for damage. Outside, a heavy fog shrouded the courtyard, making the world an eerie, unfriendly place. He walked to the door and peered out, barely able to see the light from Sir Ollerund's room.

He wondered if the steward had died yet.

He had seen death too many times not to recognize the mark of it on a man's face. The gray skin, the flaccid mouth, the labored breathing . . . it was merely a question of when.

He had wanted to stay, to offer what little comfort he could to Fritha, but it was not his place. Fritha didn't need him there, not when Lord Gervais was with her.

He was outside her grief. Better to take himself away and leave her alone with them.

He picked up a sword and began to rub it with an oiled cloth. He thought he heard something outside and as he got up to see what it was, the door to the storehouse opened. Lady Adela Gervais, covered in a cloak, came inside.

"My lady," he said, trying to mask his surprise, "how is Sir Ollerund?"

She took a step toward him and his heart began to pound. He didn't know what she wanted here with him, but he wished she would state her business and leave.

"Sir Ollerund is dead."

"I'm very sorry, my lady."

"He was an old man."

Her voice was cold, distant, as if Sir Ollerund had been nothing more than a dog. Then she smiled. "Tell me, Sir Urien," she asked softly, "are you happy here?"

He couldn't understand why she was asking. "Yes, my lady."

"There is nothing you lack?"

"No, my lady."

She was very close to him now. Too close. He suddenly felt as if he were facing an assassin.

"I like you, Urien."

He didn't reply.

She smiled, and there could be no mistaking the lustful gleam in her eyes. When he had first come to Bridgeford Wells he had dreamed of a moment like this, but now he wanted her to be gone.

"We must do everything in our powers to ensure that you stay," she said. "Especially now that Sir Ollerund is dead. My husband will need people around him he can trust."

"I'm happy you consider me trustworthy, my lady."

"Oh, I do. And most discreet, too." She slowly ran her hand up the shaft of a lance leaning against the wall. "I would like to help you, Urien."

He waited, feeling as he had when he faced Sir George in the tournament—only this time the battle was not with swords, but with words. "Where is Lord Gervais?"

"With the body. But let's not discuss that unpleasant business."

Urien made no effort to keep his disgust from his face at the way she spoke of her husband's oldest friend. He desperately wanted to know where Fritha was, but wouldn't risk revealing his concern to Lady Adela.

"I should like to ask you something. May I?"

He remained motionless.

"Are you as good a lover as I imagine?"

He stared at her, not knowing what to answer. Or if he should even try.

"Shall I tell you what I imagine, Urien?" She began walking toward him again and he began to back away. "I imagine you naked in my bed, your hands caressing my body—" his back hit the wall "—your lips tasting mine, like this..."

Just as her mouth touched his, he put his hands on her shoulders and pushed her away. "What are you doing?"

"Come now, Urien. I think you know. We both know you've wanted me since we first saw each other. Do you deny it?"

"I don't want you now."

"Are you certain? *I* want *you.*"

Her hands glided over his chest and he stepped away. "I will not commit adultery."

She gave him a sly, sidelong glance that chilled him to the marrow of his bones. "But you have no qualms about seducing a virgin."

He said nothing.

"Oh, I know all about you and Fritha. It's a pity the girl will be disgraced when it becomes known what she's done."

"She hasn't done anything wrong."

"No? Then she's still a virgin, despite that meeting in the stable with you? You disappoint me, Urien."

He didn't answer.

She smiled coldly. "I thought so. I must say I had credited you with better taste." She ran her tongue over her lips. "Shall we discover your tastes, Urien?"

"Good night, my lady." He began to march toward the door.

"Aren't you forgetting something, my bold warrior? I am your lord's wife. One word from me, and you are gone from here."

He stopped and turned around slowly. "I will tell him everything."

"You will tell my doting husband that I tried to seduce you? I'll claim you tried to seduce *me*—and who do you think he'll believe?"

"I'm leaving."

"Oh, please, not yet, my dear. I've been thinking about you for so long, I'd like you to...linger...awhile yet."

"No." He was at the door.

"Poor Fritha."

He halted and looked back at Lady Gervais over his shoulder.

"It's a pity she'll have to suffer for your stubbornness."

He turned to face her. "What do you mean?"

"I mean, you can either satisfy our mutual curiosity and make love to me, or I'll be forced to reveal your seduction of the poor girl to Lord Gervais."

He took one step toward her. "Would you?"

A look of fear came into her face at his cold, calm words.

"Why are you doing this?" he demanded, pressing his momentary advantage. "We've done nothing to harm you."

The fear disappeared, replaced by another emotion. "I have my reasons."

At that instant, Urien saw the reason in her eyes. "You are *jealous!*"

"Me? Jealous of her?" Adela cried, her voice harsh and mocking, no longer the dulcet tones of Lady Gervais.

"Yes."

"Perhaps I am jealous of Fritha because she's had you."

He marveled at how quickly she resumed her mask of gentility. But too late. "God's blood, I pity you! You have so much—beauty, grace, a loving, rich husband, and yet you begrudge us happiness. Fritha was right. You are a selfish, evil woman."

"How dare you say such things to me!"

"It is the truth."

Adela pulled her cloak around her. "I'll give you one more chance, Sir Urien Fitzroy. Gervais will be at Sir Ollerund's estate for a few days. Come to my bed, and I will not only see that we find the experience mutually satisfying, but I will also do all in my powers to see that you are given an estate. If you don't come to my bed, I will tell Gervais that you have callously seduced Fritha and tried to seduce me.

"The choice, my bold, handsome, virile warrior, is yours."

Urien looked at the beautiful golden-haired woman. "I may be a bastard, my lady," he said coldly, "but I am not a whore."

Chapter Sixteen

Fritha stood on the battlements and sighed wearily. The fog surrounded her like damp, clammy fingers. A chill wind blew over her and she shivered, hugging herself tightly.

But what chilled her more was Urien's continuing absence and her own nagging guilt. To think that while she had been enjoying herself, Sir Ollerund was ill. How could she have abandoned her duties so completely?

Her gaze fell on the glowing chapel windows. Sir Ollerund's body had been prepared and now Lord Gervais kept a vigil. He had asked to be left alone, and so she had come here.

She sighed again, then turned when she heard footsteps on the parapet.

Urien stood nearby. She had missed him before, but suddenly she didn't know whether she wanted to see him or would rather be by herself.

He came toward her, but stopped before he reached her. In the fog she couldn't quite see his face.

"He was a good man," he said softly.

"Yes, a very good man."

"How is Lord Gervais?"

"The last time I saw him like this was when Lady Eleanor died."

"He'll get over it in time."

She nodded, hoping that would be true.

Urien took a step closer. "And you, Fritha? How are you?"

She shrugged her shoulders as he took another step closer. Then he embraced her, his warm arms tight around her.

She clung to him desperately, as if he were a strong tree on a windswept plain. He said nothing, but stroked her hair tenderly as she wept.

"I should have seen that he wasn't well," she said after several minutes, her voice choking.

"He kept telling everyone he was only tired," Urien said quietly but firmly. "If he felt ill, he should have stayed in bed."

She raised her tear-streaked face to look at him. "He might have, had I attended more to my duties. But I didn't. I was..."

"With me."

She nodded slowly. "Yes, with you."

"It's not your fault he died."

"If I hadn't been so selfish, I could have helped him more these past few days. All I've been thinking about is my own pleasure."

"You are not everyone's keeper, Fritha. He was a grown man, not a child."

She sighed, wanting to believe him as she held him tightly. "I needed you this afternoon," she whispered. "Why didn't you stay?"

"I had no place there."

"Yes, you did! Wherever I belong, so do you."

"And where I go, you will go?"

She heard something in his voice that made her look up at him questioningly.

"We must leave here. At once."

"What?" She stared at him, uncomprehendingly. "Why?"

"For our safety."

"What do you mean, Urien?"

He looked away, his face suddenly flushing. "It's Lady Gervais. You were right all along, Fritha. She is a very dangerous woman."

Fritha felt as if a huge wave had washed across her, leaving her struggling for air. She fought to keep panic at bay and concentrate on Urien. "What has she done?"

"Nothing, yet. It's what she's going to do. She came to talk to me."

"When?"

"A little while ago. I've been trying to find you."

"What did she say?"

"It doesn't matter. All that matters is that we have to leave here."

"Are you in danger?"

"*I'm* not."

So, the time had come. So soon! She had known that without Sir Ollerund, she was more vulnerable to Adela's schemes. But she had hoped for some time yet!

"Am I to be sent to the convent?"

"No."

"Betrothed, then, to Sir Tallentine?"

He didn't say anything.

"Not Sir Giles!"

"No."

"Then what has she planned?"

To her surprise, he let go of her and walked to the stone parapet. "She wants . . . she's asked me to make love to her."

"*What?*" she cried, staring at him. "Adela's full of evil, but she wouldn't risk committing adultery!"

"She says I either come to her bed, or she will expose your shame."

"I've done nothing . . ." She paused, realizing that she herself had given Adela a very great weapon to use against her. "But we're going to be married."

He turned around and looked at her. "Don't you understand? This woman is *dangerous*. She hates you. If she can't harm you one way, she'll find another."

Fritha gazed out over the town. "Either Adela wants you very much, or she's trying to make you run away."

"It doesn't matter what exactly she's planning. I don't want *her* and we're in danger unless we leave." He ground his fist into the palm of his other hand. "God's teeth! A fair fight I can understand, but this! She makes me feel . . . unclean."

Fritha straightened her shoulders and raised her eyes to Urien, finding strength in his presence. "I think she murdered Sir Ollerund."

"I'm beginning to think she's capable of anything. That's why we *must* leave."

Fritha shook her head. "And leave Adela to win? Never."

"It would be foolish to stay." He put his hands on her shoulders. "We should go at once," he repeated.

She shook her head. "Urien, please try to understand. I owe Lord Gervais too much to leave him, especially now when I think he needs me the most. Adela is a patient woman. If she has chosen to come to you now, she must feel it's time to set other plans in motion.

"*Everyone* is in danger. I can't go. I won't go."

He saw her grim, stubborn determination, and his heart faltered. He wanted her. Needed her, as he had never needed another living soul. She had the power to make his life a joy, or tear it apart with pain.

With her he had found something he had thought he would never have. He couldn't believe she didn't feel the same way, that she would refuse to take what he offered her.

That he wasn't enough.

So he did what anyone who had ever known him would have considered impossible. He pleaded. "Please come with me. You can't stay. Adela will find some way to hurt you."

It didn't change the look on her face. "Maybe she will. But I can't leave Lord Gervais to Adela."

"Fritha," he whispered, desperate now as he pulled her into his arms. "Fritha, don't you understand? I'm asking you to come with me and be my wife."

She gently pushed him away, her heart feeling as if it were being torn in two slowly. "Urien, I love you. But I cannot run away. This is my home. They *need* me here."

"I need you, too."

His eyes! How they seemed to be burn into hers. She saw that he meant everything he said. He was determined to leave. Oh, how easy it would be to go with him. To take the happiness and love he offered.

But at what price?

The safety of the man who had been a father to her and the people who were her friends. If anything happened to Lord Gervais, she had little doubt that Adela would drain the townspeople dry of money, of goods, of hope. They were her family, and this was her home. If Urien didn't understand this about her, perhaps she had been deluding herself that he understood her at all. "I can't go, Urien. Don't ask me to."

He stepped back, and the pain on his face struck her like a physical blow. "I mean what I say, Fritha. You have to choose between this place, or me."

She lowered her head, knowing she had already made that choice. "I'm staying, Urien."

His voice when he spoke, so filled with misery, stabbed at her. "I thought you loved me."

"I *do* love you, more than my life. If you stay, we can fight Adela together."

The mocking look that she hadn't seen for a long time appeared on Urien's face. "Obviously I made a mistake falling in love with you. You were already in love—with the whole damned town!"

She reached out to touch him, but he yanked his arm away. "It's my duty, Urien. Don't you understand?"

"No, I don't. I don't understand why you should martyr yourself for the sake of duty."

She walked up to him so that she could see his face clearly. "As a soldier, you should understand duty and responsibility, Urien. But it's not only a duty for me to care about the people here. They're my family, and my friends. Yes, I do love them—but that also means I must protect them.''

"To stay would be foolish.''

"It's not foolish to keep safe the people you love.''

"You'll be a lot of help when you're sent away in disgrace. Or dead.''

"Adela will have to succeed to do that. I mean what I say, Urien. I won't run away. I'm no coward.''

"And I am? I knew it was a mistake to tell you . . .'' His expression turned so cold and cruel his face seemed to belong to a stranger. "*I* would call leaving an act of wisdom.'' He bowed stiffly. "I am extremely grateful that you were able to spare a few minutes from your many duties to make love to me.

"But of course, a whole town can't perform that function, can they? Perhaps I should be grateful you saw fit to share your favors with an unworthy bastard.''

At his mocking words she felt a hurt so terrible and deep that for a moment death would have been preferable. As she stared at him, part of her knew he was lashing out at her because he truly couldn't understand her decision. But whatever his pain, he had no right to say such things, not when she was feeling an anguish equal to his.

She lifted her hand and slapped his face.

He didn't flinch or move a muscle. For one brief instant his eyes changed, but in the next they became as hard and unyielding as the stones of the castle. "Clearly, my lady, we *have* made a mistake.''

With that he turned and walked away, leaving her standing alone.

Fritha clenched her hands into tight fists, fighting the sorrow in her breast. Then she lost the battle, sinking to her knees with a moan like a wounded animal.

"By Jove's jewels, you don't mean it! You're not leaving!"

It had taken Urien only a few minutes to pack his few possessions and saddle his horse. He had intended to ride out of Bridgeford Wells without saying a word to anyone, but Bern had seen him and called out.

He stopped, and even though he didn't say anything, Bern saw his pack and guessed that he was leaving.

Urien kept his face expressionless. "It's time to move on."

"Surely not! Lord Gervais has made you a knight! You can't just leave."

"I can and I am."

"Come in and have a drink, then, anyway."

Reluctantly Urien got down. He had few friends in the world, and he realized he didn't want to lose one.

Lurilla was busy stirring some stew, but paused and straightened when Bern told her Urien was leaving.

Perhaps it was well he was going, Urien thought bitterly. He couldn't get used to the idea that his business was anybody's but his own. "I've been offered work in Wales. By Baron DeLanyea. The pay's very good," he said. The words began as a lie, but after he said them, he decided that plan was as good as another.

Lurilla looked as if she had questions to ask, but apparently thought better of it, which suited him fine. The children came crowding in at the door, smiling and greeting him.

God, he should never have come to Bridgeford Wells!

When Urien finished his ale, Bern nodded at the door. "We'll say our farewells outside," he said heartily, leading the way past the disappointed children.

The moment they were outside, Bern shoved Urien against the wall. "Now, then, what about Fritha?"

Urien glared at him. "What about her?"

"Everybody's been talking about you two. Lurilla and Meara's been planning the wedding feast, for God's sake."

Urien clenched his teeth and shoved Bern back. "I'm sorry to disappoint them, but perhaps they should have inquired of the intended bride and groom."

"Are you saying nothing happened between you and her?"

"I'm saying it's nobody's business."

"By God, Fitzroy, I'm making it my business. We all care about Fritha around here, and don't want to see her hurt."

"Then I suggest you take care of her and let me alone."

Bern planted his feet firmly, his hands on his hips. "Fitzroy, I want your word that you didn't take advantage of her."

Urien, his nerves raw with the strain of the past few hours, was in no mood to explain anything to anybody. "To hell with her, to hell with you and to hell with this whole damn place!"

He took a swing at Bern, who caught Urien's hand in his huge one, his grip tightening like a vise. "God's teeth, something has happened! By God, Fitzroy, if I find out you've done anything to hurt her, anything at all, I'll find you and you'll be sorry! And you'd better believe I'm not the only one you'll have to worry about."

He let Urien go. "Get on your horse and get the hell out of here. You're not the man I thought you were! I'm ashamed I ever knew you!"

He stalked back into the alehouse, slamming the door behind him.

With a muttered curse Urien mounted his horse and rode away.

Several days later, Adela watched her husband as he sat in their bedchamber, his shoulders slumped, his eyes covered by his hand. He looked very tired and very old.

She got up and walked over to the window. Outside, it still rained as it had for the past few days, a dismal, misty rain that never fell harder or showed any signs of stopping.

One of the squires ran across the courtyard, swathed in a cloak. The big one, Seldon, she thought. With the death of Sir Ollerund and the abrupt departure of Urien Fitzroy, the squires had been left to their own amusements.

She smiled slowly. Fitzroy hadn't said a word to anyone at the castle, but simply packed up and left, leaving his lover behind.

It was a pity that he hadn't taken her offer, although she had suspected from the first that he might not be as unscrupulous as most hired soldiers. Of course, had he come, afterward she would have screamed and called for help, then claimed that he had raped her.

Nonetheless, the main goal had been to have Fritha abandoned, and in that she had succeeded admirably.

Now that Sir Ollerund was dead, the only person who could impede her plans was a young woman with no one to aid her.

She subdued the one tiny pang of guilt that lay in her heart. Perhaps the dose of gentle poison that created Ollerund's first illness only made the inevitable arrive a little sooner.

Glancing at her husband, Adela wondered who would take the steward's place. That was the next part of her plan, to have a person of her choosing in that position. Perhaps she could even make some kind of monetary arrangement with the likely candidates, as she had with the miller. He paid for the privilege of working the mill, used false weights and paid her a percentage of the illegal profits. The only people who lost were the peasants, who were too ignorant to find any evidence of cheating.

Adela managed to squeeze out a decorous tear and sighed softly. "I've been thinking of poor Ollerund, my dear," she said mournfully, turning to her husband. "I'm sure we'll miss him very much."

"He's been my friend for forty years," Gervais said quietly. Slowly he raised his head and looked at her. "I'm getting old, Adela."

She went toward him and knelt beside him. "Oh, not you, my dear. He had been ill not long ago, remember. You haven't been sick as long as I've known you." After a few minutes of silence, she said softly, "Have you decided who to make steward in his place?"

"No."

"Perhaps Sir Tallentine."

"I don't know. I still think he let that boy take his place in the tournament. I don't trust him."

"I believe you're mistaken about that incident, my love. After all, the boy has never implicated Tallentine. And I must say it isn't fair to forgive the boy and blame Tallentine. Why, you haven't even sent that Seldon fellow home!"

Gervais stood and poured himself a goblet of wine. "Maybe I should have, but Fitzroy didn't think it necessary. The boy seems to have mended his ways." Her husband ran his finger around the rim of his goblet, a rather unusual expression on his face. "If only I knew what had possessed Fitzroy to leave so suddenly!"

She had a moment of dread, but decided his look was no more than a compound of grief and disappointment. "Well, my dear, he was only a hired soldier, after all. I'm sure we'll find someone to replace him."

"I had hoped he would marry Fritha."

"She would be wasted on someone like him, don't you think? Whereas, if she married Tallentine, she would be a wonderful influence on him. Don't you agree?"

"Maybe he needs the proper wife, but I'm not convinced Fritha is the one."

"He's rich, young and handsome. What more could any girl ask?"

"Some sense, for one thing."

"Fritha has sense enough for ten men."

"You may be right, my dear," Lord Gervais replied with a tired sigh.

Bern, Lurilla, Meara and Dunstan sat in the alehouse, looking at one another despondently.

"I tell you, I don't like it one bit!" Lurilla said forcefully. "Going away like that, all at once! What does it mean?"

"Have you seen Fritha lately?" Meara asked softly. "I want to cry just looking at her."

"Maybe she sent him packing. She's done that before," Dunstan suggested hopefully.

"Not this time. I've seen the way she looked at him. If he's hurt her, I hope he rots in hell and soon, too," Lurilla said. She looked at Bern, her mouth a thin line. "What do you think? He's *your* friend."

"Not after this. I mean, he was always one to move on quick, but I thought ... well, the way he looked at *her*..." He shrugged his shoulders. "Blackguard," he muttered into his mug.

"Well, somebody's got to help. Poor Fritha looks like death walking upright," Meara said.

"Somebody should ask her what happened," Dunstan said.

"It isn't our business," Meara replied.

"Yes, it is!" Bern said. "We all care about her." His fist slammed on the table. "By God, I hope he *does* comes back."

They all turned to stare at him.

"Because when he does, I'll gladly rip his guts out."

Meara stood up. "I'll go speak with her. She was good to me when John died and I think she might talk to me about this."

"Yes, you're the best one," Lurilla agreed. "Be sure to tell us if there's anything we can do."

Meara nodded and hurried outside.

The innkeeper's widow found Fritha in the kitchen, checking the food for the evening meal as if nothing untoward had happened, until she called her name and Fritha turned toward her.

"Have you a moment?" she asked quietly.

Fritha looked about to say no, but seemed to think better of it. "A moment."

Meara nodded toward the door and they went outside. The rain had finally stopped, and the sun shone feebly. "Can I do anything?" Meara asked immediately.

"What do you mean?"

Meara sat down on a nearby bench. "We all know Fitzroy's gone. For good, it seems."

Fritha sat beside her like someone not quite awake. Meara faced Fritha and took the girl's hands in hers. "Tell me what happened between you."

Fritha hesitated, then seemed to collapse as if the weight of the castle had fallen on her. "He wanted me to leave with him."

"Why would he want to leave Bridgeford Wells? Lord Gervais was pleased with him. He could have stayed as long as he liked."

Fritha sighed and looked away. "It doesn't matter why. He wanted to go. I wanted to stay. You know what he decided to do."

"Well, he's a fool then. Leaving you like that! When we all thought..." Meara paused when she saw the burning anguish in Fritha's eyes. "Oh, my poor dear!" She put her arms around the girl's shoulders and embraced her. "I'm so sorry!"

Fritha stayed resting in the comfort of Meara's arms for a brief moment, then drew back. "Perhaps I should have known this would happen. He's never had to stay anywhere. Maybe I was asking too much of him."

Meara tried to think of something comforting to say. "You'll forget him soon, I'm sure."

Fritha shook her head sorrowfully, and Meara found herself wishing the girl would cry. Scream. Curse. Anything, to wipe the agony from her face.

"I may not be able to forget him, even if I wanted to." She looked at Meara with a mixture of hope and despair. "How soon can a woman be sure she is going to have a baby?"

Chapter Seventeen

Cold, wet and tired, Urien came to a small inn at a crossroads.

The building wasn't much, but at least he could get a little drier, and hopefully have some ale.

It had taken him days of riding slowly over muddy roads to get this close to the northern borderlands between Wales and England; DeLanyea's castle lay only another day's ride away.

Shivering, Urien dismounted and entered the low wooden doorway. The smoke from the fire made his eyes smart. There were a few men drinking inside, probably local farmers. Glancing around, he spied a man he assumed was the innkeeper, and after a few minutes of haggling, secured lodging for the night.

He hoped he wouldn't find the bed filled with bugs. Or other travelers.

A young woman came into the main part of the building, carrying tankards of ale on a tray. She sauntered over to him, and he took one of the mugs from the tray and began to drink.

The brew tasted like mare's sweat, but he was thirsty. He doubted a place like this would have wine that tasted any better than vinegar, either.

"Can I get you something else?" the serving wench asked, leaning forward so that he had a very good view of her ample bosom.

"Perhaps," he said, sitting back and surveying her. She was not bad looking, with long dark hair, clear skin and, he saw when she smiled at him, good teeth.

Maybe all he needed was a night with another woman to drive Fritha from his thoughts. And his dreams. "For now, the ale will have to do."

She grinned slyly and walked away, swinging her hips, undoubtedly for his benefit. Wide hips, not slender like Fritha's. And her smile was as false as only a whore's could be, completely different from the secret smiles Fritha gave to him alone.

He cursed softly and took another drink. And another.

Ever since he had ridden out of Bridgeford Wells he had spent his days in the saddle and his nights getting drunk. That had been the only way he could get any sleep and almost forget the ache in his heart.

A short time later another man, older and quite dirty, came into the room. He looked about for a while, and when the serving wench came, whispered something in her ear. Then they went out the door together. Some minutes later, the wench was back, adjusting her bodice as she tucked what appeared to be money into her clothing.

So, she *was* a whore.

Urien stared at his ale for several more minutes. *Why not?* he asked himself. He had plenty of money.

He beckoned to the wench and she sauntered over to him.

"How much?" he asked.

She smiled seductively. "For a man like you, five pennies."

"That's expensive."

"I'm worth it. You'll see."

He nodded. "Where?"

"Follow me."

She walked toward the door and glanced back over her shoulder to make sure he was following.

She went across the yard to a small building opposite. With deliberate steps he made his way through the mud, ignoring the rain.

The wench led him inside a dark, dingy room. In one corner was a pile of none-too-clean straw covered with blankets.

She began to undo her bodice. He yanked off his tunic. She wiggled out of her dress. Glancing at her large, pendulous breasts as she slipped under the blanket, he stripped off his *chausses* and pulled off his boots, then joined her. She wasted no time, but began to kiss him, and as she did so, he felt her hand moving beneath the sheet.

Her kiss was cold, her hand unwelcome. Urien lay unmoving, his eyes closed, but in his mind's eye he saw Fritha, smiling. Laughing. Then ready for his kiss. Then in the midst of lovemaking. And then standing before him, willing to sacrifice herself for the people she loved.

While he—he had run away, ignoring another cry for help.

It had been the wisest thing to do, he had told himself countless times. Not cowardly, for now he was not afraid of any man. Or woman, for that matter.

But, as he lay in the whore's bed, he realized the truth. He *had* been a coward—and as selfish as Adela Gervais, demanding that Fritha give her love only to him and abandoning her when she would not.

Fritha was right. What *did* he know of duty and responsibility and love?

Only what she had taught him.

He rolled over and got out of the bed.

"What's the matter? Forget to do something first?" the woman asked coyly.

"No." He tugged on his *chausses* and grabbed his tunic, belt and boots. From his purse he took five pennies and tossed them to her. "I made a mistake."

A mistake. Oh, God, he'd made a mistake! He put one hand out against the wall to steady himself. He hoped he was not too late.

"Are you sick?" the woman asked, sitting up.

But Urien was already gone.

"You look tired, my lord," Fritha said to Lord Gervais as he sat near the hearth in the great hall. The flames made the pale oak paneling glow warmly, driving away the chill of the windy, rainy evening, although it was still summer.

Fritha, too, felt exhausted, but she smiled and hoped Lord Gervais wouldn't notice, just as she hoped he didn't notice the large helpings she was taking at mealtimes. Her appetite had become ravenous.

"I am tired, my dear. I knew Ollerund did many things as steward, but I have to say I didn't fully appreciate his efforts until I had to find another to take his place."

She sat beside him. "Have you chosen a new steward?"

"Adela thinks Tallentine would be a good choice."

"Tallentine?"

"I know he's not a very good knight, but he does seem to manage his own estate rather well." He gave her a wry grin. "How else could he afford all those clothes?"

"But still, my lord! Tallentine!"

Lord Gervais gave her a sidelong glance. "I wouldn't hesitate to make him my steward if he had a certain wife."

There could be no mistaking his meaning as he looked at her.

She gazed at the floor, feeling as if a cold wind had blown into the room. Tallentine's wife! She would rather...

But if she were with child and unwed, Adela would surely compel Lord Gervais to send her away, no doubt under the pretext of sparing her shame.

Lord Gervais was looking at her.

She raised her head. "Has Sir Tallentine asked for me, my lord?"

"Not yet. Adela thinks he will."

"Oh."

"There's no one you would rather have, is there, my dear?"

She shook her head. No, there was no one. Now. She blinked rapidly to hold back the tears.

"I've also been thinking about Sir George," he said.

"He lives so far away." To marry him would mean she had lost Urien for nothing.

"That's true. I wouldn't want you to be too far from home, either, my dear."

She tried to stifle a sorrowful sigh as she stood up. "I will consider Tallentine. You may tell him so, if he asks for my hand. Good night, my lord."

"Good night, my dear."

Lord Gervais stroked his chin thoughtfully as he watched her walk away.

Fritha felt as if she were going to be ill, but she forced herself to smile at Sir Tallentine. She had no wish to go riding, but Lord Gervais had suggested it, and the weather had kept everyone indoors so much lately, it *was* a pleasure to be outside.

Lord Gervais, Adela and most of the other knights were far ahead.

Tallentine kept smiling at her in a manner that bordered on a leer, and she was certain Lord Gervais had told him of her change of heart. He reached out and took hold of her horse's bridle, forcing it to come to a halt.

"What is it?" she asked, wishing they were not so far behind the others.

"It's a beautiful day. I thought you might enjoy a walk beside the river."

The river! She wanted nothing less than to walk beside the river with *him*. The riverbank only conjured up sweet and bitter memories for her.

"That might lead to gossip," she warned.

Tallentine dismounted. "I don't think we need be concerned about peasants' talk," he said with a smile.

Fritha sighed and allowed him to help her down. Considering that she might already be bearing a man's child outside of wedlock, gossip might not be the worst thing that could happen. If people troubled to count back the months when the baby was born, they might believe it was Tallentine's, should they marry.

They walked a little in the shade of the trees, and to her surprise Tallentine said nothing. She wondered if he had changed his mind about marrying her, and couldn't decide if she cared or not.

"Fritha," he said suddenly. "Lord Gervais told me . . . he implied that . . ."

She looked at him. Now, here in the shade of the trees, away from the castle, he didn't seem to be quite the same person, as if he were no longer trying to be more than he was. "Yes?"

"He gave me to understand that if I were to ask you to marry me, you might say yes."

She took a deep breath. "I told him so."

Tallentine stopped and faced her, but he made no move to touch her. "Why?"

She hadn't expected this. She had expected that he would be as he had always been—vain, arrogant, sure of himself. But something had changed him and she needed time to try to discover what. "I . . . I don't understand. I thought you wanted to marry me."

He suddenly looked lost. "I did. But then when Fitzroy came, I thought . . . that is, I supposed you cared for him. And I acted like a dishonorable rogue. I mean, I could understand it if you never wanted to even speak to me again. But nothing would make me happier than if you would consent to be my wife."

She had been prepared for everything but honesty from him. How could she deceive him? "Tallentine, I must tell you something, and if, after hearing it, you no longer wish to wed me, I will understand." She took a deep breath. "I believe I am going to have a baby."

He stared at her, disbelief on his face. Then his eyes narrowed. "Fitzroy's?"

She nodded. "I only ask that you respect my confidence in this. If I am right, people will find out soon enough."

"That despicable blackguard! That...that..."

"Please, Tallentine. It was as much my fault as his."

"I see. So that is why you've suddenly given your consent." He walked away, his back to her. She didn't know what to do or say, so she waited. After a few minutes, he turned to her. "I thought, of all the women I have met, you would be the most chaste." He came toward her, and she didn't like the look in his eyes. "You disappoint me, Fritha, but I suppose I should have known better. All women are lying, scheming creatures. However, there may be certain advantages."

She backed away. "What do you mean? I wanted to be honest with you."

"Oh, I will still marry you. Otherwise Gervais won't make me steward."

She took another step away, suddenly frightened of him, of the loathing in his eyes, the hard line of his mouth.

"Don't run away, my future bride. After all, now we need have no concern about your chastity, so we need not wait for the ceremony."

"Tallentine, please..." She backed into a tree and could go no farther.

"Don't refuse me. I'm going to save you from shame, you little whore, so don't you *dare* refuse me."

There was a moment when she almost gave in. Almost let him do what he wanted, almost believed she owed him the right.

But the memory of Urien, holding her so tenderly, his gentle words of love echoing through her memory, gave her the strength to push away from the tree.

"No!" she cried, shoving him back. "No! I'm *proud* that I was his lover! I'm proud to bear his child!"

She picked up her skirts and began running back to the horses.

"You're proud to be his whore!" Tallentine called after her.

"I won't marry her. She's going to have that...that *bastard*'s child!"

Adela frowned as Tallentine pouted petulantly. She pointed to a chair, glad that the great hall was empty. "Are you certain?"

"She told me herself."

"That is very interesting. And absolutely shameful, of course." Adela kept a beaming smile from her face, but she was delighted. Fritha had sealed her own fate with such a shame. And Fitzroy had gone. Things couldn't have taken a better course if she'd planned it for years. "Unfortunately, I don't think Gervais will appoint you steward unless you marry her."

"Surely he won't expect me to marry her if she's carrying another man's child!"

"If he finds out."

"Of course he will."

Adela fingered the bracelet on her slender wrist, her other hand resting on her rounded stomach. "Well, my dear, that depends upon you. How much do you want to be steward?"

He frowned. "Are you saying the *only* way I can become steward is to marry that harlot?"

"The idea was rather appealing a little while ago, wasn't it?"

"That was before Fitzroy had her."

"My dear Tallentine, it was all I could do to get Gervais to agree to let you marry Fritha! If you don't, then I simply cannot do any more for you."

He scowled darkly, and she wondered if it would be better to have another steward. On the other hand, there was a chance another man would not be so amenable to her suggestions. "You realize," she said quietly, glancing around to make sure no servants were lurking about, "that as steward you will spend much of your time here. With me. Away from your wife." She watched his face as the implication of her words dawned on him.

"I'll marry her."

Fritha stared at Adela, not quite believing what she had just heard. "What do you mean, the banns will be announced tomorrow? What banns? For whom?"

Adela's smile was as cold as a smile could be. "Why, my dear, don't act so surprised. For you and Tallentine."

"I'm not going to marry him."

"Don't you think that would be most unwise?"

Fritha's heart sank. Adela knew! Tallentine must have told her about the baby. "Why do you say that?" she asked, determined to be sure that her secret was a secret no longer.

"He's doing a very generous thing, you know. Marrying to give your bastard a name."

"Even if I am with child, I don't want his 'generosity'!"

Adela gazed at her calmly. "Really? Would you rather Lord Gervais found out the truth about you?"

Fritha stared at her enemy. Adela had found the weakest part of her armor. No, she didn't want Lord Gervais to be ashamed of her.

But then she lifted her chin proudly. She *wasn't* ashamed that Urien Fitzroy had loved her. "I shall tell Lord Gervais myself. And I will not marry Tallentine."

"You disappoint me, Fritha. I thought you were a clever girl."

Fritha walked slowly toward Adela. "I may not be as clever as you, but I know how to love, Adela. And the people here love me. You will *never* make me leave. Understand *that*." She spun on her heel and marched from the room.

Adela frowned and went to her chest. She pushed one of the decorative figures and a drawer sprang open, revealing a small vial. "There are many ways to leave," she whispered.

Chapter Eighteen

Something was wrong. The fields were empty, though it was not yet dark on a warm, sunny day. There were only one or two travelers on the road, which should have been filled with people on their way home from the market of Bridgeford Wells.

Urien didn't like it.

Spurring his horse, he made for the inn and found the gates barred shut. Dread began to fill him, an uneasiness that somehow he was already too late.

Too late to tell Fritha he had been wrong. Too late to keep her safe. Too late to tell her that he loved her more than his own life.

He halted outside the alehouse and jumped down from his horse. Inside he could hear several voices raised in argument. He entered the building.

The place was hot and stifling, and crowded beyond belief. As his eyes adjusted to the dimness, a cold, chilling silence descended on the room. All the people turned to stare at him. He could see Lurilla, Meara and Dunstan, Donald and Seldon, and even old Peter, with his dog by his side.

"What's happened?" he demanded, seeking Bern's face among the many.

Bern stepped out of the corner, his mouth hard and his eyes as cold as ice. "What's it to you, Fitzroy? Why don't you just go back wherever the hell you came from? We take care of our own. We don't need you."

Urien's dread grew. He pushed his way through the crowd, ignoring everyone else. "Tell me."

"It's none of your business, seeing as how you left her."

He reached Bern and grabbed his tunic at the throat, glaring at him. *"Tell me what has happened."*

"It's Fritha. She's been accused of trying to murder Lady Gervais."

He gasped and let go of Bern. "What?"

"Adela Gervais claims Fritha tried to poison her."

"That can't be true."

"There's not a soul here believes it," Bern said. "But we can't do anything till the king's men get here. Lord Gervais' put her in the custody of Sir Nevil, and they're not letting anybody see her."

"How did this happen?"

"What do you care? You left her—rode off and left her—even though she's going to have your child."

Urien felt as if he'd been punched in the stomach. For a moment he couldn't breathe, or think. A child! His child! "She didn't tell me," he whispered.

"Like hell she didn't."

"I don't think she did," a woman said quietly.

Urien turned to Meara, who stood up and came forward. "Can't you see it? He didn't know," she said to Bern. "He left before Fritha herself even knew for certain." She cocked her head and looked at Urien. "Why did you come back?"

"I love her." Simple words, but he had never said anything more true in his life.

Meara nodded, apparently satisfied. Others in the room began to mumble, but it was not with scorn or anger.

"What is everyone doing here?" he asked Bern.

"Trying to think of some way to help her, of course."

"I think we should storm the castle!"

"That's right!"

Urien turned toward the voices he recognized as Donald's and, more surprisingly, Seldon's. "Shouldn't you be there, in the castle?"

Donald's gray eyes flashed with defiance. "I won't serve someone who treats his own like that!"

Seldon nodded, and Urien took note that now Seldon seemed to follow Donald's lead. As it should be.

Urien turned back to Bern. "Who accused her?"

"Lady Gervais herself."

"Lying, evil Jezebel!" Old Peter called out.

"Is that all the evidence?"

Bern frowned. "No. They found a bottle of poison in Fritha's things."

Urien sat down. "I want to hear everything."

The others let Bern tell him. "First thing odd that happened, Tallentine comes back. Then we start to hear rumors—from the ones in the kitchen up at the castle first, wasn't it?" Lurilla nodded. "People up there was talking about Tallentine and Fritha being wed," Bern continued.

Urien's hands bunched into fists, but he didn't say a word.

"Well, we couldn't hardly believe it. I mean, she's never so much as looked at him. But then, considering the way things was—" he looked hard at Urien, who stared back without a change in his expression "—we thought there might be something to it.

"Next thing we hear, Tallentine's off for home and tryin' to make everybody think *he* had refused to marry *her*, when anybody with an ounce of sense knew it was likely the other way."

Urien smiled briefly, then frowned. "I want to know about Lady Gervais."

"Yes, well..." Bern cleared his throat. "It was five days ago. Lady Gervais had been poorly, but nobody thought much of that, not since Lord Gervais said about the baby. But she didn't seem to be getting much better. So they sent for a monk from a monastery a ways off. He's famous, this priest, for being very skilled at healing.

"So he comes. Then next thing we know, Fritha's taken and locked in the tower room. Meara went right up to the castle to find out what it was all about. Lady Gervais had accused Fritha of something terrible, was all anybody would tell her."

"Aye," Meara said quietly. "I knew Fritha thought she was with child, so I wondered if that was it, even though I didn't think Lord Gervais would lock her up for that, especially when you ran..." She caught Urien's eye. "Well, anyways, it turned out to be a lot worse. Hylda was very upset, poor girl, but I finally got her to tell me what had happened.

"Hylda had gone to the women's quarters to fetch some laundry and saw a vial in with Fritha's things. She'd been sent out of Lady Gervais' bedchamber by the priest and Lord Gervais, but she'd overheard some talk of poison. She thought they meant poisoning from the food, especially since Lady Gervais always seemed to eat such odd things.

"The poor thing was terrified when she found that vial. She didn't know what it was for sure, but was too scared to keep it herself, in case somebody should think it was *hers*. Finally she decided to take it to Godwin, the cook, hoping it wasn't anything bad. She didn't tell him where she found it.

"He didn't like the smell of it, so he took it to the priest. Seems it *was* poison. Godwin's a good man, but I think he'd been worried that perhaps something had gone amiss in the kitchen that made Lady Gervais fall ill, or that Lord Gervais would think it had. Right away the priest took it to Lord Gervais, who made Hylda tell him where she found it.

"He didn't act surprised or shocked or anything. She didn't know what to make of it. He just took the vial and said not to tell anybody else about it.

"Later that night, when Hylda was taking Lady Gervais her evening meal, she heard Lord and Lady Gervais talking. She listened at the door."

Everyone in the room nodded. Urien knew he would have done the same, too.

"It seems Lady Gervais knew all about Fritha's state. She kept saying Fritha was insane with shame and jealousy. Hylda couldn't hear what Lord Gervais said, but she didn't think he was so willing to believe such evil of Fritha."

"Good for him!" Peter said loudly. "I always said he was a fine man."

"Just when Hylda thought she'd better knock, she heard Lady Gervais come right out and accuse Fritha of trying to kill her.

"Fritha's been locked up ever since. They're waiting for somebody to come from the king, since they're nobles."

Bern put his hand on Urien's shoulder. "Sir Nevil's lookin' after her. She'll be well treated."

Urien looked around at the people. "Does anybody, not least of all Lord Gervais, think Fritha capable of poisoning someone?"

"We don't know what Lord Gervais thinks," Dunstan said, "but nobody else had been serving Lady Gervais her food except Fritha, and lots of people ate the same dishes as Lady Gervais. The poison had to be put in her food after it was ready to be taken to her in the bedchamber—and the only person who had a chance to do that without being seen by someone else in the kitchen was Fritha."

"Does Lord Gervais believe that she would be so completely stupid as to leave the poison lying about where anybody could find it?" Urien demanded. "This is ludicrous."

"We all know she's innocent," Lurilla said. "That's why we're here. That's why we're going to get her out."

Urien surveyed them all slowly. "What do you mean?"

"We're going to demand that Lord Gervais release her."

"And if he doesn't?"

Bern's expression told Urien that if Lord Gervais did not agree, the townspeople had every intention of using force. "You would all risk your lives for her?"

One and all they nodded. "We love her," Meara said quietly.

Urien drew in a deep breath. Just as Fritha had wanted to protect these people, so did they wish to protect her. Here was another kind of love she was teaching him.

He stood up abruptly.

"Where are you going?" Donald asked.

"To the castle."

Fritha sat by the window, wondering how many more days she would have to spend inside the tower room. It had already been five, and she had little idea how long it would take before she could be brought to trial.

She had nothing to do to pass the time except sew— which she hated—and think. And remember. And wonder if she had made the right choice staying behind, especially now when it seemed Adela would win after all.

She got up and began pacing the room. Perhaps she should have agreed to marry Tallentine.

No. Never. She had done the right thing refusing him.

Still, she was certain that was what had made Adela come up with her daring scheme, but who would have guessed Adela would go to the lengths of poisoning herself to accuse her? No one else had had the opportunity to administer poison, for lately Adela had insisted that only Fritha serve her. Fritha had thought Adela meant to keep an eye on her at all times, but now it was clear the woman had had a more sinister purpose.

When Adela fell ill, Fritha had assumed that Adela's latest illness was the result of her pregnancy. When it lingered, Lord Gervais had sent for the learned priest.

Fritha had had complete trust in the priest, as did Lord Gervais, so when the priest whispered that he thought the illness was the result of poison, even naming the likely kind, they had both been shocked and horrified.

She closed her eyes, trying to block out the memory of Lord Gervais' face when he summoned her to show her the small vial Hylda had found among Fritha's things. She had simply stared at him, too dumbfounded to speak.

Lord Gervais had been kind, even then, telling her she would have to stay in the castle under the supervision of Sir Nevil until the matter could be settled in the proper court. Lady Gervais remained in her bed, although Hylda had confided in Sir Nevil that she seemed very well indeed.

Fritha sighed. It was not a hard imprisonment, except that she was completely innocent and could think of no way to prove it.

She heard a commotion in the courtyard and went to the window to look out. Someone was calling for Lord Gervais.

She stared—and could hardly believe her eyes.

Urien! In the courtyard, standing there shouting!

He had come back. She hadn't cried once since she had been imprisoned, but tears sprang to her eyes now. She wiped them away impatiently, not wanting anything to cloud her view of Urien.

As she watched, the courtyard began to fill with people, until a large crowd milled about.

Lord Gervais came out of the great hall. "Fitzroy!" he said, surprised, then wary. "You've come back?"

She strained to hear his reply.

"Yes."

Lord Gervais walked closer to him. "Why?"

"Fritha is innocent."

"That is for the court to decide," Lord Gervais replied. "Why did you leave?"

"Your wife tried to seduce me."

Fritha gasped. Everyone in the courtyard fell so silent she could hear every word as if the two men facing each other were inside her room.

Lord Gervais' hands clenched tightly. "How dare you say such a thing to me?"

"It is time you knew the truth about her. Your wife is a lying, scheming, evil woman, my lord, who may very well deserve to be poisoned. But everyone here knows that it is ridiculous to think Fritha capable of such a crime."

"Who, then, are you accusing?"

Fritha listened in horror. She knew when Lord Gervais' voice had that particular cold, resounding tone, he was beyond anger and had reached smoldering fury.

"I think your wife administered the poison herself, so that Fritha would be accused."

For a moment she feared Lord Gervais was going to strike Urien down, although he had no sword. Urien didn't move, but watched Lord Gervais steadily.

"Do you formally accuse my wife of this?" Lord Gervais asked slowly.

"Fritha is innocent," Urien said firmly. "I would stake my life on it."

Lord Gervais frowned. "And so you should, for making such accusations against my wife. And so you shall." He crossed his arms. "We shall not wait for the king's men. We'll decide this matter tomorrow. Trial by combat."

"Name your champion."

"*I* will fight for my wife's honor."

Urien turned and marched from the courtyard, leaving behind a stunned, muttering crowd. Lord Gervais went back to the hall. Fritha drew back from the window, her hands on her cheeks.

Urien and Lord Gervais! To fight over her—and only one man to win.

What had she done by staying? She hadn't protected Lord Gervais, but only brought more trouble. Now she might cost him his life.

To think she was the cause of this battle between the man she loved and whose child she carried, and the man who had been a father to her. She knew Urien would fight to win, and he was a well-trained, strong warrior in his prime. Lord Gervais would be fighting for his wife, and for his pride. He would be a formidable opponent.

She stared at the stone walls, unseeing. There must be some way she could stop it.

Some way to save them both.

* * *

Adela lay in their huge bed, staring at her husband. "Trial by combat? But surely that's not legal! You have to have a proper trial. I am too important."

Levander shook his head. "No. Now this is between Fitzroy and me. It's a question of honor."

Adela realized she had heard only part of the story. "Isn't this about Fritha trying to kill me?"

"She didn't."

Adela's throat went dry. "What do you mean? You don't believe her lies, surely. I tell you, Levander, she's been making my life a misery ever since you married me. I didn't tell you because I knew you thought of her as a daughter. I was trying to spare your feelings. And now that I'm having a child, your child, and she's bearing a bastard—"

"So you keep telling me, my dear."

"That's *why* she did it. She's mad with jealousy."

Levander turned to face his beautiful wife. "Is she?"

"Yes, yes, of course."

"Did you ever ask Urien Fitzroy to make love with you?"

"Is that what he said? The lying scoundrel!"

"Did you?" He asked the question so calmly it scared her.

"No, I did not."

"Is the child you bear mine?"

By now Adela was more frightened than she had ever been in her life. "Yes, Levander. I swear it!"

"I hope so, for your sake, my dear. Because if I ever find out otherwise, I will send you as far away from me as I can."

Shocked by the vehemence in his voice, Adela fell back against the pillows. "Levander, I swear by the Blessed Virgin, the child is yours!"

He gave her a long, scrutinizing stare. "I believe you," he said at last, and Adela began to breathe again. "But a man in love is only so blind. I *don't* believe Fitzroy would make up a story like that, and I *know* Fritha is not the sort to use poison. That's the weapon of a devious, scheming woman. Isn't it, Adela, my love?"

"You must believe me, or why would you fight Fitzroy?"

Levander looked at her, his eyes filled with both a cold hatred and helpless despair. "Because whatever else you are, you are still my wife."

Late that night Urien stood underneath the willow by the riverbank.

As the water lapped gently nearby, he sighed softly. He was glad he had returned, but he had not expected Lord Gervais to issue such a challenge. He had expected . . . what?

Contrary to the habits of a lifetime, he had not been patient. When he had heard all that had transpired in his absence, he had gone at once to the castle without first thinking of the consequences.

And now he would have to kill Lord Gervais.

He bowed his head as he turned to go back to the inn. He liked the lord of Bridgeford Wells, but he loved Fritha, and she was innocent. Tomorrow he would fight the most important battle of his life, and he would win.

* * *

The next morning dawned gray and damp, and the morning air was cold. Fritha shivered in the tower room.

She had spent a sleepless night knowing what she had to do to protect the men she loved, and she was determined to do it, even though that meant her own life would be forfeit.

Not only that, but she must forfeit the love and respect of everyone who knew her. She would have to convince them that she was guilty of the shameful, monstrous evil of trying to murder her lord's wife.

There was a brief knock at the door, which opened to reveal Sir Nevil. The poor man looked as if he had spent a sleepless night, too.

"It's almost time," he said apologetically. "Are you still certain you wish to be there?"

"Yes."

She had asked to be present at the combat. There she would announce her guilt—but at least she would see Urien one last time before she was completely disgraced and taken away from him.

Clasping her hands to still their trembling, she walked toward the door and followed Sir Nevil down to the courtyard. Sir Nevil led her to one side of a rough square, marked off with ropes.

The crowd stirred uneasily, small murmurs of wonder and discontent filling the air.

Fritha straightened her shoulders and lifted her chin as she prepared to see the curiosity and speculation on everyone's face as they looked at her.

Her steps faltered. On each face she saw concern and respect and...and love. Hot tears burned her eyes and for a moment she had to look away.

Oh, how hard it was going to be to take away what she saw in their faces and replace it with hatred and disgust!

But she must. For Urien and Lord Gervais, she must.

She blinked and lifted her head, searching for Urien.

He had not yet arrived, but with surprise she realized Lurilla and Meara were in the courtyard. She had hoped her best friends would stay at home.

Donald and Seldon were hovering across the courtyard and her eyes widened when Donald winked at her. Old Peter stood near the gate, a fierce expression on his face and his dog at his feet. Far at the back of the gathering, she could see Bern, and beside him, Dunstan. They looked grim, but she had expected them to be there.

"Where is Lady Gervais?" Fritha asked.

"Too ill to attend," Sir Nevil replied.

Fritha bowed her head, thankful Adela would not be there to witness her humiliation.

And then she saw Urien. Garbed in mail and carrying his helm under one arm, his plain black tunic made him look like a creature of shadows as he entered the courtyard.

She moved forward, but Sir Nevil restrained her with a gentle hand on her arm.

Urien had seen her. She wanted so much to call his name. She wanted to tell him that she loved him, that she had been wrong, that she should have gone with him. Dearly, dearly she wished for a second chance. But it was too late.

His expression didn't seem to change. His mouth stayed hard and determined, his face ruthless. Except for one brief moment when their eyes met, and she knew that he understood. Everything.

Then Lord Gervais came forth from the great hall. It had been a long time since Fritha had seen him bearing weapons. His face was equally grim and determined.

He stepped into the fighting area. "People of Bridgeford Wells," he said, his powerful voice carrying to every part of the courtyard, "this battle will determine the innocence or guilt of Lady Fritha Kendrick, who stands accused of attempted murder. It is also being fought to refute the charges against my lady's honor, brought forth by Sir Urien Fitzroy. May God reward the just, and punish the guilty."

Urien put on his helmet.

Fritha took a deep breath and stepped forward.

An arrow flew through the air and the courtyard erupted into pandemonium.

Chapter Nineteen

Urien heard the familiar hiss and called out a warning. Lord Gervais twisted, but the short arrow, shot from a crossbow at close range, pierced the mail of his left leg. With a cry of pain, he fell to his knees.

Fritha hurried toward him, wrenching herself away when somebody grabbed her arm. Someone else called out to her, but she ignored everything and kept going.

Urien was beside him. Fritha knelt on the ground and put her arms around Lord Gervais, supporting him. As she did so, she realized Meara was with her. Sir Nevil ran up, puffing for breath. Donald and Seldon appeared, looked at each other and moved away.

Urien looked at Fritha. "He'll be all right. It's not bleeding much."

She managed to smile at Lord Gervais. "I'm so glad!"

"Adela," Lord Gervais said, one hand on his knee. "Find her."

Fritha glanced at Urien, who nodded and stood up. Suddenly a woman screamed, and across the courtyard people were crowded around something...or someone. Old Peter shouted and waved a sword, his dog barking loudly.

Hylda came running up to them before anyone could move. "Lady Gervais—she's gone."

"When?" Urien demanded.

"I don't know! I left her sleeping."

"She's run away," Lord Gervais said calmly.

Fritha turned to stare at him. His mouth was grim, but there was anguish in his eyes. "I've known for some time what she was, but I could not stop loving her, even then."

He looked at Urien. "I was not planning to kill you, Fitzroy. I was planning to lose. Fritha would be declared innocent and I would have at least defended my wife's honor, such as it is."

"I didn't want to kill you, either."

Lord Gervais steadied himself with one hand as he sat up a little more. "I must confess I was counting on that."

Fritha bit her lip and looked at Urien. He had been right. Lord Gervais didn't need her to protect him after all. Urien said nothing, but helped Lord Gervais to his feet.

Dunstan rushed up, shock and dismay on his face. "They're after the devil who did this," he said. "He was amongst the squires. Donald and Seldon had hold of the fellow's cloak, but he squirmed away and fled."

"It was Lady Gervais," Lord Gervais said softly. "I saw her."

Dunstan was too surprised to reply.

"When you find her, bring her to me." The sadness in Lord Gervais' voice brought new tears to Fritha's eyes.

Dunstan nodded and walked quickly away. Fritha realized Meara was no longer beside her and looked around the courtyard, her gaze coming to rest on the small crowd. "Urien," she gasped, "I think Bern's been hurt."

He saw where she was looking and turned pale.

"I'll help Lord Gervais," she said softly. "You go see to Bern."

With a grateful nod and a look full of love, he left her and dashed across the courtyard.

Adela ran as fast as the long cloak she wore would allow.

She had failed. Completely and utterly. Her only hope had been to kill Gervais. If he knew everything, she would be forced to live like every other wife, in her husband's shadow, doing only what he wished, having no power of her own. Even worse, he would be suspicious of her and watchful of her every move. It would be like being in a prison.

She would not live that way.

She would get away from this place. She would go to France, or Germany perhaps. She was a beautiful woman, and there were always ways for beautiful women to find powerful, wealthy men.

She hurried down an alley. If she could get to the river and find a boat, perhaps she could escape the people chasing her. There had been much confusion when she'd shot the crossbow. If only that old fool's dog hadn't barked and those two stupid boys laid hold of her cloak, she would have been even farther ahead by now.

Then that brewster had come between her and the gate. Fortunately she had had the narrow dagger tucked up her sleeve. He had tried to stop her, but she had been taught to use a dagger well. She had ducked and jabbed, the knife piercing the skin of the man's side. He had fallen to the ground, though whether or not she had killed him, she didn't know. Nor did she care.

She staggered a bit, a sharp pain in her stomach. If only she weren't with child, she would be able to run faster.

She heard the sounds of the chase coming closer. It spurred her on, regardless of her rasping breaths and the pain.

As Adela reached the river she clambered into a small boat and used her dagger to cut the rope holding it to the bank. It swung out into the current.

There was a long oar at the stern of the boat for propelling it through the water. She could see people running for the riverbank.

Standing, she began to push on the oar.

Unfortunately, Lady Adela Gervais, who had learned many things, had never learned how to row a boat. She leaned too far, lost her balance and fell into the water.

The long cloak she had worn to hide the crossbow pulled her down as if it were a millstone about her neck. She struggled and tried to grab the oar or the boat, but to no avail.

The water closed around her, cold and merciless.

Fritha and Urien sat side by side and hand in hand in Bern's bedchamber at the alehouse. Lurilla sat silently beside them. Meara and Dunstan were in the kitchen with the children.

Lord Gervais had insisted that Fritha and Urien go to their friend. Fritha had been unwilling to leave Lord Gervais, but she knew that if Bern was seriously hurt, Urien would want to be with him.

And her place was with Urien. She knew that now.

Urien stared down at his friend's pale, drawn face, then at Fritha. "I should never have left you. This is my fault."

Fritha tried to smile. "You came back."

"Almost too late."

She sighed and laid her head on his shoulder. "Almost."

"I'm sorry."

"No, *I'm* sorry," Fritha said. "You were right. Lord Gervais didn't need me to protect him."

Urien turned to her and ran his finger along her cheek. "I was wrong. This is your home, and you belong here. I want to belong here, too."

Bern groaned. Lurilla was at his side in an instant, her face full of fear and worry. "Oh, my dear," she whispered, laying her face on his chest as she wept.

"Ale. I need ale," he said groggily.

Lurilla sat up abruptly, then laughed as the tears fell down her cheeks. "I'll give you ale, you big oaf! Scaring me like that!"

Urien began to laugh, a deep, rich booming laugh that made Fritha laugh, too.

"What's all the fuss? All I need is a good drink." Bern opened his eyes. "What the hell..." He stared at Urien. "That's not *you* laughing like that, is it?"

Urien glanced at Fritha and winked. "You look like a boar waiting for an apple in its mouth."

Bern looked around the room, smiled at Lurilla, then tried to sit up. "Oh, dear sweet Lord, what's happened?"

"You've been stabbed," Urien said, becoming serious again.

Bern felt his side and sat up, swaying a little. "By Jove's jumping...whatevers, it's just a scratch. And where's Lady Gervais got to? I tried to stop her—"

"Lie down!" Lurilla commanded. "You'll start to bleed again!"

"I've had slivers worse than this." He looked from his wife to Urien to Fritha.

"Lady Gervais is dead," Urien said.

"God's teeth!"

"She drowned," Fritha said softly.

"That's a more merciful fate than she deserves, too," Lurilla began angrily.

Fritha shook her head. "It's not right to speak ill of the dead. And we mustn't forget that Lord Gervais' child died with her."

Lurilla sighed. "You're right. But when I think what might have happened..."

Urien took hold of Fritha's hand and squeezed it tightly, and she knew he too was thinking about what might have happened.

Urien stood up. "Since you're obviously not dying, I think I'll take Fritha home and ask Lord Gervais for her hand in marriage, as a gentleman should."

"About time, too," Bern said.

Fritha grinned slightly, happy and yet subdued by the events of the day. She had what she wanted most, but she was also thinking of her foster father's pain.

Once outside the door, Urien pulled her to him and kissed her gently. "I give you my word that I will never leave you again," he promised. "This place will be my home. *Our* home. Our children's home."

Fritha held him tightly, then lifted her face and kissed him. "I love you, Urien," she whispered. "We should get back to the castle. Lord Gervais—"

"Doesn't need us right this moment."

She was about to argue, until she realized he was probably right. Lord Gervais had always preferred to be left alone in his grief.

Tears returned to her eyes, but Urien took her chin in his hand and tilted her face up. "I think I fell in love with you that first day, when you threw the honeycomb at me."

She had to smile. "Really?"

"Yes." He nodded, his face serious but his eyes twinkling with merriment. "I couldn't help admiring your..."

She cocked her head and eyed him dubiously.

"...aim."

She knew he was trying to make her feel better, and it worked, as much as anything could that day.

Gently she kissed him again.

After a long moment, she pulled away. "This is not the best place..."

"No," he agreed, taking her hand in his, "I suppose we must wait some more."

She smiled at his choice of words, but nodded as they entered Lurilla's kitchen.

They looked at each other and grinned. Meara and Dunstan were sitting suspiciously close together on the bench by the table, like two lovers whispering secrets. The twins were tugging on a piece of rope, arguing over who had legal possession of said valuable. Adelissa stirred the contents of the pot on the hearth, her face a study in concentration. Hildegard and the baby were both in the cradle, asleep despite the snug nature of their accommodation.

The couple moved apart quickly. Dunstan's face turned bright red, and so did Meara's, but she smiled broadly.

"We beg your pardon," Urien said, his face now a mask of seriousness.

"We didn't mean to interrupt," Fritha said, but she couldn't stop the giggle that bubbled up and burst out.

Meara tried to look serious, too. "We were just discussing—"

"Sir Tallentine," Dunstan said suddenly.

"What about him?" Urien asked, and Fritha's brief moment of lightheartedness seemed at an end.

"He's sold everything he owns and joined a monastery," Dunstan said, his face breaking into a beaming smile.

"What?" Fritha and Urien cried together.

Meara chuckled and nodded. "Maybe it's only a rumor, but it seems he's disgusted with women, for some reason."

When they had all managed to subdue their laughter, Urien turned to Meara. "I'm going to need a squire, Meara," he said. "I was thinking of Tom. Would you be willing to part with him?"

Meara sighed and looked at Dunstan before she spoke. "I had hoped he'd help me at the inn, although he's always been set on being a soldier. Still, I won't be alone in looking after the inn soon..." her hand crept into Dunstan's "...and you won't be living very far off, will you?"

Urien shook his head. "No, we won't. I promise."

"And if you have to fight for Lord Gervais or the king, you'll look after him, won't you?"

"I give you my word."

Meara sniffed loudly, then wiped her eyes with the corner of her sleeve. "Well, then, I can't hope for a better master for him, that's for certain."

Fritha smiled and patted her friend's hand. "That's for certain, Meara."

"What's all this?" Lurilla demanded as she came into the kitchen.

With more tears and laughter on the part of Fritha and Meara, and a few mugs of ale on the part of the men, Lurilla learned the whole story.

By now Hale and Lud had stopped arguing over the piece of rope and were listening unnoticed by the grown-ups. They didn't understand much, except that Tom was going to get to be a squire—oh, fortunate boy!—and that Urien Fitzroy and Fritha were going to be married sometime after morning but before somebody had a baby.

Hale nudged Lud. "See, he got made a knight. I knew he would."

Lud frowned. "Do you think he'll go looking for dragons now?"

"Don't be daft. He doesn't have to. He's already got his lady."

*   *   *   *   *

Harlequin® Historical

WARRIOR SERIES

The WARRIOR SERIES from author
Margaret Moore

It began with A WARRIOR'S HEART (HH #118, March 1992)—the unforgettable story of Emryss Delanyea, a wounded Welsh nobleman who returns from the crusades with all thoughts of love put aside forever...until he meets the Lady Roanna.

Now, in A WARRIOR'S QUEST (HH #175, June 1993), healer Fritha Kendrick teaches mercenary Urien Fitzroy to live by his heart rather than his sword.

And, coming in early 1994, look for A WARRIOR'S PRIDE, the third title of this medieval trilogy.

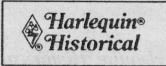

Harlequin® Historical

T E X A S

TEXAS HEART—A young woman is forced to journey west in search of her missing father.

TEXAS HEALER—A doctor returns home to rediscover a ghost from his past, the daughter of a Comanche chief.

And now, TEXAS HERO—A gunfighter teaches the local schoolteacher that not every fight can be won with a gun.
(HH #180, available in July.)

Follow the lives of Jessie Conway and her brothers in this series from popular Harlequin Historical author Ruth Langan.

**Relive the romance...
Harlequin and Silhouette
are proud to present**

by Request

A program of collections of three complete novels by the most requested authors with the most requested themes. Be sure to look for one volume each month with three complete novels by top name authors.

In June:	**NINE MONTHS**	Penny Jordan
		Stella Cameron
		Janice Kaiser

Three women pregnant and alone. But a lot can happen in nine months!

In July:	**DADDY'S HOME**	Kristin James
		Naomi Horton
		Mary Lynn Baxter

Daddy's Home... and his presence is long overdue!

In August:	**FORGOTTEN PAST**	Barbara Kaye
		Pamela Browning
		Nancy Martin

Do you dare to create a future if you've forgotten the past?

Available at your favorite retail outlet.

HARLEQUIN Silhouette

REQ-G

THREE UNFORGETTABLE HEROINES
THREE AWARD-WINNING AUTHORS

Untamed

MAVERICK HEARTS

A unique collection of historical short stories that capture the spirit of America's last frontier.

HEATHER GRAHAM POZZESSERE—over 10 million copies of her books in print worldwide
Lonesome Rider—The story of an Eastern widow and the renegade half-breed who becomes her protector.

PATRICIA POTTER—an author whose books are consistently Waldenbooks bestsellers
Against the Wind—Two people, battered by heartache, prove that love can heal all.

JOAN JOHNSTON—award-winning Western historical author with 17 books to her credit
One Simple Wish—A woman with a past discovers that dreams really do come true.

Join us for an exciting journey West with
UNTAMED
Available in July, wherever Harlequin books are sold.

MAV/93